LEAVING *Eden*

LEAVING *Eden*

a novel

by Amber Esplin

BONNEVILLE BOOKS
Springville, Utah

ISBN: 1-55517-807-3
e.1

Published by Bonneville Books
Imprint of Cedar Fort Inc.
www.cedarfort.com

Distributed by:

Typeset by Natalie Roach
Cover design by Nicole Shaffer

Printed in the United States of America
10 9 8 7 6 5 4 3 2 1
Printed on acid-free paper

Library of Congress Cataloging-in-Publication Data

Esplin, Amber.
Leaving Eden : a novel / by Amber Esplin.
p. cm.
ISBN 1-55517-807-3 (alk. paper)
1. Brothers and sisters--Fiction. 2. Parent and child--Fiction. 3. London (England)--Fiction. 4. Teenage girls--Fiction. 5. Sick children--Fiction. I. Title.

PS3605.S64L43 2004
813'.54--dc22

2004020354

Dedication

For Lauralyn and LuAnn

Acknowledgments

The school described herein is ficticious, but it is modeled after a real school known as Christ's Hospital. More information about the history of Christ's Hospital is available at

http://www.virtualjamestown.org/christs_hospital

Part One: Judith

London, December 2002

Chapter 1

As it turned out, Guildwell Hall was not at all as Judith had imagined it, not gracious or dignified, just immense and dark and cold. She had hoped for something warmer. All during the drive from the airport, as the car sped along into the city, she had kept her face turned to the window, searching through the confusion of lights for the one that would matter. She had imagined something yellow and welcoming shining out through the winter twilight, something to dispel the grayness that hung about all of them. But as it happened, no one waited to greet them, and the hall itself seemed unused to visitors. Three rows of windows, the only interruption in the vast stone façade, blinked out blindly, revealing nothing of the interior. Near the door an ancient stone plaque still announced: "Disciples of Christ Schoole for Boys and Girles."

There was nothing extraordinary about the place, really; its age was not unusual in London, and the architecture lacked any outstanding features. Its outline jutted straight and sharp against the pale December sky—no curves, no ornaments, no beauty in the somber gray stones. But it stirred something in Judith, a thread of fancy. The wrought iron gate gaped like a portal into a dream world, and nothing on the other side could be counted on to be exactly what it seemed. The tangle of chimneys, with their weird shapes silhouetted against the gloom, could have been goblins caught in a dance. The empty windows stared out like eyes from a soulless face. Even the barren trees didn't seem like ordinary trees: with their thin branches thrust upward, they resembled groping hands, contorted and desperate, unable to get hold of what they wanted. Everywhere she looked, Judith had a sense of frozen motion, of stilled life. Somehow, between one breath and the next, time had stopped, and the world inside the gate had iced over. The dancing goblins had turned to stone. Judith shivered and shrank deeper into the puffy down coat that had been made for a Utah winter. It seemed inadequate here, against the chill of centuries of winters.

"It's old," Judith muttered as her parents emerged from the car and glanced casually toward the inhospitable lodgings. What she meant was, *Couldn't we stay somewhere else? In a hotel, and just come here to work?* But her mother had never been afraid of anything, least of all anything old. Her green eyes flashed disapprovingly in Judith's direction as she bent to retrieve a snarl of duffel bags from the trunk. "Actually, by British standards, this is pretty new," Judith's father told her. "I'm a little disappointed, aren't you?" He gathered up luggage and strode easily through the gate, across frost-coated blades of grass that gleamed like needles. The notes of a whistled tune drifted back and hovered in the cold, damp air: "True to the faith that our parents have cherished . . . " Judith watched, suspended. What would happen when he disturbed the spell on this place? Would he turn to ice? Would the stones suck the color out of his hair and clothes? But there he was still—tall and confident and normal, heading to the side door that was supposed to lead into the family's quarters.

"This is a good place for ghosts, isn't it," chirped the small boy in the back seat.

Judith glanced at her brother sharply, but she could see immediately that he hadn't meant anything by it. His pale face, glowing out from inside the shadows of the car, manifested a childlike curiosity and excitement—nothing else. "Yes, you'd think so to look at it," Judith replied. She hoisted her own bag across her shoulder, then held out her hand to accept her brother's thin, cool fingers in her grasp. Gabriel climbed gingerly out of the car and stepped onto the sidewalk. Judith could see him mustering his strength as he stood there, squaring thin shoulders and savoring deep breaths of air.

"Well, let's go," said their mother. "We'll get the rest later." She walked off without waiting for an answer, leaving Judith and

Gabriel to follow more slowly in her wake. Judith braced herself to support her brother's weight, which always surprised her—he looked like he would float. Moving carefully, clinging together, the pair passed through the gate, crunched across the stiffly frosted lawn, and finally arrived at the side door. Judith felt her body sag as she took in the narrow entryway and the long, winding staircase spiraling up in what looked like an endless series of turns. "You'll have to go piggy-back," she told Gabriel. She dropped her bag and stooped near the wall for him to mount, and then they were climbing up and up into darkness. The daylight from the open side door grew weaker and weaker until Judith was lost in a deep gray gloom. She couldn't remember how long she had been climbing. The air in the stairwell had a damp, heavy quality, and moving through it was like pressing against a curtain. Judith began to wonder if the place had electricity . . . had anyone thought to ask? Finally she saw a dim light shining from somewhere overhead, and after what seemed like several more turns around the circular stairwell, she cleared the top step and let Gabriel slide down. The two stood blinking at a short hallway lit by a single bare bulb, which coated the ancient stone walls with an incongruous orange glare.

"Oh, you're here." Their mother leaned out from the doorway of what Judith took to be the kitchen. The first thing Lori Casey always did in a new place was inspect the kitchen. It was her way of confronting the practical necessities of life: organize your resources, plan your attack. If, as mortals, the family had to eat, so be it. Lori would figure out the most efficient way to meet the need. Sometimes the places they stayed in were equipped with a dishwasher and garbage disposal. Sometimes they had no refrigerator and the family fished damp, lukewarm packages of string cheese out of a cooler. Mostly they lived on cereal, yogurt, and sandwiches wherever they went, but the more modern appliances a place had, the more variety in their diet. Judith would never admit it to her mother, but she sometimes admired Lori—or at least, she owed her a grudging sort of respect. She was the true leader of the family, and throughout their changing circumstances, she had kept them all healthy and safe for a long time. A long time, but not forever . . .

"How does it look?" Judith asked, stepping to the doorway and surveying the cramped, shadowy room where her mother was now rummaging through a drawer with one hand and holding an array of utensils in the other—slotted spoons, a soup ladle, and a couple of metal spatulas. *We'll never use any of those,* thought Judith. This kitchen looked decidedly unpromising. She ducked back out through the low doorway and wandered through the other rooms, her eyes gliding over furniture that looked like it was standing at attention, plain metal bed frames, and the ubiquitous dark stone walls. In the living room her father was spreading out equipment across the seat of a stiff blue couch. As usual, the thick yellow pad he used for notes and his favorite pencil received as much tender care as the fragile camera he would use to put Guildwell Hall's records on microfilm.

Gabriel had chosen a bedroom with a tiny round window up near the ceiling—"like an eye," he explained—and Judith dug his bag out of the tangle of luggage in the hallway and pulled it in by his bed. The boy lay stretched out on the mattress, one arm behind his head, his eyes fastened on the small round patch of sky that seemed to hang on his wall like a picture. "I can't see any trees or anything," he murmured without looking at Judith, "just clouds." Judith knelt on the hard floor, still clutching the handle of Gabriel's bag. She felt suddenly too tired to move. One of Gabriel's hands rested idly at his side, close to Judith's face. In the gray light the narrow fingers appeared transparent, as insubstantial as mist, and Judith imagined that if she blew on them they would float away.

She was not angry at God because her brother was going to die. She was not even truly angry at her parents—at least, she couldn't blame them for what was happening. But she could blame them for bringing him here. They baffled her sometimes: what were they thinking? To lock him away in ancient stone, as if he were already sealed in a tomb! To let him waste away, becoming less real, less solid every moment while they pored over the names of people who had been dead for so long that nobody cared anymore. History, thought Judith with an inward scowl, had warped them. Maybe if you spent all your time reading about dead people, being alive didn't seem all that important.

Her hand trembled as she gripped the zipper on Gabriel's bag. She glanced at his face, and saw that his eyes were closed. He had fallen asleep during her silence. She stared at his chest, waiting for the slow rise and fall. He stirred slightly, his fingers moving on the blanket, and Judith relaxed. Her gaze roamed absently around the room and finally fixed on the window. *Not like an eye*, she thought. *Like something from a cartoon, when characters see holes around themselves and fall through the floor. Like a chunk from an iceberg that has broken off and is now drifting aimlessly at sea.*

She thought of the night last fall when her family had still been in Utah, her brother still in the hospital. She had gone to the church with her mother. It was Enrichment night, and the women of the ward were grouped around long tables in the cultural hall gluing dried flowers and sticks together. Judith had come to help in the kitchen, but now and then she wandered out, gliding ghostlike between the knots of women whose voices combined in a low hum. Once in a while a few words stood out distinctly.

As she passed a table near the door, she stopped. She had heard her mother's name.

"Lori," someone was saying, "is dealing with it so well. She has such a strong testimony."

"That last treatment didn't work then?" someone else asked.

"No, it's really final now."

"Oh, that must be so hard, especially after what she went through with Elijah."

"She'll get through, though. She's strong."

"What a great example to everyone of how to accept the Lord's will. To have that kind of faith—she makes me think of a pioneer mother, losing her children like that," the woman said as she stuck a dead pink flower onto her wreath with hot glue.

Judith eased out of the doorway and steered quickly back to the kitchen. She worked silently next to her mother, watching Lori slice

French bread and arrange cheese according to color, as if it were the most important thing in the world. A few days later Gabriel was home, gray and shrunken, and Judith's father had announced that they were spending the winter in England.

What bothered Judith about that night was the ordinariness of it. People talking about really awful things—about death—and all the while their faces were scrunched in concentration as they pondered what and where to glue next, as if a stupid decoration they would add to already perfect-looking kitchens deserved as much consideration as a dying child. They watched the cartoon saw, watched the hole being cut out of the floor, and instead of reaching out to grab the victim about to fall away into nothingness, they simply stood there and chatted. "It's a shame," they would say, shaking their heads and clicking their tongues, as the last piece of wood groaned and began to give way. "Oh, by the way, can I get your recipe for cottage cheese casserole before you go?"

Judith shook her head determinedly. She would not cry now. But she couldn't stop thinking about that night. What would she have wanted them to say, she wondered, if not what they had already said? What would she have wanted them to do? People had helped them, brought them dinners during those long cold evenings they spent camped out at the hospital. People had offered to do their laundry, wash their dishes, take over all those nagging, necessary chores that piled up whether your child was about to die of cancer or not. But all along Judith had really been waiting for them to . . . to acknowledge that things like this weren't supposed to happen, that her family had the right to be devastated. Instead everyone made it sound like a blessing. To listen to them, you'd think it was Thanksgiving and the Caseys had just won a free trip to Hawaii. "You should be grateful for this chance to prove your faith," they seemed to say. Didn't anyone understand that little boys weren't supposed to die?

"Judith." Her mother was standing in the doorway, and she sounded irritated. "Why aren't you unpacked? It's almost time for family home evening. Go get your bag, hurry up."

She had left it at the bottom of the stairs when she brought Gabriel up. Back down the spiral staircase, round and round too many times to count, and then back up to the dreary orange-lit rooms at the top. Flushed and warm from the climb, Judith spilled the contents of her bag onto a narrow bed in an unclaimed bedroom. She stared down at the pile of clothes, interspersed here and there with books, a toothbrush, an old photograph of the family on vacation in Ocean City. This pile was most of what Judith owned, and it didn't look like much when you threw it all together and stood staring down at it. "Travel light," her parents always said, and they didn't just mean on trips, but through life.

Judith tried not to let her parents notice, because they wouldn't approve, but she got attached to things. Like the pair of rainbow-plaid Keds she'd had a couple of years ago. She wore them until they had so many holes they looked like sandals. Lori was embarrassed to be seen with her when she had those shoes on. She kept telling Judith to go and get a new pair, and then one day Lori took matters into her own hands and threw the Keds into the Great Salt Lake. Judith laughed along with the others, but for weeks afterward, she felt a vague sense of disappointment every time she happened to glance down at her feet. She liked the comfort of familiarity, and there was never much of it around. Even the city her parents considered home was barely less foreign to Judith than the dozens of other places her parents' research had led them. But that old pair of Keds had seemed . . . friendly.

Well, now she had one thing, a single treasure that no one was allowed to throw away. She grasped the chain at her neck in a habitual, nearly unconscious gesture. The little roundish shape on the end felt cool in her hand. She believed the shape was meant to be a heart, but her father, who had given it to her, wasn't sure. "To be honest, honey, all I see there is a lump of metal—but it probably is supposed to be something, and if you see a heart in it, that must be what it is." He was giving it to her, he explained, because she would take better care of it than he or Lori would. That little lump of metal was a family heirloom; nobody knew how old it was, but it went back several generations at least. It was a piece of silver, somewhat tarnished, that had been worked into a shape and then pierced so it would go on a chain. Before Judith's father had it, it had belonged to her grandmother, who had received it as a wedding gift from her mother-in-law. "Traditionally, it goes to a bride when she marries into the Casey family," her father had told her. And she had studied his face for signs of sadness, because there would be no brides for the Casey sons. But he only looked a little preoccupied, as he always did, and then he said he had work to do.

Judith let go of the necklace and folded up the clothes on the bed. A few minutes later her mother's voice was calling to her from the living room.

"Judith, we're all waiting for you."

She went in and sat down on a wooden chair with a straw seat. Her parents faced her from the blue couch, and Gabriel was on the floor at their feet. Lori's hand rested on his shoulder. Judith noticed that her mother's fingernails were freshly painted—the polish was a pale spring green, the same color as the long-sleeved knit top her mother now wore. Judith studied Lori out of the corner of her eye, an unconscious frown tracing creases across Judith's forehead. How did Lori do it? She carried hardly any luggage and never seemed to spend any time on personal grooming, and yet she always looked so perfectly put together. Her hair seemed to stay put by the sheer force of her will. Not a strand would have dared fall out of place.

Judith's father offered the prayer, and then he picked up his triple combination. "When the angel Moroni appeared to Joseph Smith in the fall of 1823," he began, his voice warm and full and alive as it always was when he spoke of the past, "he quoted from the writings of the Old Testament prophet Malachi. I want to read some of that right now, even though I know the words are already familiar to us." He let the book fall open on his knee, and his eyes found the place automatically. "'Behold, I will reveal unto you the Priesthood, by the hand of Elijah the prophet, before the coming of the great and dreadful day of the Lord.'" He paused, made sure everyone's attention was focused on what he was about to say: "'And he shall plant in the hearts of the children the promises made to the fathers, and the hearts of the children shall turn to their fathers.'"

Judith knew the verse as well as anything—she had heard it all her life. It was more than a scripture—it was a theme, the purpose and direction of her family's existence. "Lori, Judith, Gabriel," her father continued, meeting each of their eyes, "the Lord has work for us to do. I believe He led us here, that this is where He would have us be." He stopped again, and looked down at the open book in his lap. When he looked up, his eyes shone with excitement. "In this place, we can learn about our fathers. I know we're going to find answers here. Nicholas Casey, the first Casey to come to the New World, attended school here as a young boy. If we can find his records, we can continue the chain, seal him to his parents and them to their parents. I'm also hoping we can discover the name of his wife."

He took a deep breath, and his voice trembled slightly under the weight of his emotion. "Children, in doing this work, we serve the Savior, and in a tiny way, we become like Him. We participate in the plan of redemption. We are taught that without us, our ancestors could not be saved . . . neither us without them. They look to us to help them secure the blessings of eternity."

In bed that night, shivering from a cold that seemed to seep through her body from somewhere in her bones, Judith considered her father's words. For a moment when he was speaking, she knew she had felt the Holy Ghost. She knew the work her father spoke about was important. But almost before the feelings of warmth and peace could envelop her, she had begun to diffuse them with confusion. Her father's comparison with the Savior bothered her. Christ's atonement was infinite; His mercy embraced anyone who would believe in Him and keep the commandments. But how did her father decide who was worth saving? Because he clearly had decided, long ago, who was important and who was not.

Never mind, tonight . . . she was more exhausted than she had realized. She lay in the darkness listening to the rushing sound of the wind and watching the waving shadows of bare tree branches blowing in the garden behind the hall. She was sinking into unconsciousness, already beginning to dream, when she saw something pale between the black forms of trees. It might not have been real, but the idea of it stayed with her through a series of twisted images that made her toss and turn in her sleep. It hadn't been anything that should have been in the garden. It wasn't snow or an animal, or moonlight reflected on water. It was a human face.

Chapter 2

It was 9:22 a.m. and Lori was hunched over the sink in the dreary kitchen. With no windows to let in the morning sunshine, the room was dimly lit—only two bare bulbs substituted for the sun, one in the middle of the room, over the table, the other above the sink. The artificial light gave Lori a strange, disoriented feeling, as if she were trapped inside a dream. Time seemed to have stalled in its linear progress and turned back upon itself—the whole shadowy scene, stuck in a night that went on and on, exuded an air of unreality. The dark walls, the ancient cabinets, the green linoleum might all dissolve before her in an instant.

But right now the chipped enamel sink felt pretty solid. If she examined it very closely, from just the right angle, she could make out thin traces of mildew snaking around the edges and joints of the faucet. She had already scoured the main part of the sink the night before, but now she attacked this mildew with a vengeance, an old toothbrush clenched tighter than necessary in her fist and the sleeves of her coral sweater rolled up past her elbows. Although the kitchen was cool she was sweating slightly; her jaw was clamped tight and her forehead creased with the effort. She was putting enough muscle into the work to scrape away the mildew and the enamel beneath it. As she paused to bat impatiently at a lock of hair, she heard her husband come in behind her. She tensed involuntarily. He eased himself into a chair, and she heard the crinkle of newspaper. For a long time he said nothing, but she knew what was coming. She scrubbed more slowly, listening to the rhythmic *whoosh, whoosh* of the bristles against the enamel.

"Lori." She didn't turn but kept scrubbing. "What is it? Just tell me." Still she didn't respond. He exhaled rather loudly, whether in exasperation or despair she didn't know. "If it's about coming here—well, I thought it's what you wanted, too. So if it's something else . . . " He paused, apparently waiting for her to fill in the gap. He still seemed to believe that if he simply asked her how she was feeling, she would tell him, though it had never worked in all these years.

The clock ticked away the silence. Lori worked as if she were alone, and imagining that wasn't difficult. But soon his voice intruded again into her private thoughts; he had decided on another approach. "If you hate these quarters, for example. We could do something about it. Or, if you don't like the schedule. Well, we don't have to be here the whole winter, you know. If you wanted to go somewhere else, that is. Or, if you don't like the shirt I'm wearing, I could change it." Lori smiled in spite of herself, because David was always a professor. He asked questions the way he wrote tests—some short answer, some multiple choice. He'd expect an essay before he was satisfied.

Why did he have to pry like this, she wondered. Was he so against having a mildew-free sink? Couldn't he let her work things out in her own way, as she always did? She stopped scrubbing and said, as casually as possible, "I don't know what you're talking about. I'm just trying to clean up this kitchen. It's a real mess, David. You never notice these things, but I do, and I won't have us a living in a filthy place."

He had been sitting at the table, but now his chair screeched and scraped across the linoleum as he rose and came to stand beside her. He peered down at the spot she had been scrubbing. "I have to be honest, dear, I've never seen a cleaner sink in my life."

"Well . . . you don't even have your glasses on."

"Lori—"

"Now, David, I know you don't care about cleanliness, but I do. I've got to get this mildew off."

She went back to work, and he watched her for a while, saying nothing. The only sounds were from the toothbrush and the two of them breathing, and Lori wondered how many moments of life went by in just this way—empty, waiting, used up by the most mundane actions of mortal existence. She wanted to scream, but she couldn't, so she scrubbed harder. If only David would move out of the way. But he was determined to keep digging at her, to keep drilling into her until she burst out. When at last his voice broke into the stillness, she could hear his resolve. "Lori, I know you're upset. You're angry. You may care about cleanliness, but you only clean with toothbrushes when there's something on your mind."

Lori was suddenly too tired for this. She knew how the whole conversation would go, as if they had already had it. They had had it, in fact, dozens of times—whenever Lori wasn't as chipper and bouncy as David wanted her to be and he took it upon himself to fix things. But there was no point now; she wouldn't stand for it today. She tossed the toothbrush into the sink, peeled off a pair of yellow rubber gloves, and stalked out of the room, flinging an explanation over her shoulder: "I'm going for a walk." As she steered down the hall toward the staircase, she smiled ironically to herself. *David Casey*, she thought, *absent-minded professor*. That's what she had expected when she married him. And she had wanted it that way, had wanted the space and the privacy that a marriage with him seemed to promise. All the other men she had dated tried to hold her too close. They asked too many questions: "*Why* can't you go out with me tonight?" They monopolized too much of her time, as if they really believed they could be the center and focus of her life. She didn't think David would be that way, and he wasn't. She remembered their first date: David arriving an hour late, nervous and flustered, because he had happened onto the very quote he needed for his thesis and had lost all track of time.

"I'm so sorry, Lori, really I'm just . . . so sorry," he had muttered as they stepped out her front door, and his hands kept moving from his pockets to his jacket front and back again, as if they couldn't figure out where to stop. And then, in desperation, he had blurted, "Are you a fan of Edwin Sandys? I mean, well, have you heard of him?"

Lori grinned and tilted her head to one side so she could see his face. This was one question no man had ever asked her before. "Edwin Sandys?" she repeated. She knew she had heard right, but she was savoring the moment. "You mean the head of the Virginia Company of London who kept shipping people into Jamestown Settlement? That Edwin Sandys? Well, I wouldn't actually say I'm a *fan*. I've read an article or two that has tried to vindicate him, though."

David was so surprised—and impressed—that he forgot to be nervous. He began to talk about the things he thought about most, things girls didn't usually want to hear about on a Friday night. But Lori was aiming for a Ph.D. in history, just like David, and she figured what he had to say might be worth listening to.

After that date Lori had made up her mind to marry him. She felt pretty confident that he would go along with the plan—it would save him ever having to go on a first date again. Not that she had been the one to propose. He had done that on his own. And, slowly, Lori had come to understand that he was more complicated than she had guessed. He wasn't like other men she had dated, but he wasn't absent-minded, either, at least not the way she had believed. It took him a while to notice things—if you came home with purple hair, he might not say anything for a few days. But when he did notice, he saw things for what they were. It had taken him a year or two to learn to read Lori's expressions and actions. Before that, she could retreat behind a solid wall whenever she tired of his company. After that, he saw through her. Their marriage had never been the same since, and she had never quite forgiven him for figuring her out.

Lori grabbed her coat from a hook in the hall and started down the spiral staircase. She wasn't sure where she was going, she only knew she needed fresh air. And she needed to be alone. From the outside door she turned left, heading into the back gardens. It had snowed the night before, and the grounds crew had shoveled off paths through the trees. Lori stepped onto one of the walkways but quickly veered off into the drifts and fought her way through, feeling the snow seep in through the tops of her shoes. She thrust her hands deep in her pockets and bit her lips together until she had hurled herself deep enough into a grove of white-laced trees to be hidden from the windows of the hall. Then she felt her anger explode out of her. "You promised me, you *promised* me!" she cried. She couldn't say anything else for a long time. Her fists shook in the air and her heart banged in her chest; the ferocity of her own emotion frightened her. Wrapping her arms around her body to steady herself, she gulped in air and struggled to regain control. After a few moments of silence she continued speaking, now in a tight, quiet voice. "Is this what you meant when you promised me another son? When you promised that my posterity would help spread the gospel? Is this a joke? Because, honestly, that's what it seems like to me. A cruel joke."

She reviewed the words of the blessing in her mind. No one had written them down for her, and it had been nearly six years since she had heard them—longer than Gabriel's whole life. But she knew them by heart. She had said them to herself so many times that they had become a sort of mantra, promising a peace and a power that extended beyond the meaning of the words themselves. "Lori, the Lord is aware of your sacrifice. He knows your suffering. . . . I bless you that you will have another son . . ." Standing there in the frozen, empty garden, Lori thought of her firstborn. Amazing, she reflected, how well she could remember tiny details: the smell of his baby shampoo as she bathed him, the slick feel of his soccer uniform as she scrubbed out the mud, the way the sunlight had glinted off his yellow hair when they got out of the car at the MTC. And she knew that one reason she remembered was because he *was* the first, and part of the thrill of motherhood had worn off by the time Judith came along. But more than that, Elijah had been . . . extraordinary.

If she had been a less confident person, she might have wondered what she had done to deserve him in the first place. Her mother had predicted that Lori would raise a family of troublemakers, but her prophecy had not proven true. Elijah was one of those children who rarely needed correction. Explain something to him once and he understood. Lori never worried about him running into the street or playing with the kitchen knives or drinking something toxic from under the sink. And when it came to the gospel, he seemed to know it was true from the time he was born, as if he'd managed to slip through the veil without letting it close all the way behind him. Sometimes, when he was a teenager, she would sit and watch him without letting him know it, and she would try to guess what his future held. Who would this boy turn out to be? What plans did his Father have for him? Was he a prophet waiting to grow up? She knew, without thinking about it much, that he was more deeply spiritual than either she or David and that, while he might have inherited his strength of will from her, his humility had come from somewhere else altogether. He was precious, the most perfect thing she could ever have given the world.

And now he was gone. No—she shouldn't think of it that way, as irrevocable. He still existed. He would be with them again someday, she knew that. But even in her most unselfish, most spiritual moments, she couldn't quite reconcile herself to this temporary separation. She couldn't make it seem right. Why did he have to leave so much undone? Sometimes, when her mind had no immediate problem to gnaw on, she would find herself listing all the experiences that Elijah would never have. Among other things, death had cheated him out of his homecoming. They'd already picked out the balloons. They'd painted a banner. His girl would have been at the airport with them. She had already flown in from Washington, where she was going to school. If Lori didn't stay focused on the here and now, these images would flood her: the girl's face, red paint dripping from the freshly formed letters, David standing in the hallway clutching the telephone. And she couldn't help it, she kept coming back to one question: WHY?

Lori never talked about these feelings, not even with David, though he probably guessed how she felt anyway. She knew people thought she was strong, stoic, even cold. It wasn't her way to blubber in front of a crowd the way other people did. What could it help to show everyone her vulnerability—her private heart? Her self-restraint was all she had to rely on. In those first few days after the mission president had phoned to tell them about the accident, she had promised herself she would not cry. She would hold onto her control, she *would not let go.* And gradually the pain had swelled up within her. It wasn't finite like physical pain; she could fall into it and never find the bottom. It was the fear of drowning that kept her going—if she stopped for one instant, she might sink forever. Her house, though generally neat, had never been so immaculate as it was in the season after Elijah's death.

One day David had offered to bless her. She hadn't asked for his help; she'd been pushing him away, as usual. But he bypassed her arguments, sat her down, and said maybe the only thing that could have pulled her out of her despair: that she would have another son. She hadn't known it, but she was already pregnant with Gabriel then. He wouldn't replace Elijah—he was a whole new hope, a new mystery to watch unfold. Now he was five-and-a-half years old, and he probably wouldn't make it to six. It was too much, too much.

"I don't get the punch-line," she shouted at the branches. "Is someone going to pop up and tell me this is all a big hoax?" She waded deeper into the trees and stood watching the little white clouds that were her breath—here and then gone. She felt calmer now, and she waited for the guilt to take over. "I'm sorry," she whispered, because she was beginning to feel it. "I know the verse, no one has to quote it to me. 'Thine afflictions shall be but a small moment . . . ' I know all about the value of adversity. I've read the Relief Society manuals. The scriptures. As an abstract concept, it all makes sense. Oh, Father, I'm sorry, but—it's my son." *And You did promise*, she thought. Though she was pushing it down now, the anger was still there. She began to walk slowly back toward the hall. She had had her say, and there was nothing else to do now but go back to work.

She was near the side door when she glanced off to the left. Several yards beyond the end of the building, between two trees, stood Judith. The girl was looking around as if she had lost something, though how she had managed to lose something in a tree on her first day here Lori couldn't fathom. How long had she been there? What had she heard? Lori strode off in Judith's direction, shouting in a voice that sounded more irritated than she intended,

"What are you doing out here? Where's Gabriel?"

Judith whirled around wearing a startled expression, but before she could answer, a thin voice piped up from somewhere deeper in the trees, "I'm here, Mother, and we're looking for ghosts. Only, I don't think they come out in the day." Lori caught sight of the small, bundled up figure moving slowly toward her through the snow. Gabriel had on so many clothes that he could barely move, but his face was not quite so ashen as usual and he looked happy. "And plus, everything out here is white," he explained, "so they'd be hard to see, anyway. I told Judith we weren't going to catch any. She thought maybe, though."

Lori turned a stern gaze on her daughter. "Ghosts, Judith? I hope you haven't been telling him any silly stories." Judith's face took on a familiar, closed-up look. She had on an old black peacoat that made a shocking contrast to her pale blond hair and light golden skin, and as she hovered there in the trees, eyeing her mother warily, she resembled nothing so much as a young deer on the verge of leaping away into shelter. Lori sighed. Judith was a puzzle to her—not in an exciting way, like Elijah. She was just outright confusing. She was so silent, so aloof, except when she opened her mouth to complain. She saw everything, and judged everything, and found it all lacking, without ever participating in life herself. She was too weak, always needing reassurance, always wanting to be held up. She was a thin little reed swaying in every breeze. Like yesterday, standing there in front of Guildwell Hall for the first time, and all she could say was, "It's old." Well, of course it was old, that was the point! Where did she think they would go to look at three-hundred-year-old records? Judith was seventeen years old; it was time for her to stop acting like a mewing kitten. Why didn't she appreciate her opportunities to travel? Why wasn't she interested in anything?

When Lori had been Judith's age, she had known well enough what she wanted. The only thing that stood in her way was her mother. Sometimes Lori imagined that she and her mother inhabited parallel realities—close enough that they could see each other, but never intersecting. Her mother believed certain things, expected certain things, and the funny thing was these beliefs seemed to work in her world. But in Lori's world, everything was different. Once, during her sophomore year of college, Lori had gone home for a visit, and among her mother's first fifty or so words of greeting were, "I pray every day that you'll meet that special man." Lori had fought down a wild impulse to laugh. *You can stop praying*, she had wanted to say. *It's pretty futile for now.* And suddenly angry words had formed themselves in her mouth almost before she could think to stop them. She bit her tongue, literally, and focused on the sharppain instead of on her mother's slightly anxious face. She went into the bedroom and began to unpack her bag, smoothing the clothes and making things neat. Her mother followed her into the room and lingered silently on the other side of the double bed. The cream-colored tricot spread gleamed like a gulf between them. But as Lori ordered her surroundings, her mind became more ordered too, and she knew she could speak to her mother without screaming.

"Mom, I appreciate your prayers. Really, I do." She sighed softly, thinking about Alma in the Book of Mormon, how his parents' prayers, their faith and righteousness, had helped save him. Her mother was in earnest; no doubt she was worried, no doubt she had thought about Alma herself, because if Lori was going in an unconventional direction, it surely couldn't be the right one. Lori glanced back at her mother, caught between anger and laughter. Ridiculous, all this trouble over dating! But it was time to make her case. "I don't want to get married yet, though. Even if there were anyone remotely interesting around, which I assure you there isn't. What I really want to do is go on a mission."

Her mother's eyebrows drew together, and she tilted an ear toward Lori. She didn't think she had heard right. "What? What did you say?"

"I want to go on a mission."

She considered this for a moment. "Lori, you don't need to do that. Now, dear, I know you haven't been dating anyone really special this year, but that's no reason to give up hope. Even if you think there isn't anyone interesting around. Well, these things can happen so fast. He'll come along before you know it." She came around the bed and patted her daughter's arm reassuringly.

Lori rolled her eyes toward the ceiling in a plea for patience. "Mom, I'm not saying this because I'm afraid I won't get married. It isn't like I don't have anything to do with my time until I get a husband. School is probably easier single, and I have a long way to go. I really want to go on a mission. I've wanted to for a long time. This doesn't have anything to do with whether or not I've been dating, or who I've been dating, or how 'special' they are."

"But Lori, missions are for young men."

"There are lots of sister missionaries, more all the time."

"Yes, but . . ." her mother wanted to say something but didn't know how to say it. She couldn't keep it from sounding just a little bit cruel. "You know the kind of women who go on missions—they're not like you."

"What do you mean?"

"You know."

"No, you'll have to spell it out."

Her mother looked pained. "They're not . . . well, the truth is, they're not pretty."

"What?"

"They're women who have a hard time getting husbands. They aren't good-looking or stylish. Lori, you're not like that; you're beautiful—don't sell yourself short."

Lori had started a mental list of all the things her mother did that she would never do to her children. Most of all, she promised herself, she would never try to run her children's lives. She would encourage them to think for themselves. She would let them become whoever they were meant to become instead of trying to force them into some ideal she had for their futures. But the trouble with Judith—the really incomprehensible thing about her—was that she didn't seem to want to be left on her own. Sometimes Lori wanted to shake her and scream, "Go out into the world! Go do something!" She didn't say that now. She only said, "Don't keep

Gabriel in the cold too long," and then she turned her back and retraced her steps to the hall. Did she imagine it, or did Judith really murmur behind her, "I'm surprised you would care"?

Inside the main doors of the hall a very old woman sat at a huge desk in front of a sign reading: "Gooding-How Historical Society Archives, Guildwell Hall." She eyed Lori suspiciously and took a long time examining her ID. First she inspected it with her glasses on, then with them off, then on again. Lori leaned one arm on the desk and drummed her fingers impatiently on the wood until the woman shot her a silent reprimand. *These archivists are all the same*, Lori thought, *they really don't want anyone else looking at this stuff. They'd keep everyone out if they could.* Finally the woman acknowledged, "Your husband is already here working. I've set him up in a back room." She led Lori down a short hallway into an open space filled with row after row of shelving. Lori sensed the familiar smells of dust, mold, and old paper, and she could *hear* the silence. It always happened when she immersed herself in old records: the quiet was no longer a lack of sound, but an anticipation of it. There were voices buried beneath—listen close enough, and you might hear them whispering. She followed the woman across the room to the opposite wall, where an open door led into a small workroom with a desk and chair. "If you'll make yourself comfortable here, I'll bring you one of the records. Your husband is filming the first book—would you like to look at the second one?"

"What dates does it cover?"

"It begins around Easter, 1645."

"All right then, that will be fine." Lori took a seat at the desk and waited, listening to the muffled sound of the woman's shoes. *She must wear pads on the soles to keep them from tapping*, Lori thought. After a moment the footsteps returned.

"Here it is, then, and you may use this so you don't have to touch the pages." She handed Lori a scrap of purple velvet. "The oil from your fingers, you know." She went out and closed the door, leaving Lori alone with the remains of fifty or so years of the building's history. She began to turn pages, reading names, skimming bits here and there. When she reached a page headed "Dyed this yeare, in the Sick Ward," she stopped. "Dead from a fall," she read, "from the measles," "from a feaver," "dyed this day of the Dropsy." Line after line they went on. It was just a list of names, it was just ink on paper. Nobody mourned for these children any more—maybe nobody mourned them even then. And because they were so distant, and their pain could never really hurt her, she spared them two tears. The drops made splotches on the yellowed pages. The archivist would not have approved.

Chapter 3

Judith scooped up a handful of snow and began patting it to pack it down. "Ghosts? You told her we were looking for ghosts?" She tossed the snowball at Gabriel's feet and poked gently at his arm, which she couldn't feel beneath his laye rs of clothing.

"Well, aren't we?" Gabriel retorted. He leaned back against a tree and tilted his head up, mouth open, to catch the bits of snow shaken off by his movement. Judith smiled as she watched him. It reminded her of another winter day—it must have been two years ago now—when they had climbed up into the hills to celebrate the first snow of the season. They were two dots of color in a vast field of white as they rolled giant snowballs and stacked them up, one by one, until they towered six feet high. A carrot, two bits of coal, and Lori's red scarf, and the snow became a man with dark, winking eyes. A wind had sprung up, stiff and sharp, and the scarf billowed out merrily. They were all alone in the world. The only noise was from Gabriel whooping, and the wind caught at the sound and carried it up, up, past the hills that surrounded them on three sides, and flung it against the steep slopes of the mountains. They danced about, skidding and tumbling in the deep, soft snow, and the prints of their feet and bodies traced wild patterns across the hillside. The cold air moved cleanly in and out of Judith's lungs as she ran. It was one of those memories that belonged to the Before.

Funny how that worked. You'd think the past couldn't change, but it did. Or at least the memories did, once you knew what everything had been leading up to. Images of the Before got shot through with an orange glow; they grew extra glossy, but with fuzzy edges—like scenes from an old home movie. You watch the movie and you already know the ending, and the carefree smiles are sadder than tears. You didn't know it then, but you were hurtling toward this event that would change your life forever. You were stuck on a speeding train all along, plunging ahead toward this moment, and there was no way off. Even on that winter day . . . on that day, the cancer was there inside, silently growing.

Today Gabriel couldn't dance about. Just staying alive tired him. Studying him as he leaned there against that tree, Judith thought she could *s e e* the energy leaking out of him in a constant stream. It was sort of like bleeding to death, only slower. She would have to take him in now.

"I didn't bring us out here to go ghost-hunting," she told him.

"But you said—"

"Never mind. I only said I saw *something*. I don't know what it was. I probably just dreamed it anyway."

"Yeah. This place makes funny dreams." He frowned up at the looming stone walls.

"Did it give you bad dreams?" Judith asked as she wrapped an arm around his waist and began to tug him toward the side door.

"I don't know. Nothing about ghosts. Just a boy."

"What boy?"

"I don't know. He didn't tell me his name."

Upstairs Judith helped Gabriel out of his clothes. It took a long time because they had to stop and rest between layers. Exhaustion had overwhelmed him, and when Judith got him down to his sweat-shirt and jeans, he lay still and quiet on the bed. She covered him up and rubbed his back until he fell asleep.

In her own room a stack of schoolwork awaited her. She had been home-schooled most of her life because her parents never stayed in Utah—or anywhere else—for an entire school year. She remembered being maybe four years old, on a plane, with Lori holding up a drawing of two men in jester costumes forming the letter A. "What sound does this letter make, Judith?" And in the next breath, "Who wrote the Declaration of Independence?" "What words start with the letter E?" (This drawing involved three jesters.) "Let's name the thirteen original colonies." David and Lori had owned a house in Salt Lake City for almost twenty years, ever since they both got teaching positions in the history department at the University of Utah, but the house, in Judith's opinion, had no idea who its owners were. "It thinks it's orphaned," she told her mother the year she was seven. "Houses don't have feelings," said Lori. "I think it liked the renters better than us, and it's sad they're gone and we're back," Judith said the year she was twelve. "Houses don't have feelings," said Lori. Once, they did stay at the house for ten months straight. That was the year Judith was fourteen.

They'd just returned from a whole year away. David had taught in Germany as part of a teacher exchange in the fall, and Lori had been invited to England as a visiting scholar for the winter and spring. They could have split up and done it all in one semester, but that was unprecedented. They were a team. So Lori began microfilming records for the Church while she waited for David's Germany assignment to be up, and the next semester David microfilmed in England. The extra funding helped out. "You don't get rich as a scholar," David had explained to Judith once. "Except in ways that don't count with the bank." They spent the summer in Rhode Island, poking around archives for some reason or other, and came back to Salt Lake at the beginning of September. The house was empty and echoing. There were crayon marks on one of the walls of Judith's room where the tenants' child had expressed her creativity. The marks looked ugly and out of place now, or maybe it was Judith who was out of place.

One night she was in the kitchen helping Lori make dinner. The two of them took turns microwaving canned veggies and chicken nuggets. Lori was taking out a dish of peas when she asked suddenly, "How would you feel about going to public school this year?"

Judith had never thought much about it before, so she didn't answer right away. It seemed sort of exotic, like something only people on TV did. Of course, the other girls in the ward went to school, but she didn't know them very well, just their names, mostly. "I guess it would be all right."

Lori began talking fast. "You know I have serious reservations about the state of public education. The whole ideology is wrong, the method, everything. I mean, just look at the students coming into college now. All they have to go on is natural talent. The system needs a major overhaul." She paused and met Judith's eyes. "But there may be something you can learn from it."

So Judith went to the high school on Grant Avenue: "Home of the Wildcats," it said. She learned a few things quickly, and one was that her teachers had certain expectations of her that had nothing to do with her actual abilities. They just assumed that the daughter of two prolific historians would naturally be a top student, and some of them graded her accordingly. It showed on essay questions: if Judith's answer didn't quite match what they wanted, they gave her credit for thinking outside the box. Leave it to her to discover a more profound meaning. Judith tried a few times to make things right: "Mrs. Thomas, if you'd just look at this again, I'm pretty sure I shouldn't get full points." But that didn't really change anything, because then they were so impressed by her honesty that they saw her as being almost infallible.

It didn't work that way with everyone. Her geometry teacher had expectations of her, too, but he grew more disappointed as the year went on. It was harder to justify an answer that was mathematically impossible. At the end of the first term Judith brought home a report card with a B minus. She worried all through dinner about what her parents would say. What were *their* expectations? She wasn't sure, but it seemed quite possible that they included straight A's. After all, her parents had played Mozart for her from the time she was a baby—she had to develop into a genius, right?

But—"Oh, fine," Lori said when Judith asked her to sign the report card. "But you haven't told us yet if you've made up your mind what clubs to join."

By Christmas Judith had figured it out. This was basically a social exercise, and the "something" Lori meant for her to learn didn't involve academics. Knowing what her parents wanted put an end to her guessing game, but it didn't necessarily make things easier. If she was supposed to understand how to fit in, they might have to give her a lot more time. So far she felt like an anthropologist recently deposited in the midst of an alien tribe. Almost everyone acted according to rules she didn't comprehend; they were caught up in a complex social dance, and she kept tripping. There were a lot of people she liked, people she might chat with before class or on the way to lunch, but only one or two girls she ever spent time with outside of school. She heard the same appraisal of herself several times—"stuck up"—and what hurt was that it came from people who had never bothered to meet her. She also heard that people thought she was pretty. It was a new thing to think about herself, since she had always felt like the ugly duckling next to Lori, but it didn't really make her feel much better. Both judgments were based on what she looked like from across the room, and neither one had anything to do with what she said or did or thought. But everyone had a label. It didn't take long to learn that.

In January she tried out for the swim team and set a pool record. She loved swimming: she loved the silence of it. When you were in the water, you were in a separate world. Even when you could hear people cheering you on, it seemed far away, coming at you muffled through all the water in your ears. It was you and the clock and the water, all alone. At the regional competition in May she won a medal, and her parents cheered and snapped photographs and took her out for pizza. After that they must have decided she had gotten what she could from public school, because in June they told her they were going to Virginia in the fall.

When she told one of her friends from the swim team, the girl was mutinous. "They can't make you do that! Maybe it was OK when you were younger, but this is high school. Tell them you're not going."

"I don't think I have a choice," Judith protested. "My parents would never stay in one place for four years. I think it's physically impossible."

"They don't have to stay," the girl insisted. "You could live at my house, or with anyone on the swim team. We need you! And lots of people have extra rooms."

Judith suggested it to her parents only to receive an "absolutely not!" response. She considered pressing the matter, but then she thought about Gabriel. She had taken care of him more than Lori had ever since he was a baby. She didn't think she could stand to be away from him for nine months at a time. So the issue was dropped, and Judith had never gone back to public school, and now she was almost ready for college.

She picked up a paper from the top of the stack of schoolwork and flopped down on the bed. "A History of Disciples of Christ Schoole," she read. She rolled her eyes—there was no one to see her, so what did it matter? She knew Lori considered this a special treat, to get to read the history while sitting in the old school itself. The thought that her mother had planned it out for ultimate effect annoyed her, and what annoyed her even more was that she would probably fall for it.

"Founded by the London city fathers in 1604," it said, "Disciples of Christ Schoole served as a refuge for 'the innocent poor,' children whose parents were either dead or unable to provide for them. Students were taught reading and writing and a few other basic subjects, then apprenticed out to a reputable master who would teach them a trade and make it possible for them to get a good start in life. Contributions from the local parishes, as well as funding from private donors, provided the resources to feed and clothe the children.

"Throughout the first century of its operation, the school rarely enrolled more than 100 children at a time. Under the leadership of Samuel Chadwicke, the school's fifteenth headmaster, however, the effort was greatly expanded, with enrollments swelling to a height of 1115 students in 1709. It was during Chadwicke's administration that the school took up quarters in Guildwell Hall, whose large rooms and spacious grounds made such expansion possible.

"Chadwicke's successors apparently lacked his enthusiasm for the school's mission, and enrollments fell sharply after his death in 1725. A scarcity of funds forced the school to close in 1804. Guildwell Hall was used for a number of purposes in the following years: it served as a hospital several times throughout the nineteenth century and again during World War I. In 1923, the Hall was purchased by the Gooding-How Historical Society and converted into a library housing one of London's most impressive collections of archives. A small suite of rooms on the top floor, once occupied by the headmaster's family, is now available as a guest quarters for researchers whose work brings them to the archives for an extended period of time."

It was that last sentence that sunk deep. Judith reached out and pressed her hand against the wall. It felt cold and rough beneath her palm. Who else had touched it? If she pressed long enough and hard enough, could she draw out the warmth of other hands that had lain against this stone? She laughed suddenly—it was a stupid thought. But her gaze flicked involuntarily to the window, to the spot in the garden where that pale face had shone out from the shadows. Gabriel was right—this place made funny dreams. And then she scowled to herself for being influenced by something her mother had left for her. She tossed the paper aside and resolutely opened her calculus textbook.

At dinner that night everyone seemed strangely quiet. The silverware clinked noisily in the long minutes of silence. Of course, it may have been because of the concentration required to chew up the soggy fish sticks and swallow them without gagging. It *did* take effort. When Judith finally downed the last one on her plate, Lori glanced over and asked, "Would you like more?"

Judith held up her hands, palms out, in a gesture of protest. "No thanks, I'm stuffed." She imagined for a moment that her father was staring at her intently, but with the light reflected in his glasses, she couldn't be sure. He may have been gazing absently at some indistinct spot above her head, and that would be nothing unusual. "Did you get things straightened out with the gardener this morning?" Judith inquired into the silence, and she was unprepared for the way her mother's head snapped in her direction.

"What?" Lori gulped. "What are you talking about?"

Judith took a breath. This was the kind of thing that made her nervous. *Subtexts*—maybe that's what her English teacher would call it. Subtexts at work here, and Judith was oblivious.

"I just wondered if everything went OK today. I heard you yelling in the garden this morning, and I just thought maybe the gardener did something stupid and you were explaining what's what." No one spoke. Her father continued to stare in her direction.

Finally David questioned in a low voice, "Yes, sweetheart, what *did* you say to the gardener this morning?"

"Let Judith tell you," Lori answered shortly. The two of them had been looking at Judith all along. She didn't know what they wanted. She shrugged.

"I didn't hear what she was saying," she told them. "I just heard her voice." She pushed her chair back and stood up. Usually she would ask to be excused, but not tonight. She made a beeline for her bedroom and shut the door behind her. Safe in her own space, she pulled out *Macbeth* and began to read.

Several hours later she heard a knock. It was her father. He came in and perched uneasily on the edge of the bed, took his glasses off, and began to clean them with a shirttail. "That looks stupid," Lori had complained before. "It works," he had answered.

"Judith," he began quietly, not looking at her, "did you talk to your mother this morning?"

"A little."

"What did she say?"

"The usual." Judith gave an exaggerated imitation of her mother's voice. "'I hope you're not being dumb, Judith. You should know better, Judith.'"

"Did you see her talking to the gardener?"

"No," she said.

"Did you see a gardener out there?"

"No."

David finished wiping the glasses and put them back on. Now he turned to face her. *Almost as if,* thought Judith, *he doesn't want to look at things without having the glass between.* Even close-up things that he could see without help. "But you heard her yelling at someone?"

"I thought I did," she admitted, but hesitantly.

"What did she say?"

"I told you before, I didn't hear. I just assumed she was telling someone off."

"Hmmm." David sat farther back on the bed and folded his arms across his chest. He seemed to change the subject abruptly. "How well do you remember your brother Elijah?"

Judith's brow furrowed in confusion. "Not that well," she said. She had been eleven years old when Elijah died, but he had left home long before. First there had been a year-long study abroad in Australia, then two years at an English boarding school, then Oxford. He hadn't visited them all that much, even when they were in England. He was busy, her parents told her. He couldn't spare a day's round-trip travel. She remembered seeing him off at the MTC, and he had seemed very tall and very grown up, and she had felt more than a little shy of him. "Be good, Judy," he had said when he got through hugging Lori and David. He tugged playfully at her ear and then walked away. He was the only person in the world who had ever called her Judy.

David was speaking again. "It may seem like a long time ago to you that he died, but not so much to us, do you understand? Because you're young. It's been more than a third of your life. But for us, six years is hardly anything."

"What exactly are you trying to say?"

"You don't know how your mother feels—"

"No, and she makes sure of that," Judith interrupted. "If you mean to say she's sad or something, she does a good job of hiding it. And she wouldn't want you to go telling on her either." The hardness in her voice surprised her. She didn't usually speak to her father this way, but she was frustrated. She watched him go, still feeling a tenseness in her body, wanting to burst out with all the things she believed about her mother. After he had closed the door behind him, she reached for her Book of Mormon and opened it to 2 Nephi, hoping it would calm her down. *"O wretched man that I am! Yea, my heart sorroweth because of my flesh; my soul grieveth because of mine iniquities. I am encompassed about, because of the temptations and the sins which do so easily beset me. And when I desire to rejoice, my heart groaneth because of my sins; nevertheless, I know in whom I have trusted."* Judith had read that as a young girl and thought, "If *he* does things wrong, if he's worried about forgiveness, what chance do *I* have?" But she saw it differently now, as a mixture of courage and tenderness, humility and faith. Nephi was brave, she reflected, much braver than Lori, who would never confess to anyone that she had faults. Everyone said her mother was strong, but maybe they couldn't tell the difference. Maybe Lori wasn't strong at all, just unfeeling. Maybe she really didn't care.

It was late. Judith undressed quickly and snuggled down beneath the covers. *"He hath filled me with his love, even unto the consuming of my flesh."* She imagined warmth spreading through her, banishing the cold that lurked inside and out. She seemed to be floating, drifting, spiraling. She opened her eyes and found herself standing in the garden.

She knew she was dreaming this time, but the dream was so clear that she could feel tiny puffs of air against her arm as a breeze blew by, and she could trace the intricate shadow patterns cast by the spindly trees. The moon was out, and the snow-covered garden was light enough to read in. A boy about her own age stood across from her. He wore an odd assortment of clothing, with pants made from a very course material, boots with cracks in the sides, and a jacket and shirt made from something almost as course as the pants. He had very clear green eyes, and they were focused on Judith's face.

"Do you know my name?" he asked, stretching out a hand entreatingly.

"No," Judith replied. "Should I?"

"No, of course not," he sighed, looking very disappointed nevertheless. "There are so many."

He caught sight of the silver heart dangling against the neck of her pajamas and took a quick step toward her. She clutched at the heart protectively.

"Where did you get that?" he wanted to know.

She surveyed him warily. Should she pinch herself now, and be back in her bed? She noticed vaguely that the shadows of the trees didn't fall across his face. "It's been in my family a long time. Longer than anyone remembers."

His face took on a visible glow. He smiled at her. "Then you are the ones," he declared.

"What ones?"

"The ones he told me about."

"Who told you?"

"The missionary. You are the ones I've been waiting for."

Chapter 4

When David Casey exited his daughter's room, he hesitated a moment before turning left and walking the few steps down the narrow passage to the room he shared with Lori. His wife was seated on top of the bed covers with her back against the wall and her legs stretched across the mattress. She had opened a bottle of mauve nail polish and was applying it with great attention and precision, with very quick but very neat strokes. She didn't look up when he came in, and he stood for several moments in the doorway staring at her without receiving the least acknowledgment. He took the opportunity to study her face, to watch her movement without interruption or reproach. She would turn fifty-one in the spring, and he couldn't help but be amazed when he thought of it. He was amazed at his own age, also—fifty-three in June—but for a different reason. Somehow, his inner picture of himself had failed to keep up with the passage of time. It had gotten stuck somewhere back in his early thirties and had never changed much since. He was vaguely surprised whenever he caught sight of his own reflection: who was that old, gray-haired man? He looked his age, to the world if not to himself.

But Lori, fifty-one? No one would have believed it. She had been a beauty for as long as David had known her, and probably for her whole life, and her softness, her luminescence, seemed outside the laws of time. She had very fine, delicate features, beautifully defined; large green eyes, lush as a rain forest and lined by lashes two or three shades darker than her hair. Whether she now colored that hair at all, or whether its dark gold shade had yet to give way to gray, David couldn't be sure. But he thought as he contemplated her that she still resembled a porcelain doll, just as she had when he first met her.

She must have hated her looks at times. She was so determined, obstinate even, and so obsessed with making everyone believe she was strong. But her face, her petite figure, belied her personality and gave everything that she said and did a certain softness. Who could gaze into that sweet countenance and believe her capable of anything harsh? Even David, who must now know her best in all the world, could not overcome a desire to shelter her, wrap her up in a fluffy blanket and hold her close, protect her from exposure to anything on earth that could possibly prove unpleasant.

He took a step across the room and eased down beside her on the bed, careful not to jolt her into making a mistake on her fingers. He laid a hand gently on her shoulder. He could tell from the speed of her strokes and the undivided attention she had fixed on her task that the tension and anger he had perceived in her still smoldered beneath the surface. What could he say to her that he had not already said? Twenty-eight years of marriage seemed to offer him no more answers. He had come to the end of his ideas. They had now lived together for six years without mentioning to each other the name of their older son; they may live for many more years without mentioning Gabriel. Whose fault was it? He had blamed Lori for a long time. If she had been brave enough to face the intensity of her own feelings, they might have found comfort in each other. But maybe it was as much his fault for growing weary of the effort it took to try to be close to her. He had had two great loves in his life, and when the second one disappointed him, he sought solace in the first.

He had known from the time he was born that he wanted to study history. At least, he couldn't remember ever consciously deciding on it, so the idea must have come into the world with him. He loved everything about the past, and the people in it were alive to him—they were better company, sometimes, than people in the present. He had never been popular. He wasn't good at relating to people on a superficial level, which meant that he rarely had a chance to relate to anyone more deeply. He was bad at small talk. He was bad at details of social ritual. He couldn't remember names until he had heard them seven or eight times.

"How can you remember every date of every battle of the Revolutionary War, which has nothing at all to do with anything and is completely useless information, but you can't remember the name of the girl who sits next to you in math class?" his father had wondered once, asking more of the universe in general than of his son, so great was his bafflement.

"I don't know every date of every battle in the Revolutionary War," David protested. "There's a lot more to history than that, you know."

"All I mean is, couldn't you find some place in your brain to keep that girl's name long enough to ask her to the dance?"

"But, Dad, I'm not sure it's a good idea anyway. You know she won't want to go."

"Not true. Girls always want to go to dances. It gives them an excuse to go shopping."

"I didn't mean she won't want to go to the dance. I mean she won't want to go with me."

His father tried vainly to protest, but since underneath he agreed with David, he wasn't very convincing.

Lori was the first girl David had ever gone out with more than once. He was so amazed when she accepted a second date that he took a step back and ended up falling down her porch steps. "Is there any chance you could overlook what just happened?" he called up to her when he had steadied his balance. She smiled sweetly and said, "I'll see you next Saturday."

He would never have dared imagine that someone like Lori could want to be with him. He would never have asked her out himself—it had been his friend's doing, and he had been told about it only after Lori had accepted. It wasn't exactly a blind date, because David had noticed her before at the university, but whether she had seen him before he never knew. He only knew that when she regarded him with those green eyes, when those eyes smiled on *him*, and no one else, he believed himself the recipient of such a high honor that every potential future accomplishment—Ph.D., Nobel Peace

Prize, whatever—appeared insignificant in comparison.

The night before their wedding he had been seized with an acute case of anxiety. What was he about to do? Could he ever make her happy? Whatever delusion she was under, she must soon find out that he was just plain old David Casey, and not the man of her dreams. He went to her and held her. "I have nothing to give you," he whispered. "And you deserve to be treated like a queen."

She smiled her sweet, otherworldly smile. "I don't need you to give me anything," she assured him. He didn't understand what she meant then. He thought she intended to soothe him—probably she did, but she also spoke truth. She didn't need him. She didn't need anything he had to give.

Tonight was no different; she was guarding every crack in her fortress. He left her side abruptly without saying anything and wandered out to the kitchen. He began rummaging through the cupboards for a snack but was too distracted to focus on the search, so he sat down at the table instead. From there he could see across the hallway to the three closed doors that shielded his family from view. How had he come to be here? The now familiar feeling of confused dissatisfaction spread out from his stomach into his chest and throat, making his breathing uneasy. In the past year or so he had experienced several moments like this, moments of complete stupefaction at the present state of his life. How had things progressed to this point? Somewhere along the line he had grown complacent or inattentive, and now he awoke to see everything off course and himself trying too late to right it. The first time he had felt that way, he had been in the middle of a conference. Gabriel's cancer had been recently diagnosed, but he had gone off to Michigan anyway to intellectualize about eighteenth-century power and patriarchalism. He was on the stand expounding upon the dynamics of the family in early Massachusetts when he had suddenly been struck with such a strong sense of disorientation that he stopped midsentence and clutched at the podium for support. He stared out over an audience of strangers while his stomach lurched dangerously. *My son is going to die*, he thought incredulously. *My son is going to die, and my other son is already dead, and I don't know my daughter. What am I doing here?* He didn't know how long his silence had lasted. Too long for people's comfort, at least. They had shifted restlessly, murmured questions, fanned themselves nervously with the pages of their programs. Somehow he concluded his remarks and sat down without inviting questions. When he got home Lori asked him, "How was the conference?"

"Fine," he told her. "Just fine. Only I . . . " But she had already turned away from him and was no longer paying attention.

David hid his head in his hands. What was there to be done? Nothing, nothing at all, the doctor had informed him. It had been an uncommonly cold night for October, and even from inside the hospital he could hear the wind shrieking around the buildings.

"What if we go back to that specialist? We can pack up and go right away."

"I'm sorry," repeated Dr. Finch, "but he'll just tell you the same thing."

David stood there marveling at his own powerlessness. *You never realize it until something like this happens,* he thought. *You think as an adult you can take care of things. As a parent, you think your judgment means something. But you're always on the edge of disaster.*

He went to the pay phones and called his home teaching companion. "I want to give him another blessing," he explained. Brother Drury was sympathetic. In a few minutes he was at the hospital, dressed in his suit and carrying a vial of consecrated oil. They had done this already a few weeks ago, back when there was still a shred of hope. They went quietly into Gabriel's room and positioned themselves on either side of the bed. The child between them was unrecognizable—just his own shadow. David laid his hands on Gabriel's head and waited for words of healing. "You'll get well," he ached to promise. "You will run and jump with your friends. You will serve a mission and marry in the temple." He fought and fought with the Spirit. Finally he took his hands away.

"Brother Casey?" whispered Brother Drury.

Tears were streaming down David's face. "I can't do it," he whimpered, sounding almost like a small child himself. "You'll have to say it."

Brother Drury prayed for all the Caseys to be filled with peace. "You know what that means," Judith had said once when someone in sacrament meeting had given a similar prayer about a sick member. "She's going to die."

Now, sitting there in that quiet kitchen, David let out a long sigh, trying to cleanse the feeling from his chest. He seemed to have two options. He could go to bed and lay next to his wife in the dark, close to her but separated by a barrier she would never allow him to cross. Or he could go over the notes he had taken today in the archives. He went into the next room to retrieve his yellow notepad. It was nearly dawn before he went in to bed.

Chapter 5

At breakfast the next morning, Judith and her parents sat around the table in the gloomy kitchen eating cereal with evaporated milk. This meal, like the one the night before, began in silence, but now Judith was as preoccupied as anyone else. Whenever she blinked, she saw a pale face plastered on her eyelids. The boy in the garden had stretched out his hand as if he wanted something from her. She had nothing to give him. She would have told him that, if she had had the chance to. But she didn't know what had happened after his startling declaration. She must have fallen into deeper sleep.

"Judith," called Lori suddenly. "Did you read everything I left for you yesterday?"

Judith took her time answering. She stirred her cereal slowly, trying to transition into this morning's reality. "Yes," she finally responded, examining a corn flake with the vague intention of figuring out what made it taste so different from an American one.

"Good. I was afraid you wasted all your time standing around under trees looking for ghosts. Well, let's see if you remember what you read. When was this school founded?"

Judith glanced up from her cereal. "The year 1604," she answered smartly. The promptness and precision of her reply surprised herself almost as much as it did Lori.

"Yes," continued her mother when she had recovered from the shock, "but how many students did it enroll at its peak?"

"About a thousand."

Lori appeared half impressed, half disappointed in this missed opportunity for criticism. She narrowed her eyes and cast about for a more difficult question. "And what was its purpose?"

"I haven't the faintest idea." Judith took a bite of corn flakes and chewed thoughtfully. "Here's a question, though. You know how everyone back then was named John, William, or Henry? How can they ever be told apart? It seems like the spirit world must be awfully confusing, and we should be encouraged to pick unique names for our kids so as not to add to it."

Lori rolled her eyes. "Judith, when you have kids, their names will be the least of their problems."

Judith thought that was a little harsh. After a few moments of unbroken silence, she snapped, "Why don't you ask me something about calculus? Why don't you ever test me on that over breakfast?"

"Ah, because we are not training you to be a mathematician," David chimed in from the other end of the table. "Learn to integrate an equation, if you will, but that stuff's all for show." He grinned from his wife to his daughter.

"Ugh," said Judith. She stared down at her corn flakes, peering up furtively now and then. This morning's test seemed to be over. Lori had lost interest. She would look at Judith's written work later, but even then she wouldn't spend much time assessing Judith's calculus assignment. What David said about math being just for show may have been a joke, but the truth was neither of them really cared about it. And that's why Judith wished she could excel at it. She had this fantasy of majoring in math and then landing some important and spectacularly complex job doing . . . whatever it was that math majors took jobs doing. She would turn away from everything that her parents loved, and while they locked themselves up with moldy records, she would pursue something they had no talent for. It seemed poetic, somehow.

She wanted to show them. To shock them, frustrate them. Lately she found herself wondering why she had tried so hard all her life to please them. She had always worked to figure out what they wanted and keep the peace. But after all, maybe she needn't have bothered, for what difference would it make in the end? Maybe she had spent all this effort trying to build something that wouldn't last, anyway. Since Gabriel's prognosis had become so bleak, she had avoided thinking about the future, but she knew next year everything would be different. She would be at college, living a life like nothing she had ever experienced before. She would be settled in one place for four years, she would interact with people outside her family and not have to say good-bye to them when two months of research came to an end. Meanwhile, David and Lori would keep roaming the earth. What would they talk about with each other? With no children to feed or school to criticize, maybe they would never stop their research long enough to say anything at all. Would they keep in touch with Judith? She didn't know. But she felt that whatever glued them together as a family was too fragile to last, and if they met four years from now, they would be little more than strangers.

And yet, they had spent more time together than most families. With their lifestyle, they had no choice. Their constant movement ensured that they had few ties outside the home. How could they have lived so long together, with hardly anyone else to talk to, and not know each other? Judith thought of all the years of family home evenings, the picture of the Salt Lake temple that David carried in his wallet and would show around while they sang "Families Can Be Together Forever." It was one of his favorite songs, and they'd sung it thousands of times.

Well, the test was now. Maybe there was still time for them to love each other before they drifted too far apart. Judith looked up from the soggy corn flakes. She could see a gray hair glinting among Lori's golden curls. *So she* is *mortal.* "Mom," said Judith softly. She got out of her chair and went to stand beside Lori. She wanted to put her arms around her, but she was too afraid. It was awkward. What was she doing? "Judith, I can't see. You're blocking the light." Judith sat back down.

That afternoon she went in to Gabriel's room and helped him bundle up again. "We need fresh air every day," she explained as she pulled a sweater over his head. "Otherwise, we'd wilt." The air inside the hall seemed unhealthy, very stale and thicker than air ought to be. It was no place for a sick child. If Judith had been Gabriel's mother, she would have taken him someplace warm, with soft, mild air that flowed easily in and out. She would let him lounge in the sun all day, taking care to put enough sunscreen on that he never burned.

When Gabriel was dressed, Judith pulled on her own coat and carried her brother downstairs. She retrieved his wheelchair from the trunk of the car and helped him get settled. When he was all tucked in and she had taken her place behind him, she began to feel better about things. The wheelchair had never bothered her—it was so much like pushing him in a stroller, and it wasn't long since she had done that. She had taken him for walks all the time when he was a baby and a toddler. "See the rosebush?" she would coo. "See the robin?" He said his first word to her. "Tat, tat!" he called excitedly when a fat tabby cat crossed the sidewalk in front of him. She had hurried home to tell her parents. They listened politely, if distractedly, to her exuberant account, but when Gabriel failed to produce an encore performance, they returned to their work. Gabriel said "tat" every time they saw the tabby, and soon he added more words: "dog," "tree," "bird," and a version of her name that sounded like "juice." But it was a long time before he said anything at home.

Today the weather was not what Judith would have hoped for. A pale fog made it difficult to see more than a few feet, ruling out any sort of sightseeing or even an opportunity to get more familiar with the neighborhood. But her long strides and deep breaths felt good.

"Run, Judith," begged Gabriel. "Run fast." She used to do it with the stroller, racing down a long stretch of sidewalk and whooping as if they were riding a roller coaster.

"Do you really want me to? Are you up to it?" she worried.

"Yes, please, please, I want to go fast." She began to jog cautiously. Gabriel laughed happily. "Faster, faster!" She broke into a run, and her laughter mingled with his. The cold air made her face tingle, but the warmth of her movement spread throughout her body. For a moment, life seemed full of joy. "Faster," Gabriel called again, and then Judith tripped. The wheelchair jerked out of her hands, and she fell heavily as the fog swallowed up her brother. She lay still for a moment trying to breathe, but her chest refused to let in the air. "Gabriel," she tried to say, her lips opening and closing in silence. She thought she might black out, but finally her lungs expanded with air. "Gabriel," she screamed as soon as she found her voice. She pulled herself to her feet and began jogging forward, but the fog had disoriented her. After a moment she stopped and turned around, frightened and confused. She was lost in a sea of white. "Gabriel! Gabriel!" She put out her hands like a blind person, groping through the fog, but she felt nothing. Panic gripped her. She began to run again.

"Judith." It was a small voice, coming at her through the fog, but relief poured over her. She slowed to a walk, and gradually the wheelchair came into view. Gabriel's face was as white as the fog, but as she gripped the handles and turned him around, he said, "Run fast."

"No. Everything is going fast enough for me already."

She put him to bed again when they got home and sat next to him thinking about her old rag doll Lucy. Her grandmother had made it for her as a gift for her third birthday. Judith thought the doll was the most beautiful thing she had ever owned, with its starched white bonnet trimmed with lace, its black button eyes, and its neat calico dress. She took it everywhere and fussed over it like a mother. Never would she allow Lucy to be too hot or too cold, to be hungry or thirsty. Lucy liked animal cookies best, which was very lucky, since Judith liked them best, too.

When Judith was nine she lost Lucy at the zoo. She had been carrying her in a sling on her back, and Lucy slipped out without anyone noticing. Her father spent hours helping her look for the doll, but they never found her. Judith was inconsolable. Lucy may have been only cloth and stuffing, but she was also Judith's best friend. "I don't think I can ever be happy again," she told her mother.

"Of course you will, Judith," Lori promised. "Don't be silly. You'll forget all about it in a day or so." But Judith did not, and in fact the idea that she *could* be happy again, even without Lucy, distressed her almost as much as Lucy's disappearance. It seemed disloyal not to be permanently upset at the loss. She grew interested in other toys soon enough, but she sometimes reflected on Lucy with sadness and even pangs of guilt. What did it mean to love something, to lose something you loved? Where was the line between compassion and melodrama, strength and coldness? She gazed down at Gabriel and felt as if she would choke from emotion. Love, tenderness, a desire to protect—they were all there. And part of her believed, as she had when Lucy disappeared, that she would never be truly happy again. Another part of her feared that she would be.

That night, when she dreamed again of the boy, she resolved to ask him a question. She felt bold in this dream world, confident of her own safety. So before he had a chance to speak, she said, "What is it like to die?" He stared at her mutely, so she continued, by way of explanation, "My brother is dying."

He hesitated a moment before replying, "It's like floating on a snowflake. Very light, and very cold, and very silent."

"Does it hurt?"

"Yes, a little."

She considered this. He watched her with his green eyes, but she seemed destined to lead the conversation tonight.

"Why are you here?" she burst out. "What *is* your name? Can't you tell me?"

"I can't."

"Why?"

"I can't remember it."

Judith gave a short laugh. "You don't remember your name? I would think, being dead, you'd be cured of amnesia."

His face remained serious. "It's been so long since anyone called me by it. It was never very important to me, until now."

"But aren't you called anything now? Isn't there someone who knows your name?"

"No one who remembers. It was never very important to anyone else, either. Now I am called by a different name."

Judith backed away from him and sat down on a stone bench that her dreaming mind had conveniently placed there. She studied his earnest face. She could not feel afraid of someone with such kind eyes.

"You said we were the ones you were waiting for. And you recognized my necklace—the silver heart."

"Yes. It was mine."

"Maybe you'd better tell me the whole story from the beginning."

Part Two: Nicholas
London, 1709-1715

Chapter 6

The boy's mother had given him a name, of course, but she rarely used it. She preferred frothy pet names like "Buttermilk," "Sweet Cream," and occasionally "Pudding." When he was a small boy, she would hold him and rock, cooing the names at him in a sing-songy way. "There, there, Buttermilk, you see there is nothing to fear, nothing to fear, little Buttermilk." He would lay pressed against her chest, feeling the even vibration that was her heart and staring up at the curve of her face. Now and then a stray lock of her dark hair would tickle his forehead. He remembered once reaching up to stroke her cheek, which felt smooth and soft under its thin layer of grime. But she jerked away from his touch, almost dumping him out of her lap, and studied him with a pair of startled blue eyes.

"What is it, Mama?" he asked, half frightened.

She regarded him silently for the space of two breaths, then pulled him close against her and began to rock again. Many years later, when he reflected back on that early part of his childhood, he suspected that she had forgotten him completely even as she cuddled him, and the soft murmurings had not been meant for him at all but for a memory she had of herself. Once a plump, healthy girl, she had spent her days perched on a stool in her father's dairy, surrounded by the homey smells of hay, fresh milk, and warm cows' breath. She had as many clothes as she needed. She lived, in fact, in a sort of paradise. "There is nothing to fear," the boy's mother lied to that little girl, "nothing, nothing, nothing at all."

When the boy grew too large to sit on her lap, which happened early since he was tall for his age and his mother small, he would kneel on the floor at her feet and beg her to tell him stories about her past, which he pictured as taking place in a sort of dreamlike, golden otherworld. “Tell about the farm, Mama, and the animals. What is cream, Mama?”

“I’ve told you a thousand times already,” she would protest. And if he could sense her reluctance, which usually came from fatigue, he would go to his corner and lie down without further argument. When she was tired, she grew bitter also. Her anger was ice cold and it was deep, like an ocean, and he feared that it would break over them both like waves and wash them away. But she had so many other moods to bury the anger that it stayed hidden most of the time. She could be gentle and sweet and playful, and then he would press her until the light in her eyes flared up and rivaled the brightness of the fire.

“Tell me again, Mama,” he would plead. “You know what it’s like, but I have to imagine. Tell me over and over so I don’t forget.”

She would look up from her pile of mending, which never shrunk no matter how long she worked at it, and stare dreamily into the shadows at the corner of the room. He would see the pink tip of her tongue slide hungrily across her lips. “It is white, and it is very soft—like eating a cloud. That’s what I always thought of.”

He would coax her to tell him about the cows, about the smell of soil and the chores she had done at her mother’s side. And finally—

“What happened to the farm, Mama?” The question seemed inevitable. It displeased her to answer it, but he wanted to know. It took him a long time to understand what she meant when she replied, “They took it away, of course. They came and took it away, as they do everything, in the end.”

“Who is ‘they’? How could they take it? No one can carry a farm away.” But by this time her impatience would begin to show through at the edges of her calm. She would stand up abruptly and sentence him to his mat in the corner. It was long after these evening chats had ended forever that he figured out who “they” were, the gentry family who owned the land her father had worked. They had decided, as many others had around that time, that the land would prove more profitable if put to other uses. Providing food was all very well, but the real money was in sheep.

The boy had seen a few farms himself. He and his mother never settled in one place for long, and though she kept to the cities as much as possible, they crossed farmland on their way in between. Sometimes they crept into barns and slept curled up in the hay, and the boy would lie awake listening to the sounds of cattle and horses and sheep. He tried to imagine what it must be like to live in one of those trim white farmhouses with the yellow thatched roofs and the neat windowboxes blooming with sprays of colorful flowers he couldn't identify. What would it be like to get up in the morning and settle warm and secure next to the kitchen fire while you savored a tumbler of fresh milk, to know that the day and the land were yours and no one would come with fists ready to hurt you? He felt as if he were peering into a different world, a more true and beautiful world from which he would always be separate. He and his mother wandered across England, through endless villages and cities, and yet they never left their own tight little realm. They walked in a transparent tunnel, with all kinds of landscapes and people flashing past and themselves never part of it. Once, at night, he reached up and waved his arm in the air around him, trying to feel the barrier. But it wasn't so far away as that. It was on their faces and in their clothes.

The cities looked much the same, dreary and crowded, and the same people seemed to live in all of them. Everywhere the boy saw the same array of faces, the greedy, the shrewd, the hopeless, the pock-marked. And the men were no different anywhere.

They represented the whole spectrum of fashion, of course, for men of all classes came to see his mother. But the boy wasn't fooled by superficial differences. They all trailed darkness—they spilled it out of their hats and swung it in on their cloaks. And though they stunk of a variety of things, underneath it all they smelled of hunger and fear and cruelty.

"Some mothers make money selling hats and clothes and running inns," his mother would explain. "Well, I never learned any of those things. And still, you and I must survive."

He mostly kept quiet in his corner when the men were there, for his mother would scold him if he made a sound. But once one of them had hit her over and over, and the boy had begun screaming. Before he knew what he meant to do, he had picked up the heaviest pot he could manage and slammed it into the man's back. He was too small to reach any higher. The man's face when it turned on him was rabid and contorted. His arm was swift and his fist knew its mark, and darkness had closed in on the boy until morning. Then he opened his eyes to see his mother bending over him. There were tear stains all down her cheeks, so the part of her face that was not black from bruising was red from crying.

"Oh, Sweet Cream, you must never, never do that again. You must promise me."

With effort he lifted his hands and placed his palms on her cheeks. "But, Angeline, he was hurting you. He wouldn't stop."

"Promise me. You have to promise me—never again." He had started calling her Angeline about the time he was five. She seemed so young and vulnerable, "Mama" didn't always fit. And she *was* young, barely twenty when he was five, but life was aging her fast. If he could have remembered the fresh, childish face that first greeted him when he came into the world, he would have gasped at the change in her.

"I promise," he told her. But inside he dreamed of the time when he would be old enough and big enough to take care of her, and then he would never let anyone hurt her again.

The year the boy turned nine, a man came whom his mother seemed to recognize, though the boy could not remember seeing him before. He was tall and solid-looking and moved with an easy, unpracticed grace. His clothing was some of the finest the boy had ever seen, but he wore it unassumingly, as if he had been born in it and never given it a moment's thought. He had sandy-colored hair that fell past his shoulders and very wide, clear green eyes that gave the impression of being able to see into the soul. The first time he came, the boy's mother turned pale and gave a little gasp. "There, Angeline, do you think I'm a ghost?" he teased good-naturedly. "Is it such a surprise to see me then?" She stood straight and stiff before him, and she looked pitifully small next to him. But gradually her shoulders relaxed a little, and the corners of her mouth moved into what might have passed for a half smile.

"It has been a long time. A very long time," she breathed.

Over the next several weeks, his visits became regular and frequent. He seemed to feel at home in the bare little room where the boy and his mother lived, and once there, he was never in a hurry to leave. He liked to stretch out in the only chair with his legs crossed and his feet propped up against the wall, and from there he would chat with the young woman and sometimes even with the boy.

"What do you do with yourself these days, young lad?" he inquired once. "Keeping busy? Learning what young boys your age should know? Helping your mother, as well, I hope."

The boy stared out sullenly from his place in the corner. He could not decide if he should speak to the man, but finally his mother prodded him. "Buttermilk, you must answer a question when someone asks you."

"I—" the boy stammered. *Of course I help my mother,* he thought, *but what makes you think you can come in here and sit in our chair as if you belong here?* The man seemed to fill up the whole room, which wasn't difficult considering that even the boy could cross it in seven or eight paces. Besides the narrow bed with its lumpy straw mattress, the room held a decrepit wooden washstand, the single chair, a low fireplace, and the boy's mat, which he rolled up and stowed at the foot of his mother's bed during the day. Why didn't the man realize there wasn't room enough for three, at least not for long? The boy didn't like the man at all, but his mother acted friendlier than usual. Most of the time, when the men came, her eyes got dull and her face almost slack. She looked as much like a corpse as a conscious, reasonably healthy person could. But not with this man. There was something in her eyes that was hopeful, almost eager.

Once, as the man was leaving, he told the boy's mother he had a surprise for her. "But you'll not get me to tell you what it is, not with any of your charms. You'll have to wait until I come again."

She smiled slightly, but her eyes glowed softly with contentment.

"I will try and wait, then, but I hope it will not be too long."

The next morning she sang to herself as she did her chores, something about a knight and his lady. Her eyes shone brightly and two red spots stood out like roses on her pale cheeks. Around midday she grasped the boy by the shoulders and said, "Everything is going to be different now. Everything is going to change for us."

"What do you mean? Are we going away again?"

"Yes, perhaps. I don't know yet. But we will go away from this room, that's for certain. And you will have cream to eat."

She flitted around all afternoon, unable to sit still and soon unable to accomplish any useful task. As evening came on, she hovered by the narrow window so that she might see the man approaching. Even there, she danced back and fo rth and wrung her small hands. The boy must have caught some of her fitful energy, because he began to feel anxious. His stomach churned uncomfortably, but he could not say exactly what worried him. Only that his mother, at that moment, had never seemed more like a child.

Finally the man arrived, and true to his word, he had a surprise. He held out something silver that dangled on the end of a long chain. The dying light from the window flicked across it so that for a moment it appeared blindingly bright. And then the light was gone, and his mother sat frozen in the dim room watching the little trinket and saying nothing.

"See, Angeline, I had my silversmith make it especially for you," the man boasted, apparently interpreting the young woman's silence as stunned appreciation. "Sentimental, I know, but then I've always had that sort of disposition."

The boy moved closer to his mother so that he could see into her eyes, and he watched as they transformed from twin fires to stormy seas to dark hollows. And finally she covered their emptiness with a layer of opaque glass. "Thank you," she whispered as the man placed the chain around her neck and fastened the clasp. Her voice sounded hoarse and far away.

"It's a heart, you see. To remind you of me." The man smiled and his bright white teeth gleamed in the shadowy room.

"Yes, a heart," said the boy's mother. "All this time, all these years, and you brought me a heart."

The man puffed out his chest. "I've always been that way. I remember things, you see. I used to tell my brothers that I'd find you again someday. They thought it a great joke, but now you see I meant it. I've been hoping these many years to run into you."

"Fancy that," said Angeline. "You really do remember trifles."

When the man had gone, Angeline's anger broke. The boy watched helplessly as the waves of feeling surged up inside and beat against her small frame until she could no longer hold them in. "A heart, a heart!" she wailed. "Would that you had ripped your own heart from your chest and given it to me on a chain! Then you might know what it is to suffer!" She screamed and screamed, beating her fists upon the bed, and at one point she snatched up the sheet and tugged at it as if to tear it. But some logic must have prevailed, for she soon gave it up and let it fall, whole, across the mattress. A bed sheet was too valuable to be sacrificed, even at a time like this. Especially at a time like this, she may have thought, when all her hopes for a modest prosperity had culminated in nothing more than a little silver bauble.

Toward morning her rage spent itself out, and she lay across the bed weeping quietly and pathetically. Now the boy dared approach her. He drew near the side of the mattress where she had laid her head and began to stroke her hair. "Don't cry now, Mama. I'm almost a man now. I'll take care of us, you'll see."

She continued to weep for several moments, and he thought she had decided not to answer. But then she turned her head and gazed up into his face with eyes that were as empty of spark as the cold fireplace. The two red spots still glowed on her cheeks, but now they looked unnatural and served only to accentuate her pallor. The boy realized with a jolt that his mother was ill, that he had ignored all the signs of her decline. "Buttermilk, you know enough of the world to understand that nothing will ever be right for us. How will you ever take care of us? We have no land for you to farm. There is no way for you to learn a trade—I cannot pay anyone to take you as an apprentice." He didn't know what to say to her. He wanted to promise her that he would find a way, but he feared she would dismiss it as the prattling of a child. He wished he could prove to her that he was no longer a child, that he would no longer sit back and watch her pain like an idle spectator at a hanging. His mind cast about for alternatives.

"Perhaps we could go to London," he ventured. "In such a great city as that, there must be something I could do."

Angeline buried her face in the bedding and coughed. When she looked up again, the boy could make out a tiny red spot where her mouth had been. "London?" she repeated, sounding a little confused and very young. "Do you think there is work in London?"

"There must be," he told her. "We have already looked everywhere else."

So the two set off on the longest journey they had ever taken together. They trekked through cities they had never been in and a few they had already seen, across moors with their frightening, twisted landscapes, through farmland rich with the promise of harvest. They passed fields with great splotches of red where farmers had let their land go to poppies, and the boy stared at them and thought of the bloodstains on the sheet in his knapsack. If his mother coughed up enough bad blood, could she get well? Angeline's face paled with every passing day—with every mile, almost. The boy observed her with worried eyes. He eased her burden as much as possible, taking all but the smallest of their belongings upon himself. And each day she walked more slowly and with more pain, but she walked.

One night he awoke to the scent of hay and the sight of his mother leaning over him. "Oh, my son," she whispered, "my little son!" She wrapped her arms around herself and rocked back and forth, making choked whimpering noises that sounded like stifled sobs. Her skin shone pale as moonlight and her eyes were lost in shadow.

"Mama?" he said softly.

She stopped rocking. "I didn't mean to wake you. Go back to

sleep." She lay down next to him, but he heard her crying as his mind wandered in and out of dreams.

The next morning the boy spotted London, and by the afternoon they began catching whiffs of the great city's stench. "It isn't far now, Mama," he told Angeline. Before nightfall they were inside the city. The boy gazed around anxiously, swallowing hard and trying not to feel overwhelmed. Narrow streets, many of them muddy tracks without cobblestone pavement, wound off seemingly at random. Liberal piles of horse manure made pungent obstacles for the steady stream of pedestrian traffic, and puddles of unspecific waste lay stagnant where they had landed after being tossed out of windows and doorways. On the outskirts of the city, most of the buildings were low and sagging behind aged coats of whitewash; they huddled together as if for warmth, reminding the boy of a gaggle of fat old ladies. The farther he and Angeline walked, though, the taller the buildings rose, and each level seemed to lean out a little farther than the one below so that, when the boy looked up, he could make out only a thin ribbon of sky between the rooftops. The rows of façades showed a hodgepodge of weathered wood, red brick, and gray, brown, and whitewashed stone trimmed and criss-crossed with dark beams, and even though some of the buildings had been painted in cheerful hues, all the shades seem to run together into a single dull color. Once when a push from a passerby sent him careening hand first into a wall, a fine black dust sloughed off on his skin. "Soot," he muttered, showing his darkened hand to Angeline. The smoke from the chimneys made the sky look overcast, and beneath the gloomy atmosphere the inhabitants went about with pasty complexions.

People were everywhere. They hung out of upper-story windows, shouting into the tumult below; they stood next to stalls that bulged with vegetables or housewares, haggling and gesticulating expressively; they ploughed their way up and down the streets, hauling wooden tubs that sloshed with water and other mysterious substances; they dodged in and out with neatly tied bundles of bread and fruit tucked protectively under one arm. Colorful signs advertised the merchandise of the various shops, not with words but with pictures because most of the customers couldn't read. A painting of a long, curly gray wig hung over a window displaying the real thing. "How much for the yak hair?" he heard someone ask. One sign, suspended from a short rod sticking out over the shop door, showed a plump, red-cheeked man popping the cork off a bottle. A stream of young patrons filed out beneath the sign, all of them red-cheeked as well and patting their stomachs happily. The boy peered hungrily into the dim interior of the tavern, from which a current of warm air carried the scent of beef stew, before the door shut behind them.

"I must rest now," Angeline murmured.

"If we can only find a place to sleep—"

"No, now," she insisted. She lowered herself stiffly onto a dusty little stoop and rested against the doorway. Above her head, a picture of a long, brown coil, like a snake, waved slightly in the breeze. "See there across the road, the bakery?" The boy picked out the sign showing a bundle of fat yellow rolls. "Go and buy us a loaf of bread." She dug out a coin and placed it in his hand. It was more than necessary. He had started to cross the street when she called him back. He waited patiently, but with growing puzzlement, as she unclasped the chain that carried the silver heart. This too she tucked into his palm.

"Why are you giving me this?" he questioned. "I don't need it to buy the bread. You already gave me more than enough."

"You may need it. Sometimes . . . things can be more expensive than you expect. Go now." He continued to stand there, staring dumbly. "Go, child," she commanded more firmly. "Hurry."

He threaded his way into the middle of the street again. He wasn't sure what made him turn back to look for her, but it didn't matter anyway. The crowd had closed in between them, and he could see nothing. His errand in the bakery took only a few moments, and then he made his way quickly back toward the stoop where he had left her.

He was only a little surprised to find her gone.

Chapter 7

Judith blinked. "Gone?" she said blankly. "What do you mean?" The boy in the garden, separated from her by a few feet and a few centuries, shifted his weight from one leg to the other. "Gone, yes. She wasn't there." He met her surprised gaze openly, without embarrassment, but his eyes were dark with remembering.

At first he had felt no panic. Angeline must have gotten impatient and come after him, or perhaps she had wandered off in a delirium. Whatever the reason for her departure, she could not have gone far in such a short time. He would find her quickly, and together they would search for a place to sleep. But as he weaved in and out among the crowds of people, the difficulty of his situation confronted him. She had brought them into one of the busiest parts of the city. Even now, with darkness coming on, the narrow streets flowed with a river of bodies who jostled each other as they negotiated the cramped space. Though the boy was small and agile, it took all his effort to resist the current and keep from being carried off in directions he did not mean to go. The masses of people formed a sort of moving cage. Everywhere he turned, he found his view blocked by backs and arms and faces that bore the cramped, grayish look of strangers.

At length he changed his plan. He would return to the stoop and wait for her. Probably *she* was searching for *him*, probably she had gone off for a moment and come back to find him gone. She would be worried, trembling, lost. He imagined her pale face crinkled with anxiety and thought how her arms would feel when she held him close and whispered into his hair, "Precious Buttermilk, I thought you had disappeared forever." The thought of her forthcoming relief warmed him as he wandered through the maze of streets, so that even his difficulty in rediscovering the stoop didn't frighten him. He had formed a plan, and his mind had adjusted to the security that comes from having settled on a course of action. But when he finally did find the stoop again, and she was not there—when he had waited until the sky was pitch black and the owner of the shop behind the doorway had come out and kicked him with a gruff "Can't have no loiters here" by way of explanation—the fear began to seep like cold water up his legs and toward his stomach. Where was she? His imagination conjured up an image of her face, white and frozen, lying in the filth at the edge of a street. He thought of her weakness and exhaustion, her increasing pallor, the tiny reserves of strength that had already had to see her halfway across England, and he feared the worst.

He hovered around the stoop throughout the darkest part of the night, skulking in the shadows like a thief in order to avoid another kick. Toward morning he began to wander again. This time he had no plan. He didn't know where to go or what to do—by now she could be anywhere, and he no longer had any confidence in his own ability to find her. Still, a sense of panicked urgency drove him forward. Every now and then he caught a glimpse of dark curls or a small, straight figure, and his stomach shot up into his throat. "Mama! Angeline!" he called to one dark-haired woman, but when she turned, her face was withered and hollow, and her sinister smile revealed a mouth long since emptied of teeth. Throughout the long day he peered into the faces of so many strangers that he began to feel like a stranger himself. Why was he here? Who was he? Nobody cared. Nobody noticed him at all except to shove him aside. And gradually the great city swallowed him up. He became lost in its endless tangles of alleys and thoroughfares, in its churning sea of anonymity.

Sometime late in the afternoon, the boy stopped to rest and remembered the bread he had bought the evening before. He still had it in his knapsack, along with all his worldly possessions: a second suit of clothes, a bed sheet, two pots, and two tin dishes. He was ravenous. He tore into the bread and managed to gulp down two bites before a dog whose ribs poked out determined to do battle for it. It was over in a few seconds, and the boy had lost. Fighting despair, he sunk down against the stone wall of a cheesemonger's shop and fell into a sort of stupor. Hours of exhaustion, hunger, and fear had drained his strength; his body felt wobbly and useless. He sat staring at his hands, which trembled even after he clenched and unclenched them, and then at his mud-caked pants and shoes. He had stepped in slime up past his ankles before finally wandering onto a street paved with cobblestones. His gaze slid from his feet to the pavement. Down in the crevices a team of ants was busy packing off some morsel of food. The boy watched them idly as they labored, oblivious to their imminent danger—for he could smash them all with a twist of his heel. He was still contemplating the ants' situation when a rather gaudy carriage passed by in the street before him. He took no notice of it. All day the world had spun around him without stopping, intent on its own business. His personal misery was of no greater significance than the plight of these ants. Tired of the struggle, he allowed numbness to overtake his mind, and it spread over his consciousness like a white film shrouding thought and care. When the carriage returned and stopped directly across from him, he ignored the spectacle unfolding before him.

A servant in bright red livery who had been posing stiff as a statue at the rear of the carriage now leaped down to open the carriage door, first laying a wide piece of red cloth over the muddy cobblestones below. After a moment, a youngish man in colorful garb emerged and stepped gingerly onto the cloth. He had on a curly wig that bushed out wide at the ends, and he stood for a full half minute inspecting his clothes to make sure they had not been mussed by his ride before surveying the scene before him with slight distaste. When his eyes lit on the boy, he uttered a soft "Aha" and turned to the man who had followed him out of the carriage. This second man was older, as evidenced by his gray hair and faint spider-web of wrinkles, and he wore more sober if equally expensive clothing and a very bland expression.

The younger man raised a gleaming black walking stick and pointed it in the direction of the boy. "Now you shall see, Glebe," he boasted to his companion. "Rest your eyes upon this pathetic piece of street refuse. Why, you'd doubt the creature was in possession of an immortal soul! But just you wait. If I put this urchin into Chadwicke's school, he'll come out looking quite convincingly human. By the end of this very day, I tell you, they'll have him shined up into a very respectable picture of an orphan."

The man called Glebe yawned. "I shan't argue with that, Wight. After all, anything can be dressed up to appear as something it is not. That is no magic and no miracle."

"But it is quite enough for one day, Glebe, and when I have praised this school, I have been speaking more of the work of years. I've got three or four lads there already, and demmed if they don't know their catechism better than I do. Oh yes, they can answer any question you put to them; they're regular little theologians. I sometimes go and quiz them on it for sport. Why, they can tell you stories from the Bible that are so obscure you've never heard of them."

"To know something better than you do, my dear Wight, is also an unremarkable accomplishment. Now, let us be gone. I've more important things to think about than this Churchwell's school. And as for the orphan problem, I prefer the other way of dealing with it."

Wight put on an exaggerated look of offended honor. "It's Chadwicke, my dear Glebe, the master's name is Chadwicke. And if you think it is better to capture the orphans and ship them off to the colonies, which I believe to be the other solution you were referring to, you have not thought it through at all." Glebe made a move as if to protest, but Wight cut him off. "No, not at all. Think upon it again—what is holding us back in the colonies?"

"The Spaniards. They've long since taken all the worthwhile land, all that with gold, and still they're marauding up and down the rivers."

"Glebe, you disappoint me. The colonies will make us rich yet. And the only thing in the way, the only real problem, is the savages. Of course, it would be better for everyone if they simply weren't there, but since they are, we've got to . . ."

"Yes? What have we got to do? If you have a solution to that problem, even Her Majesty would be anxious to hear it."

"We've got to make them like us, Glebe. Why, they can't go on keeping miles and miles of the best land to themselves just so they can wander through it when they like. They've got to settle down, they've got to farm like us, and they must, above all, become Christians. We'll never be able to trust any of them until we have brought them up to our level of civilization, taught them to follow our way of life and our God."

"You believe, then, that God is an Englishman?"

"The possibility of His being otherwise has never so much as crossed my mind."

"Well, at least there we are agreed," admitted Glebe. "But how is this relevant to anything we have been discussing?"

"Well, it's quite clear, isn't it, if you only think? Round up orphans and send them over there, and they're likely to become savages themselves. Yes, shocking as it is to think what a creature born and bred in England could sink to, it is only too true. The pull of savagery is strong. But put them in this school, and where do you think they end up? Well, a third of them at least do go to masters in the colonies. But they've had some Christian teaching shoved down them first, and they'll not become savages when they get to the wilderness, oh no. They'll make the Indians into as near copies of Englishmen as any group of savages can hope to attain."

"Well now, that would be something," chuckled Glebe.

"Let me convince you to witness this miracle at work. Let us take this poor piece of street filth to Chadwicke, and while we are there you can meet my other triumphs of philanthropy—my other boys, I mean."

Glebe sighed the sigh of a man who has much to endure. "Fine, Wight, if you insist. Only let us not be late to dine. That I really cannot tolerate."

Although the boy had been near enough to hear this conversation, his brain had failed to register a single word. Even Wight's enthusiastic gesticulating and his clear references to the boy had not called the child out of his stupor. But as Wight had no intention of consulting anyone about his plans for this boy's future—least of all the boy himself—he was completely untroubled by the boy's violent surprise at being approached by three men and hauled rather roughly off the stoop and toward the carriage. Wight watched his servants thrusting the child unceremoniously through the narrow doorway with an expression of sublime serenity and satisfaction.

"In you go, there's a good lad," soothed the carriage driver, who, like both his companions, wore red bright enough for a court jester. A moment later the driver yelped in pain as the boy thrashed wildly and caught him on the nose. "Why, you young demon!" he hollered. "You'll get that back and then some."

The boy suddenly found his voice and let out a scream. "Let me go! Go away and leave me be!" He struggled more, but the men had tightened their grips. One had hold of his collar and was on the verge of choking him. When the boy opened his mouth to yell again, no breath came out.

Wight stepped close and looked down at the boy amusedly. "What is all this rumpus? Are we interrupting an important engagement? Keeping you from a meeting with the queen, perhaps?" He glanced at Glebe with an expression that showed him excessively proud of his wit. "Never fear, we will give you a ride."

The grip on the boy's collar relaxed slightly, enough for him to answer. A short pause followed as he gulped in air. "Well, say something, child," Wight commanded impatiently. "Is it your pleasure to go with us?"

The boy looked up into the man's countenance. He noticed that Wight had on a bit of rouge, and it made his features appear distorted. For an instant the boy believed he was trapped in a nightmare that would all dissolve if he could only will it, but no, no such comforting discovery as that. The pain he felt was real enough.

"I can't go with you," he said with what he hoped was an air of importance. "I'm looking for my mother. I have to find her straightaway, because she's sick and she needs me."

Wight's eyebrows floated halfway up his forehead. "Sick is she? Tut, tut, that's most unfortunate to hear. But you said you were looking for her. If she is sick, is she not at home in bed?"

"No," the boy explained, "we only just came to London, and we got lost from each other in the crowd."

"Oh, I see." Wight pursed his lips as if thinking things over. "Well, you can look for her much more easily if you accompany us. Riding in a carriage is faster than walking. Come with us and we will find her together."

The boy didn't trust Wight and would still have fought getting into the carriage if he hadn't been so dismally outnumbered. As it was, he settled into the seat quite docilely with the hope that, after he did whatever these men wanted, they would set him free, and then he could continue his search. Futile as it all was, he would not allow himself to get discouraged again. If only he hadn't stopped there to indulge his misgivings, he might have avoided this delay. His resolve, which had been melting away all day, began to stiffen again.

The carriage lurched forward over the cobblestones, and after a few minutes the boy sat up and started to take some interest in the ride. He had never been in a carriage before. He stuck his head out one of the windows and marveled at the speed with which the buildings and people flowed by. He gawked down curiously at brownish water when the carriage rumbled across the Thames, and then he stared open-mouthed at a huge, majestic church. After a while, though, Wight tapped him on the shoulder with his stick.

"Sit down, boy. The air is too close in here as it is." So the boy sat back and kept silent throughout the rest of the journey.

It ended, abruptly, before a vast building of dark stone that loomed ominously toward the late afternoon sky. Looking up at it, the boy could not suppress a shiver. "What is this place?" he asked his captors. If he had been able to read, he might have noted the sign that proclaimed: "Disciples of Christ Schoole for Boys and Girles." But the building's long façade gave nothing away. The windows may have let some of the outside world in, but they let nothing out—no hint of movement or even of habitation.

Wight ignored the child's query and Glebe scolded, "Impertinent thing, aren't you? You just speak whenever you please." The liveried servants jumped down to open the door, scooping the boy out with arms tensed and ready for resistance. Wight and Glebe followed, and placing themselves on either side of the boy, they approached the huge double doors. A knocker in the shape of a lion and another in the shape of a lamb observed their approach with unmoving brass eyes. Wight seized the lion knocker and gave three swift taps.

"Yes?" asked the young man who heaved one massive door aside and stood looking at them blankly. "Do you have business here today? It is not marked in the record."

"I have the sort of business that cannot be anticipated," replied Wight. "I have brought you a new boy."

The clerk glanced down surprisedly as if noticing the boy for the first time. "A new boy? Well, sir, you should have written ahead to inquire if there was a place open. As it is, we have no room for him."

"No room? You turn away this orphan who asks only a chance to learn?"

"We have not enough beds for every orphan in London," the clerk retorted testily. "After all, we have only this hall to occupy."

"Let me speak with Chadwicke," Wight persisted. "He may give me a different answer."

"Mr. Chadwicke is a man of uncommon ability, but even he cannot conjure up what is not there."

Wight held up his walking stick. "Do you dare speak to a gentleman this way? If you value your place here, you will do as I say."

The clerk turned away with a sullen expression and disappeared from view. A moment later he returned, still looking sulky, and said, "Mr. Chadwicke will see you. Follow me."

He led them across a high, dark hall and into a little room with a wide desk and a bookcase crammed with ledgers. He motioned for them to sit down and then left them alone. Soon another man, whom the boy presumed to be Chadwicke, entered from a side door.

The boy studied him curiously. He was a most awkward-looking person: tall, with big elbows and knees and an Adam's apple that justified reference to the fruit. His hair was such a dull color that the word color might not be properly applied to it at all; it was done up in a pigtail, which stuck out nearly straight in the back and gave him a silly profile. His face and nose were long, his skin sallow. His wrists poked out of the sleeves of his coat, which was so patched that there was hardly any of the original material left. The boy marveled. When dissected, every aspect of this man's appearance was ridiculous, and yet . . . and yet, he carried himself with a grave dignity that remained undaunted by the peacock presence of Mr. Wight. No one would have thought to laugh at him. Even the ledgers seemed to stand a little straighter out of respect for their master. The boy, too, improved his posture without realizing it.

"Chadwicke, old man, jolly to see you again," exclaimed Wight, jumping to his feet to clap Chadwicke on the back.

Chadwicke endured this greeting stoically. He stepped back slightly from Wight's exuberance and nodded politely to both men. "It is always a pleasure to see you, sir." His eyes moved to the boy, and he continued to gaze at the child while directing a question to Wight. "What business brings you here this day?" he inquired, speaking slowly as if taking time to deliberate over each word. His voice was low and sonorous and suggestive of a depth of things left unsaid.

Wight seemed finally to sense the solemn mood that Chadwicke exuded. He resumed his chair and answered evenly, "As you see, old man, I have brought you another boy."

"Yes." Chadwicke continued his visual inspection of the child for a few moments. Then he seemed to come to a decision; he turned to the bookcase, took out a ledger, and sat down behind the desk. "We have very little room here. Every bed is filled. Each day when I walk out, I see children in need of our institution. It pains me that we are capable of doing so little." His face twisted as if he really were in pain. "Often I must turn people away. But you are lucky, or perhaps the Almighty has put His hand in. One of our boys has run away this week. Usually we are prepared to be forgiving, but this young man has demonstrated such a lack of respect for this institution that I cannot allow him to return. This new boy may have his bed. I presume you are prepared to act as his presenter?" he asked, glancing up at Wight as he thumbed through the ledger's pages and dipped a quill into the ink jar.

"But of course. You know it is my favorite hobby, and you certainly cannot doubt my credit. How are my other lads, by the bye?"

"One of them will be bound to a master within the month."

Wight beamed. "Glad to hear it. Perhaps you could call him so that I might introduce him to my good friend here."

Chadwicke's mud-colored eyes met Wight's. "The boys are at their studies now. I would not disturb them."

Wight scowled like a child and Glebe uttered a loud "Huff!" but if Chadwicke noticed, he made no response. He had found the first blank page in the ledger and poised the quill for a new entry. "What is the child's name?"

Wight realized that he didn't know, so he turned to the boy, who answered shyly.

"Good, good, a sensible name," encouraged Chadwicke. "But you have not told me all of it. I must know your surname as well as your Christian name."

"What? My what? I told you my name, sir, all there is of it."

"Yes, you gave me your name, but you cannot have told me all of it. There must be more."

"No, nothing but what I've already said, unless you mean the names my mother sometimes calls me, but they aren't my real name."

"What was your father's name?" Chadwicke tried again.

"I don't know. I never knew about him. He must have died long ago."

The schoolmaster glanced significantly at Wight, who snickered. "And your mother's name?" he wanted to know.

"Angeline."

"Angeline—er . . . "

"Just Angeline."

"Ah, I see. Well, here all the boys must have two names at least. How about this: you are starting a new life, and I will give you a new name. We will not use your old one because it will remind you of your old life, and you must put that behind you." He wrote down a name and then read it to the boy. "Does that please you?"

"It's fine as far I can tell, sir, but I don't know what you mean by a new life. I don't know why these men brought me here—I told them I had to find my mother."

"Find her?"

"Yes, sir. She's sick. We came into London yesterday, and I went to buy us some bread, but when I came back she was gone. She must have got lost in the crowd."

"I understand," said Chadwicke. He seemed to consider his next words for a moment. "It is natural and good to care for one's mother. But now it is time to begin anew." He wrote several more lines in the ledger, then blotted the page and set the book aside. "Excuse me for a moment," he said to his guests. He stepped out the door and called to someone. The clerk who had let them in appeared in the doorway.

"The boy is to come with me. I will show him his bed." The boy followed the young man reluctantly, examining his surroundings forlornly as he went. From the hallway he heard Glebe say, "This place will work a miracle indeed, if it transforms the child of a whore into a Christian." As the clerk led him up a narrow staircase, they passed several boys, all walking together and in the same rhythm. They wore blue coats and matching knickers. "Do all the boys wear those?" he wondered out loud, but he got no reply. The pair climbed a second flight of stairs, and then the clerk led him into a long, narrow room lined with cots. He indicated one on the end. "This is where you sleep. We will try to scrounge up a suit for you. After all, you can't wear that." He pointed disdainfully at the boy's clothing. "Supper is in half an hour. If you are late, you will be punished." He turned to go, but the boy called him back. Perhaps the note of desperation in the child's voice convinced the clerk to turn and give his attention once more to the boy.

"Yes?"

"Are the students ever allowed to . . . to go out?"

"Of course. You'll walk in the garden for a half hour every midmorning."

"But into the city?"

The clerk looked horrified at the suggestion. "I should say not!" He whirled on his heel and sped away down the hall. Once alone, the boy sat down on the cot and stared about dismally. No one was with him for the moment. He could get up and walk outside now. But the mention of supper had reminded him of his empty stomach. He had eaten only two bites of bread in the past two days, and he longed for something to fill up the emptiness that gnawed painfully at his belly. Perhaps he could just stay long enough to eat, and then creep out into the night. He felt ashamed at the triumph of his stomach over his concern for his mother, but he was so hungry . . .

After what seemed an excessive wait, he heard a bell announcing supper, and an ensuing stampede of feet. He followed the wave of children down the stairs and across the hallway where he had first entered with Wight. There, a vast room filled with tables awaited the rush of hungry children, mostly boys but a few girls as well. The clerk who had showed him to his room appeared at his elbow and directed him to a seat at the end of the room opposite the massive fireplace. It was late enough in the day for the room to be chilly, and the fire was much too small to warm any but those situated nearest. The boy shivered in his place but soon forgot the cold as he shoveled spoonfuls of thin stew into his mouth and tried, at the same time, to inhale a chunk of bread. When he had assuaged the sharpest pangs of hunger, he took another moment to investigate his surroundings. Far down the room, close to the fire, he could see Chadwicke seated next to two homely children, a small boy and a slightly larger girl. Chadwicke, who should have been the warmest person in the room, seemed unconscious of the fire's comfort; he had a ledger open in front of him and appeared wholly engrossed in its contents. Behind him, a short row of children sat primly, watching the others eat. "Why don't they join in?" the boy whispered to his neighbor, indicating the row of silent observers.

"They were bad and can't have any dinner tonight. Watch yourself, or you'll end up there, too."

The boy finished his meal slowly, trying to draw it out. He was still hungry. Maybe he should stay until breakfast and then leave sometime during the morning. He couldn't search well at night, anyway.

After a while he saw Chadwicke stand up and walk toward his end of the room. The boy watched him expectantly as he drew near. Was he coming to tell the boy that he would help him with his search? That he would pack some food for the boy to take with him on his journey? That he had been stupid to give the boy a new name as if a flick of his quill could wipe out all that had already happened? No. Chadwicke was only heading for the doorway that led back into the hall. His eyes flicked across the boy's without acknowledgement—or even recognition.

Chapter 8

That night the boy searched for his mother through a labyrinth of twisted dreams. Staggering with exhaustion, he wandered through an endless succession of rooms—all the lodgings they had lived in during the nine years since the boy had come into the world. Some were shadowy and fuzzy-edged from their long storage in the corners of his memory, others, more recent habitations, were quite clear, and all seemed to hold out a promise. "Come home, come home," they whispered, as merry firelight danced across walls whose closeness now seemed cozy. "She is here, she is waiting." But every one was empty except for his own shadow, large and gruesome as it lurked along beside him in a caricature of companionship. Sometimes he would linger hopefully, half believing that if he only waited a moment, she would come bursting through the door with bright eyes and flushed cheeks. But she never came, and inevitably he moved on. Although in reality the various lodgings were scattered all over England, tonight they had contrived to connect themselves into a chain, so that he no more closed the door of one than he was entering another.

When he stepped from the door of the last room, he found himself on a road that stretched out straight to the horizon. At first he thought himself alone, but as he walked the scene became clearer, and forms that he had vaguely perceived as trees or hedges or shadows of animals resolved themselves into solid-looking people. Soon a multitude of silent travelers accompanied him on his journey, all with heads up and eyes focused on some distant object, though the boy could see nothing ahead but road, fields, and sky. The travelers appeared singularly united in purpose, but they shared no other characteristics; there were men, women, and children of all ages, with all sorts of features and wearing such a variety of clothing as he never knew existed. He wanted to inquire of one where they were going, but their earnest silence frightened him, so he walked on for some indeterminable space of time. And then—it was like watching something under water come slowly to the surface, shifting from a glob of wavering indistinctness to some terrestrial shape—he began to recognize the slim, straight figure off to his left. At the instant his realization became full, the figure turned. His cry of "Mama!" echoed strangely in the intense silence.

Angeline stepped out of the current of people and moved toward him. Reaching out a hand to ruffle his hair, she called him by name, and he stood very still and stiff beneath her touch for fear he would weep like a small child. "I told you to go," she chided gently, "and go you must, for you cannot come with me."

He gazed up into her face, which had somehow lost its pallor. Her cheeks looked softer than he remembered ever seeing them before. "But where are you going?"

She smiled mysteriously. "Somewhere you *cannot* go. Not now. Leave me." She began to walk again, but the boy still hung about her.

"I want to come, too," he pleaded. "You've got to let me come. You can't leave me here." He reached out for her arm but caught at empty air. "Don't leave me here!" he screamed. And then a pair of rough hands had him by the shoulders and the whole scene was disintegrating before him. "You can't leave me, you can't leave me," he repeated breathlessly, as if the words themselves could bring her back.

"What's this nonsense?" complained an impatient voice. "Argh, I haven't time for this. Wake up, boy, and speak reason." The boy opened his eyes—his real eyes, not his dream ones—and found the young clerk's face hovering close above his own in the semidarkness.

"Did you expect to sleep through the entire day? We don't tolerate laziness here." He drew back and tossed a bundle onto the cot. "There is your school clothing. Now I'll be taking these." The clerk gathered up the boy's belongings, which were still wrapped in a knapsack and deposited at the foot of the bed. "Up now!" he ordered gruffly, whacking the boy's arm for good measure. "Inspection is about to begin, and you'll not enjoy your first day here if you are caught lazing about. You'd better remember to wash your face—and good!"

Feeling disoriented and slightly sick, the boy swung his legs over the cot and eased them gingerly onto the floor, bracing for the first shock of cold stone against warm skin. He groped for his knapsack, remembered that the clerk had confiscated it, and reached instead for the bundle of school clothing. It contained two freshly laundered suits that appeared inky black in the dim light but that were really blue like all the others. The boy had not meant to dress as one of the schoolchildren. After all, he was leaving today, and he would never be coming back. He was not one of these children—not an orphan, not abandoned, not someone who had no better place to go. He pulled the clothes on reluctantly, wondering if he could find where the clerk had put his things before he left.

At the far end of the room a crowd of boys were gathered around several washstands, which had already rendered so much service that particles of dirt now swam in the water. The boy could feel them sharp and abrasive against his skin as he splashed the water onto his face and scrubbed at his forehead and neck. "It'll help loosen your own dirt," someone told him, grinning, and then the children were filing out through the long room and down the stairs like a procession of ghosts. Except, reflected the boy, that ghosts were pale and luminous, while the children in their dark clothing were deeper shadows in a pool of gray obscurity. But they were as silent as visitors from the grave, the early hour or perhaps the fear of a reprimand discouraging conversation.

On the second floor, the line of children turned down a long, narrow corridor, lit sparsely by small candles set in sconces along the wall. Following the crowd, the boy found himself in what he took to be a classroom. A set of narrow wooden tables and benches had been scooted against the wall, leaving the floor clear. Bookcases stuffed full with leather- and cloth-bound volumes lined another wall, and near the door rested a chair with an elevated seat and, next to it, a wooden stand like a pulpit. The room had no fireplace. While the boy looked around, the children formed themselves into three neat lines, and finally he ducked into one of them. Everyone seemed to wait with bated breath. Soon a man entered, carrying a candle in one hand and something long and flexible in the other. In the dim light, the boy couldn't tell if his hair was gray or pale blond, but even the semidarkness couldn't hide the shabbiness of his clothing, which was nearly as patched as Chadwicke's.

The man stalked to the far end of the first row of children and held the candle up to scrutinize the first boy's face. Now the boy could see the man's scowl; he had harsh, rugged features, and his furrowed brow poked out amazingly far. The first child in line held out his hands meekly for inspection. The man ignored them and tugged roughly at the child's ear instead. "Edwards!" he spat. "You've not washed your ears."

"B-b-but I have, Mr. Fortescue, sir," stuttered the child. The man dragged him out of line, turned him around, and brought the long, flexible thing down across his back. The man appeared to enjoy the whipping. As he moved on down the line, he thrashed three other boys, two whose fingernails weren't clean enough, one who had a tear in his coat. The boy wondered how the man could see all that by candlelight.

By the time the man made his way down the last row, where the boy was, he seemed to have grown bored with the whole thing. He stopped in front of the boy and growled, "Who are you?"

The boy opened his mouth to answer but choked on his words.

"Never mind, 'tis no matter," Mr. Fortescue bellowed, as if his voice had to project out through the windows and down to the street. "As long as you behave yourself. I suppose you're the new boy Mr. Chadwicke admitted last night."

The boy nodded dumbly.

"Well, I hope you spent the whole night on your knees thanking the good Lord, for it's a lucky beggar you are."

"Yessir," the boy managed.

After the inspection, the children swarmed down to the main level and into the long dining hall with its fire beckoning enticingly from the far end of the room. Looking longingly at the orange flames the way he used to gaze up at a farmhouse from his hideout in the barn, the boy sank down in the seat he had been directed to the evening before. The morning was chilly—hints of frost laced the edges of the windowpanes. They reminded the boy of long, thin fingers, waiting to reach out and touch the back of his neck with a chilly fingertip. He could feel his skin tense in clammy anticipation as the children recited their prayers, but he took comfort in the steaming bowl of porridge that was soon passed down to him and he ate hungrily, feeling as empty as he ever had before.

But for all the hours he had spent looking forward to it, breakfast lasted a lamentably short time. He had no sooner experienced the first waves of relief than his spoon was scraping the bottom of the bowl. He pressed his tongue against the remaining drops, dreading the moment when the dish would be licked clean. There would be no more until—well, that wasn't worth thinking about. Impulsively he groped for the little silver heart his mother had given him. Lucky he had kept it about his neck, tucked close to his skin. He still had that at least. But he hated to think of using it to buy food. He must keep it for his mother and return it to her.

With the last of his food gone, the boy grew anxious to leave and, trying to appear nonchalant, he considered his escape route. It wasn't far to the door of the dining hall, and it would take only a few moments and several long steps to be across the entryway and out the front doors. Unfortunately, he was not to be left to himself just yet. The clerk materialized at his side to inform the child in his most officious manner that he would escort him to his classroom. The boy followed as the clerk threaded his way through the lines of children all headed in separate directions, but when they had arrived and the clerk had strutted off with the air of one who has accomplished an unpleasant duty, the boy found it easy enough to slip out again and walk quite freely back down the stairs and across the wide front hall. Crowds of children were still marching about in all directions, somehow managing to keep themselves in tolerably neat processions as the lines criss-crossed one other on their way to the different classrooms. Dodging lithely between the groups, the boy felt invisible as he let himself out of the wide front doors, crossed the lawn, and turned decisively out of the gate and down the street. He walked briskly at first, but finding no pursuers, he slowed his pace and looked about him, reveling in his freedom and in the beauty of the morning. The air was stiff and fresh and cool as it filled his lungs, and he breathed deeply of it. The boy had always liked this part of the day. Something about the angle of the light—maybe just because it was still a bit slanted and got in your eyes so you couldn't see too clearly—made everything look new and unspoiled. Here was a fresh chance. If things were horrible yesterday, they needn't be so today. At least, you couldn't believe that at this hour, with everything so bright and shining. He would find his mother today—he knew it. He began to hum softly to himself as he walked along, and the school and all connected with it began to fade from his mind the way a nightmare does when the dreamer awakes to find all is right with the world.

He had not gone far, though, when he noticed that something was different today. People looked at him—not just casually, not just in passing. They eyed him with something that resembled suspicion and disapproval. Or if not himself, at least his *clothing*. Finally a man approached him and demanded, without preface, "What errand has Chadwicke sent you on, boy?"

The child ignored him and walked on, but the man would not be put off so easily. "Not one for speaking, eh? No manners. You must be new there. Why don't we make our way back there and I'll give them the report of you. They'll want to know what needs working on."

"I can't stop, sir," replied the boy at last. "I'm in a hurry. I've got someone waiting for me."

"Oh, you've a partner in crime?" the man surmised with a grin. "Who, then? A schoolmate, is it?"

"No." The boy darted to the right, intending to break into a run, but the man caught at him. "You'll not get far with this blue coat, boy," he warned breathlessly as he struggled to hold the writhing child. "Everyone knows where you belong." With a mighty effort he hauled the boy back the way he had come, loosening his grip only when he had turned the child over to a scornful clerk who promised him a good whipping. For his pains, the man received an invitation to the kitchen for a bowl of stew, which he accepted gratefully, and the boy could see that he was not really mean but only tired and hungry.

Things took a similar course when the boy escaped that afternoon, and even when he crept out under cover of night and made several miles before dawn, he ended up back at the school with hands that bled from punishment and a back covered with welts. People knew the clothing, knew "where he belonged," as the man had said. Or at least they thought they did.

The boy ran away several more times that week, but always with the same result. He had tried again and again to discover what the clerk had done with his own clothing, but the young man had taken pains to keep it from him, especially when the child proved so determined to leave. It was an odd thing, the boy mused in the rare moments when he was not preoccupied with either the plans for his next escape or unrestrained self-pity, how he could go all day feeling as if no one had the slightest idea that he was there at all, only to find himself so sought after if he ventured beyond the front doors.

After his eighth attempt, they brought him to Chadwicke. He understood from the clerk's grave manner that this was a very serious step and that few of the children were ever so unfortunate as to require it. He trembled a little in spite of his brave front as he sat waiting in Chadwicke's office for the schoolmaster to arrive, but he promised himself he would hold on to his resolve. They could not keep him there. He was not one of the friendless.

When Chadwicke entered he looked considerably less grave than the clerk had, though he bore his customary solemn dignity. He sat down in the chair behind his desk and faced the boy for a long time without speaking.

"You have tried to run away from here," he said at last. He leaned back in his chair, laced his fingers, unlaced them again. He seemed to choose his words carefully. "Many have tried before you, and some have succeeded. I make no secret of that. The boy whose space you now occupy threw his coat down on a dung heap. We would not take him back after that. You may do the same, if you choose. I cannot stop you. But . . . " He paused and sighed deeply. "It is a fault of the young that they can rarely see what is good for them. You are here not as a punishment but as a blessing. You are too foolish to understand that by rejecting it you are hurtling yourself towards your own destruction. Mind you, I don't hold your foolishness against you. Before God we are all fools, and the wisest cannot afford to put on airs. But I would that you would allow yourself to be taught. I want to help you see that this is the right path, and God would have you choose it."

The boy understood very little of this speech but tightened his brow into a scowl nevertheless. His frustration at being held against his will was the only protection he had against his fear—fear of the formidable schoolmaster, of his own future, of never seeing his mother again. "You don't even know me," he protested. "You don't know but what I might be better off somewhere else." He stared past his blue knickers to his shoes and grumbled, "I don't think you know so much. I guess you don't even remember that name you made up for me."

"What did you say?"

"I see you everyday, but you don't see anything. You don't look anyone in the face."

Chadwicke remained unperturbed. "'Is not the body more than raiment, and the life more than meat?' Do you think that if I do not know your face, I cannot know anything about you? I have your record, here," he indicated the ledger, "and in my mind as well." He tapped his forehead. "I know what you told me about yourself—the very little that you *could* tell me. I think I could tell you more. But perhaps that is for another time."

"If you remember what I told you, then you remember that my

mother is sick. She may be dying, and you won't let me go to her! How do you think she can take care of herself? By keeping me here, you're . . . you're killing her!" Emotion thrust the boy to his feet, and Chadwicke reached out a restraining arm and laid a large, clumsy hand on the child's shoulder.

"Peace, child. Be still," he murmured. Gradually the boy stopped shaking. He couldn't tell how, but a calm seemed to spread from that touch. After a moment, the boy resumed his seat, still feeling desperate but no longer violent. Chadwicke sat down also.

"Son, did your mother teach you about our Redeemer, the Lord Jesus Christ?"

The boy shook his head, and Chadwicke raised his eyes to the ceiling for an instant before continuing, "But you have heard of God, at least, the Creator and Master of the Universe?" The boy nodded dully because he could see it was what the schoolmaster wanted. "Well, son, what if you knew that God himself, the greatest of all, had come down among men to suffer as men do, to serve them and to lead them to righteousness? He is the king of all creation, but He came among the humblest of men. And it was all for our benefit, to serve us and teach us. If you knew that, wouldn't you want to learn His teachings and try very hard to do what He wanted you to do? You wouldn't want to disappoint Him, would you?"

"Well, but I don't know Him, and anyway I'm sure He wouldn't tell me to leave my mother if He was so good as you say."

"But He is good, and He did say to leave your mother. Or rather, He spoke to someone whose situation was very like yours. A young man, a good son, like you. His father died, and he wanted to do all the proper rituals. The Lord Jesus met him and asked the young man to follow Him, doing good and serving others as Jesus did. But the young man said, 'Let me bury my father first. Let me take care of him first, and then I will do what you ask.'"

The boy nodded approvingly. "He sounds sensible."

"Sensible, maybe, if this life were all there is. So many of the things that people believe are important are of no consequence at all. I told you when we first met that it is good and proper to think of one's parents. But there is One higher whose authority is more important. Do you know what Jesus said to the young man?"

"Did He tell him to take care of his father, and then come and do what Jesus wanted?"

"No, my son. After all, the father was already dead. What service could the young man render? He belonged among the living."

That afternoon, for reasons the boy could not have explained, he did not try to run away. Chadwicke's words had meant little to him; he had hardly understood them. But something about that meeting held him back. He put his hand upon the knob of the massive front door but did not turn it. Once, in the night, he pulled his feet out from under the blanket and planted them on the cold floor. But he did not rise. He sat so still that there might have been a hand against his chest, restraining him. Moments slipped by while he listened to his own breathing and the high, tooting snores of the other boys. Outside, the wind moaned mournfully and rattled against the windows. He had never been so alone.

He twisted around to gaze down the rows of cots. The other children lay still beneath their white sheets and gray blankets. He stared at them and wondered, Was friendlessness catching? Many of them had watched their parents die. If the boy threw in his lot with them, did it mean he believed his own mother was dead? Was every hour he spent here another handful of dirt thrown over her memory, so that eventually his image of her would be buried as surely as any physical body?

He shivered but didn't climb back under the covers. He thought of Chadwicke, who would always be a stranger no matter how long you knew him. He thought of Mr. Fortescue, who did the inspection for this group of boys, and how his cruel mouth had curled up into a smile when he had discovered a smudge of dirt on the boy's nose two mornings ago. And that same afternoon, when the boy had been sent to him for punishment after a failed escape attempt, Fortescue had hollered, "Who are you? Well, no matter. Every one of you could use a good whipping, that's my view."

And then there was this Jesus Christ, this man who told people to leave their parents. He was a stranger, too. *If this life were all there is*, Chadwicke had said. He stared at the tall, white-blue windows and imagined his mother floating to him through the night, pressing her face up against the glass. "Mama, you're flying," he would say, and she would answer, "I'm dead, my precious. I'm gone."

"No!" he cried aloud, starting at the sound of his own voice. The child in the cot next to him groaned and turned over onto his stomach but didn't wake up. The boy swung his feet back onto the bed and huddled into the blanket. Was it only in his head, or had the room grown colder? He made himself as small as possible and lay quietly, blinking into the darkness. There was only one other person in this world who knew him, and it wasn't Chadwicke or the inspector, it wasn't anyone at this school. No one here cared about him. They never would, and so it didn't matter—he could leave anytime, tomorrow or the next day. It didn't have to be tonight. Eventually they'd forget about him and let him go. But Angeline wouldn't forget him. She wouldn't forget his true name.

He didn't make a decision that night. He simply got up the next morning, put on the uniform, and went to class with the least advanced group of students, where he sat looking blankly at the first page of *The Book of Common Prayer*, which all the children were supposed to learn to read. That evening he went for supper in the long dining hall, where the fire embraced a small circle with its warmth and radiated a cheerful orange glow that gleamed on the rows of polished tables and danced in the eyes of everyone in the room, even those too far away to benefit from the heat. The next morning he did the same thing, and then the next and the next. Weeks and months passed, and then years, with nothing much to distinguish them. He progressed slowly in his schoolwork. Eventually he managed to stammer through a few pages of the Bible or *The Book of Common Prayer* without making too many mistakes. He could do a little arithmetic if he could get help from his fingers. And twice a week, he went in to be tested by the catechist, a short, mean-faced man who barked the questions impatiently.

"What is God?"

"God is a Spirit."

"What do the scriptures principally teach?"

"The duty God requires of man."

"What is sin?"

"Any want of conformity unto the law of God."

"Did all mankind fall in Adam's first transgression?"

"All mankind sinned in him and fell with him."

"Did God leave all mankind to perish in misery?"

"God, out of His mere good pleasure, did enter into a covenant of grace to deliver them out of sin and misery."

At this point the catechist would eye him contemptuously, as if he thought God might not have bothered.

The boy knew he was a mediocre student—none of the teachers would ever single him out for special training. Some boys were chosen for the mathematical school to learn how to be ships' navigators, and others studied for university. Not the boy. Still, he wasn't quite bad enough to be singled out for frequent punishment, either. He was inconspicuous. Even invisible.

When the first snowfall of the season marked the beginning of the boy's sixth winter at the school, his thoughts turned toward his future. Snowed in and iced over, the school might have been its own separate world, created from a palette of white, gray, and blue. But its solitude couldn't last; even during the coldest months, children came and went. It was the going part that concerned the boy now. No child remained at the school past the age of fifteen; he or she was either apprenticed out to a master to learn a trade or, if a parent or friend still lived, perhaps returned to that guardian's responsibility. In any case, once students had exceeded that magical age, the school troubled itself no more over them, abandoning them with as much enthusiasm and officiousness as it had once displayed in taking them in.

Knowing this, the boy pondered on the great blank void that loomed before him. To whom would he be apprenticed, what trade would be chosen for him, where would he go? All were matters with a substantial bearing upon his future condition, yet he knew he would have no say in any of them. One day the clerk would simply come to him with a gruff order to proceed to Chadwicke's office; there his sentence would be delivered, and as far as anyone at the school was concerned, that was the end of it, the end of him. The boy could not suppress a creeping fear when he thought of this moment. At one time, he had exerted all his strength, made use of all his resources to escape these walls. But that was long ago. Meanwhile, the world had gone on without him, and he now felt apprehensive about venturing beyond the space that had circumscribed his existence for five and a half long years.

With a kind of morbid curiosity, he began tuning in more attentively to the conversations of boys who faced a similar uncertainty. One evening at mealtime, in the early spring, he heard one boy ask his comrade, "Have you heard what happened to Gatesby?" Instantly his consciousness became focused on the speaker and the speaker's nearest companion; he waited breathlessly for the reply.

"No, I've heard nothing. Is it decided? Has a master been found for him?"

"Yes, he's to leave for Antigua the day after tomorrow."

"Antigua?" the young man exhaled expressively through rounded lips. "The poor fellow."

"Yes, indeed. You'd better go and say your good-byes, for you'll not be setting eyes on him again."

"Is he to be part of a ship's crew, then?"

"No, it's worse than that. He's staying in Antigua. His master owns a plantation there."

"The poor fellow," repeated the boy. Then, perking up as if a new thought had occurred to him, he asked, "Hasn't Chiswell been apprenticed to a planter in Antigua? That's strange, isn't it? Are they to go to the same place?"

"No, that's the worst of it. Chiswell had been apprenticed to this very master, all the details were worked out, his passage had been purchased. But when they went to his mother for final approval—she's still alive you know, with rooms over in Spittle Fields—she said not as long as she had breath in her body would she allow her son to go and live among barbarians."

"Was she afraid of the natives? There are hardly any left, you know. They might have reassured her."

"I think by 'barbarians,' she meant the planters—and all those slaves, of course. Well, they had no choice but to make new arrangements. Chiswell has now got a nice, safe position with a cobbler not three streets over from his mother's lodgings."

"And Gatesby? How did he get mixed up in this?"

"Oh, you know, they had already promised the planter, and they don't ignore opportunities like that. Not with so many needing positions. So they thought of Gatesby. There's no one to protest if he's sent to live with barbarians. They wrote that right in the ledger, in fact. 'This boy, having no friends,' they said. So that's the end of Gatesby."

That night the boy let himself into the garden behind the school. The March evening was frosty and the garden still, with patches of snow giving off a faint glow of reflected moonlight. A slight breeze brought the blood to his cheeks and made the bare trees sway gently like slender maidens in a ballroom. He strode deep into the trees' meager shelter and then stood staring up into the vast sky; the twinkling stars, the blue-black night, the graceful roundness of a near-full moon—*all so beautiful,* he thought, *and so indifferent.* He had fooled himself a long time, but he could do it no longer. That boy on his way to Antigua, the boy who had no friends, might be himself a few weeks from now. And after that? His apprenticeship would no doubt last six or seven years, but chances were that few of the boys who went to the colonies would live out the full term. Many of the colonies were notoriously rough and dangerous. They attracted people who had already used up every other possibility and had only their lives left to gamble with. And that was him, now. He had nothing else.

Five and a half years ago he had come to this school believing he was nearly a man. Somehow he would find his mother, somehow he would care for them both. Well, what if he had really found her? What could he have done? It didn't matter now, he mused, feeling the warmth of a teardrop against his cheek. His mother was dead. He had known that for a long time without ever allowing himself to think about it. A detached part of his mind reflected that he was now the only living person who knew his true name—or who cared.

He brushed at his tears impatiently. What was worth crying about? These stars, this moon, these trees never wept. What was the pain of one human being in this immense realm of creation? The stars didn't need his permission to shine. The snow would fall every winter and recede every spring, with or without him. Nevertheless, he sunk to his knees and cried bitterly, while the trees went on swaying and the moon went on glowing and the stars never missed a twinkle.

Chapter 9

They couldn't tell how long he had been in the snow before they brought him in, and by then he was in no condition to tell them, so they warmed blankets in front of the fire and wrapped him up tight like a mummy. But then his head was hot. "He's got the fever, poor lamb," confirmed Nurse Gwynn, who was second in command of the sick ward and the highest authority available during the night hours. "Perhaps that's why he went outside in this cold." So they made up cool compresses with ice folded in cloth and swathed his head with them while Nurse Gwynn stood over him clicking her tongue disapprovingly. "It's a shame," she said to the other nurses. "He should have come straight to us, like these others." She gestured to the ward's other occupants, about six in all, most of whom also had the fever and were tossing restlessly or mumbling in delirium.

"Someone should have sent him," said Nurse Jellicott.

"Oh, who's to do that?" put in Nurse Meryton. "You know what idiots men can be. All these teachers with all their fancy learning, and they can't see something that's plain as day."

Nurse Gwynn had very little hope of saving the boy, on account of his being out in the cold so long, but since the sick ward was more sparsely populated than usual and the nurses had leisure to fuss over their patients, she took up her post by the boy's bedside and kept vigil throughout the night. In the morning the doctor came round on his usual visit and Nurse Gwynn encouraged him to do all that he could for the boy, though he was in worse condition than any of the others. The doctor consented to bleed him and set about cutting a neat rectangle in the boy's elbow. When he had filled a bowl with the boy's blood, he pressed a piece of cotton to the wound and tied it up with a bandage.

"Out with the bad," he muttered soothingly. "That will soon set him to rights." Some of his colleagues were reluctant to bleed people who were too near death for fear it would hurry them on their journey to the other side—like all the best medical remedies, it had its dangers—but the doctor always argued that logic decreed it was better to do something than nothing. He looked down at his patient and noted the boy's pallor with satisfaction. Everyone knew that people with fevers had red faces, so white faces meant recovery. Either that, or death. But one way or another, the suspense was brought to an end, and the doctor sometimes felt that was all the medical profession could really aspire to.

Whether from luck, miracle, or some odd chance, the boy lived on through the next day and the next. He edged in and out of consciousness, his mind fumbling through a world deprived of time and logic, but not of pain. Something tugged at him, a nagging, shrieking presence urging him on in a futile quest. "Find this!" it commanded. "Go here!" "Hurry, hurry!" "Don't stop, don't rest!" He writhed with frantic anxiety . . . *can't be still, must hurry, must go on.* Once, he opened his eyes enough to view his real surroundings through two narrow slits, but everything looked distorted and out of place, as strange as his own dreams. Beholding the fire that burned not far from the foot of his bed, he surmised that he had died and arrived in hell. He trembled, for the flames hurt. "So hot," he whispered. And then a voice—not the urgent, angry voice in his mind, but a soft, kind, gentle voice—replied, "I know, lovey, but you'll be better soon." And then a face shut out the awful glare, a pleasant, comfortable face, and a cool hand wiped at his forehead, brushing away hair that was wet with perspiration. Ah, that was where the fire was, in his head. He clung to Nurse Gwynn as darkness flooded his vision and wrestled him back into delirium. Through the twisted dreams and illogical mental anguish, she anchored him to reality. The touch of her hand, the sight of her face not far above his own, promised a return to a world where floors and ceilings and fires were where they should be and where shadows couldn't reach out and choke you and the only faces you saw belonged to solid human beings. Whenever he became truly frightened by his feverish visions, when he felt he would lose himself in the nightmare world and never be able find his way back, he would squeeze her hand and immediately receive an answering squeeze. She didn't need to speak; the meaning came through: "Don't worry, I am here. I will not leave you."

On the morning of the third day, the fever broke, and he opened his eyes cautiously to find her still there beside him, her eyes full of something that resembled concern. "Well, so you've decided to stay with us after all," she smiled. He smiled back, or at least he tried to. The corners of his mouth moved only slightly, but he watched her eyes and felt that she understood. She sat with him a while longer, gently smoothing the bed clothes and puffing up his pillow, before bustling off to help distribute a breakfast of hot broth.

The boy let his eyelids fall closed, testing the darkness inside them. No, it didn't threaten to pull him down again, he was safe from it. The only vision floating in his consciousness was that of Nurse Gwynn as he had seen her gazing at him a few moments before. Had anyone else ever looked at him like that, as if they were cheered up by his very well-being? He tried to conjure up an image of his mother's face and found with dismay that his memory of her had grown indistinct. But he knew that she had loved him, and she must have looked at him that way sometimes. And then she had gone, and all through these cold years there had been no one—no one he mattered to, no one who mattered to him. He realized suddenly, still feeling the touch of Nurse Gwynn's hand on his forehead, that it had been this loneliness that had gnawed at his insides when he had already filled his belly with stew, that had made him shiver with cold in spite of his blanket, that had made him feel as alone and unprotected as if he were sleeping outdoors beneath the vast, indifferent sky. Somehow, just to know that one person cared, even if only a little bit, made all the difference. Perhaps the future was not so bleak after all.

After several days in the sick ward, the boy, though still very pale and weak, was proclaimed officially out of danger, and since the fever was beginning to spread through the school with greater rapidity and beds were no longer lacking in occupants, he was sent up to convalesce in his own cot in the dormitory at the top of the building. His meals were brought up to him three times each day, but aside from that brief interaction with whomever the kitchen staff had commissioned for the task, he was left to himself to recover as best he could without being a burden to anyone. He slept most of the time, a peacefully dreamless sleep that trickled gently into his mind and body like a stream of warm water. He floated and drifted through a succession of days in a pleasant state of half-consciousness, and all the while a soft gray haze enveloped him. It insulated him from his surroundings, dulled pain, fear, even the memory of real life, so that his years at the school became dim and wavery like an image reflected in a pond. If he so much as threw a pebble in, the whole picture would scatter and dissolve, and he could walk away untroubled with the breeze caressing his face and the grass swaying beneath his feet. He enjoyed this solitary paradise, this sense of peace that came of having left the harsher realities behind. Although physically he grew stronger each day, his mental attachment to the world grew more and more tenuous, until finally his mind struck upon an idea sharp enough to penetrate through the haze. He opened his eyes one morning feeling that there was something about the day that he ought to remember. He puzzled over it unconcernedly for a while, dozing off and on, until with a start he realized that it was his birthday. He was fifteen years old, and his summons would be coming.

Startled into action, he eased his legs cautiously over the edge of the cot and stood up. The cold, rough floor felt the same as always as he made his way tremulously toward one of the windows and pressed his forehead against the pane. The glass was cold and damp against his warm skin. In the garden below, most of the snow had melted and a few brave buds had popped out on the tree branches, manifesting their faith in the coming spring. Soon the whole garden would throw off the dreary deadness of winter and burst into life, replacing dull brown with green, white, pink, and yellow. "New and clean," he could hear his mother's voice saying. "In spring, the world is reborn. When you were born, you were new and clean, and I felt—I felt as though you were me, and I was new and clean again, too."

He sighed and turned away to plod back to his cot. Tugging the blanket around him, he closed his eyes again to shut out the world. But it didn't work. Reality was still there on the other side of his eyelids, and there was no hiding from it now—his paradise was lost. The old anxiety caught at his chest and beads of sweat began forming along his hairline. Tomorrow, or the next day, or the next, the future would come for him. It would snatch him away from the relative safety of Chadwicke's school and drop him anywhere it chose. The darkness inside his head looked like his life: there was no light anywhere. And then an image blotted out the blackness, the image of Nurse Gwynn's gentle face. "Do you know my name?" he had asked her on the afternoon of the day he awoke from the fever. "Did anyone tell you?"

"Yes, lovey, of course." And she had recited the name that Chadwicke had assigned him on the first day at the school, the "new name" for the "new life."

"That isn't my true name," he explained earnestly. It seemed important that she know his name, though it cost him to speak. He told her the name his mother had given him and how she used to call him "Buttermilk" and how she had gotten very sick.

"Poor little lamb," clucked Nurse Gwynn soothingly. Remembering that conversation now, the boy felt a boost of courage. At least someone here knew him, and if someone knows you, he reasoned, you can't fall into a void. If someone cares about you, the darkness can't swallow you. You'll always have a name if there is someone else to love you. Of course, Nurse Gwynn didn't really love him. She couldn't; he wasn't her son or any other relation. But at least she knew him, and for a while she had cared.

He fell asleep again, immensely comforted by the thought that she knew his name.

Two days later the clerk came to summon the boy to Chadwicke's office. The schoolmaster, who looked much the same as he had when the boy first laid eyes on him except that his coat was more patched, if that were possible, and his eyes more grave, read him the agreement he had already recorded in the ledger:

"This boy, having no friends, is by approval of Mr. Chadwicke bound apprentice for seven years to Captain Jonas Humphrey of the Hudson's Bay Company, master of the ship *Friend's Pardon* bound to Newfoundland."

When Chadwicke had finished, the pair sat in silence until the schoolmaster said, "It is quite a large ship, and you will find there is much work to be done, which is as it should be. You will see many strange and exotic places. After a time, you will come to love the sea, as all sailors do."

The boy said nothing. No comment, either of dissent or approval, was required of him. After a few moments the schoolmaster dismissed him. "You must be ready by Thursday morning," Chadwicke ordered in parting. "You will leave immediately after breakfast."

Late that night the boy crept down through the darkened school to the sick ward, where candles glowed, a fire burned, and nurses hurried back and forth. It was an island of activity in a silent, sleeping world. He hovered tentatively in the doorway, his eyes searching among the moving figures for the familiar one he sought. When he had found her, he threaded his way toward her between the beds full of restless, moaning children. He waited patiently behind her until she had finished laying a cool compress across one patient's forehead, then approached her somewhat shyly.

"Nurse Gwynn," he began, "I came to tell you . . . "

Instead of offering a welcome, she gazed at him with a puzzled look.

"Yes, dear, are you sick, too?" She laid an experienced hand across his forehead. "Hmm, you feel cool enough. Is something else wrong? Did someone send you?"

"No, I'm not sick, I'm much better. I came to tell you . . . "

"Not sick?" She looked past him to one of the beds across the aisle, where a girl about ten years old had started coughing. "Excuse me, lovey," she said, and went to take the girl a glass of water. The boy watched her work, remarking the mixture of efficiency and tenderness with which she cared for her patients' needs. He could see that she was busy; the ward was filled to overflowing. At the far end from the door, the neat rows of cots collided in one tangled mess of sheets and bodies. A few beds held two or three small children. By now the fever had affected a large proportion of the school, and the boy, being one of the first to contract it, had also been one of the first to recover. He didn't want to disturb the nurses now, but he had only a few days left here, only a few more chances to say good-bye and receive some words of encouragement in return. So he lingered, keeping out of everybody's way until Nurse Gwynn had settled herself next to a patient, and then he rushed over to her and pushed the words out as fast as they would come.

"Nurse Gwynn, I only came to thank you for taking care of me when I was sick and to tell you that I've been apprenticed and will be leaving on Thursday. And so . . . to tell you good-bye. Good-bye, and thank you. That's all."

The old nurse glanced up distractedly. "What? What about Thursday?" She turned back to her patient in a dismissive way, tossing advice back over her shoulder: "If you are not too sick, lovey, you should go back to your own cot, for you can see that we've very little room here. We can only take the most serious cases."

The boy stared at her back, half inclined to leave. But now he had gone this far, he had to finish what he had come to do. "I'm not sick. Nurse Gwynn, I've already been here. Do you . . . " A cold thought chilled his stomach. "Do you remember me? I was here a few weeks ago."

"A few weeks ago?" She twisted around again and focused her attention on him for the first time, narrowing her eyes in an effort to remember. "You've already had the fever, then? Good, very good. That's one less we have to worry about. Leave me to my work now, child."

The boy slunk away dejectedly, feeling numb but also stupid. Why should he have expected her to remember him among so many? There were over a thousand students in this school. Just to feed them, clothe them, catechize them, and finally apprentice them was all the staff could do. Why should they remember a face? The relevant information was there in Chadwicke's ledgers, in the teachers' daily records. Nothing mattered here unless it existed in ink. And because of that, everything worked in an orderly fashion; nothing was ever late, no one was out of place. It was all miraculous. And to care about one individual would mess everything up, like poking a tree branch into a carriage wheel. You had to let the wheel keep turning, and if you couldn't turn with it, you had to get out of the way.

The boy maneuvered back out between the cots and slipped through the door, turning resignedly to go up the stairs to bed. But he had not gone two steps into the dimness of the corridor when he heard a voice crying out in the darkness behind him. He froze with surprise, for though it must have been coming from the sick ward, the voice sounded very close. He paused and surveyed the blackness around him. Past the rectangle of light that was the door to the ward, he could see a thrashing bundle of white. He stepped hesitantly toward it until he could make out, in the midst of the sheets, the face of a child with tousled dark hair. The boy knew him vaguely; for a while they had been in the same reading group. The child's name was Nicholas Casey, and he was several years younger than the boy, about ten or eleven. But he was smart. He had advanced rapidly through the classes and would probably be selected for some kind of special training. Most likely, he would never go to sea—or if he did, it wouldn't be as a common sailor.

For the moment, though, Nicholas's intelligence wasn't helping him. His eyes, bright from fever, looked out uncomprehendingly, his hands groped for something they couldn't reach, and his voice cried plaintively for the two things he wanted most, water and someone called Anne. The boy wondered at his being left out there alone where no one was likely to give him much attention, but it must have been the result of the crowded conditions. Still, no one else would hear the one request that could be granted, so the boy strode back into the ward and located the long table where the nurses had set out fat pitchers of water. He went and filled up a tumbler and brought it back to the child. As he slid an arm under Nicholas's neck to raise him up, he touched the child's burning skin and recoiled a little. He had never felt anyone so hot. The child writhed as the boy brought the glass to his mouth, and a small stream of water spilled down onto Nicholas's chest. Perhaps this roused him somewhat. At any rate, when the boy pressed the glass against Nicholas's lips, the child drank. After Nicholas had emptied the tumbler, the boy set him gently back against the pillow and stood to leave. But as he turned away from the cot, a hot hand clawed at his arm. "Please," murmured Nicholas thickly. "Please help me." With his own experience of the fever still fresh in his mind, the boy sat back down and reached out a hand to smooth the wet hair from Nicholas's forehead. The child desperately needed to be cooled. Why didn't someone come to check on him? Well, if no one else would take care of him, the boy would have to do it himself. He stood up again, and Nicholas held him tightly. "No, no, don't leave!"

The boy bent close to Nicholas's ear and spoke very clearly. "I won't leave you, except for a moment, to get something to cool you." He plucked Nicholas's hand away, set it down next to the child, and stepped quickly aside. On the same table in the ward that held the pitchers of water, the boy found a few cloths that had not yet been used as compresses for other patients. He dipped two into the water, then traversed a series of dark hallways and let himself out into the garden. The night air was chilly, just as he had known it would be. He draped one of the cloths over a tree branch, then went back inside and laid the other cloth over Nicholas's forehead. The child started under the sudden touch of cold, then relaxed and took hold of the boy's arm.

"I tried to save them," mumbled Nicholas, his eyes seeking the boy's face but failing to focus. "They went one by one, until there was only me. I waited for three days." The boy didn't understand what he was talking about but listened patiently and murmured the soothing, meaningless words he had heard other people say. "Were you there?" asked Nicholas. "Did you see them?"

"No," said the boy. "But it's no matter now. You can rest."

"I tried to save them," Nicholas repeated, then tossed fitfully and clawed at the sheets. The cloth quickly grew warm against the burning skin, and the boy left to retrieve the other one from outside, where the crisp night air had kept it cold. He wiped Nicholas's face and wrists and spread the cloth across his chest. Throughout the night, he repeated the routine countless times, trading off the cloths as they absorbed the heat from the child's body. Once as he returned to the sick ward to dip a cloth in water, he spoke to one of the nurses, who was also preparing compresses.

"Why is that boy out in the corridor?" he asked. "He was crying for water earlier and no one could hear him. No one has been to examine him these many hours."

The nurse glanced over at him as if noticing his presence for the first time. She looked drawn and haggard, and a few untidy locks of hair were stuck to her face with sweat. "You can see for yourself we have too many as it is," she snapped. "We have to make choices."

"What do you mean by choices?" persisted the boy. "Surely you can still spare a few feet of floor, and then no one would have to bother to go out of the ward to tend to him."

"We've sent many home, them as have a bit of family left," she replied, a bit less sharply. "We would have sent him away if he had anyone to go to. They might have done something for him. *We* can't. He'll not pull through, you'll see. He's very bad. Some of the ones in here aren't quite so bad off. We have to choose, you see."

The boy did see. No one would be going out to tend to Nicholas. He had been shoved aside where he would be no bother to anyone while he died. Well, perhaps the nurses couldn't do anything about it, with so many others to care for, but he could. He had a few days left here and nothing to do that really mattered. He would stay by Nicholas, give him what care he could. And if the child died anyway, as well he might, at least he wouldn't die alone.

For the next two days, the boy scarcely left Nicholas's side. He kept constantly busy changing compresses, giving the child water to drink, answering the child's earnest, illogical queries. "Do you think they will pull through?" Nicholas asked him once, with apparent distress. "I'm doing all I can."

"Yes," said the boy. "I'm sure they will all be better soon." He couldn't help wondering as he held Nicholas's small, hot hand if anyone had been with his own mother at the end, to stroke her forehead and promise her that everything would be all right. "There is nothing to fear," she used to sing as she rocked him, and all the while her eyes had been big with fright and dark with the memory of sorrow, with the knowledge that security is fragile. "There is nothing to fear," the boy whispered now to Nicholas, half skeptical, half hoping it could somehow be true.

Early on the morning that he was to leave, the boy awoke from a cramped position on the floor next to Nicholas's cot. The hallway was silent. Acting from reflex, he jerked up to study the child's face and laid a hand across his forehead. He felt cool. Anxiously, the boy watched for the slow rise and fall of Nicholas's chest. After an instant that seemed more like an eternity, he saw the bedclothes stir faintly once, twice, three times in a peaceful, even rhythm. The fever had broken. Nicholas would live. Feeling suddenly drained, the boy allowed himself a smile, then got stiffly to his feet. He had only a few hours left to prepare for his journey. He needed to go, but . . . he had hoped for a chance to speak to Nicholas after the child awoke. He hesitated, gazing down at Nicholas uncertainly. It seemed strange just to walk away. On impulse, he reached under the neck of his coat and pulled out the chain with the silver heart. It was the most precious item he had, the only thing he owned of any value. When he had given up thinking that he could return it to Angeline someday, he had never imagined himself parting with it. But he wanted to leave something of himself behind for this child, something to say, "I was here, and I cared." No doubt it was a strange gift, but he had none better. He unclasped it from his own neck, knelt down, and wrapped the chain three times around the child's thin wrist. The heart gleamed in the firelight from the doorway of the sick ward. "Good-bye," whispered the boy, speaking to his mother as much as to Nicholas. Then he got up quickly and walked away without looking back.

Chapter 10

It was an overcast, drizzly day when the boy stepped onto the dock and got his first sight of the *Friend's Pardon*, the ship commanded by his new master, Captain Humphrey. The brightly painted red and blue of the young vessel stood out incongruously against the dreary background of gray sky and gray water, like a red cloak in the middle of a funeral procession. Faint tendrils of mist wafted about here and there like uneasy spirits. A sharp, cold wind blew in angry defiance of the coming spring, and despite the foreboding atmosphere the ship was alive with activity as men thronged up the gangplank hefting crates and barrels, many of the crewmen with breath enough left to whistle. The boy, like all children of that era, had heard tales of ships and adventures in distant lands, and this vessel with its cheerful crew and its colors that were almost unnaturally vivid might have popped right out of the world of imagination. The ship had three tall masts supporting several levels of square sails, and compared to some other ships the boy had seen from afar, it was a large vessel, as Chadwicke had promised. Even so, it appeared more inadequate than he had anticipated, as if it wouldn't take all that much to overturn it. With effort he pushed back mental images of waves as high as castles and green, toothy monsters emerging from towering cascades of foam.

After a bit of unsubtle prodding from his companion, an elderly clerk who had kept his hand clamped tightly on the boy's shoulder during most of the journey from Chadwicke's school, the boy approached the ship cautiously. As the pair drew near the gangplank, a man stepped out from his post on the right and gruffly demanded, "What do you want?"

The clerk cleared his throat and adjusted his cravat with one hand, still gripping the boy's shoulder with the other. "I've brought Captain Humphrey his apprentice."

"Oh, you have, have you?" grinned the man, his eyes gleaming with what the boy interpreted as something like mischievous glee. "Well, young lad, what have we got in store for you!" He turned abruptly and hollered loudly in the direction of the deck. Amid the flurry of activity now taking place there, a thin sailor put down a barrel he had been hauling and came out from among the crowd, maneuvering lithely down the gangplank around the stream of ship-bound traffic.

"What is it, Jones?" the thin sailor inquired.

"Here's the boy what the Captain's sent for from the school. Take him and show him his duties." As the boy moved grimly toward the gangplank, he thought he saw the man wink at him.

"All right, then," said the thin sailor, "first I'll show you where to sleep. You can't carry that around all day." He indicated the knapsack the boy was holding, which contained a new suit of clothes from the school. Once on the ship, the sailor led the boy through the mob of crewmen toward a gaping hole in the middle of the deck. Into this he motioned for the boy to descend. Fumbling for a foothold, the boy made his way carefully down into the hold and blinked at the semidarkness. There was a stench of shut-up air, and the objects he could see silhouetted in the dimness suggested chaos. As his eyes adjusted he saw that cargo, packed in barrels and crates of various sizes, had been crammed into every available space. Here and there a few feet of floor was surrendered to a narrow, straw-filled mattress. A rat stared at him from the top of a crate before scurrying off into the shadows.

"Get on with you boy, there's work to be done," ordered the sailor, pressing his boot against the boy's neck and shoving gently. The boy stumbled down the final step of the ladder and careened into a barrel, which did not shift under his weight—there was no room for it to move. Behind him, the thin sailor climbed down effortlessly.

"That's yours over there," he said, pointing to a mattress against the wall. "Put your knapsack down and come back up."

Back in the light, the boy took a moment to survey his surroundings more closely. He estimated that the ship was about eighty or ninety feet long, and a thick crowd of men was presently swarming over it. He wondered if they were all crewmen or if many of them would be staying behind.

"How many are going on the ship?" he ventured to ask.

"Oh, as many as that is," replied the sailor, waving vaguely in the direction of the crowd. "Help us get loaded up, now." He led the boy back down the gangplank and across the dock toward a pile of crates.

"What, all these are going too?"

The sailor looked at him with an expression of thinly masked exasperation. "What, surely you didn't think we would waste our time galloping halfway 'round the world for that little mass of cargo we've got in there already? Get to work now, we've a schedule to keep."

Back on the dock, the boy selected a medium-sized wooden crate and hoisted it up against his chest, grunting slightly at the effort. He watched other men balancing large barrels across their backs. "What's in these, anyway?" he asked one of the other sailors as he headed back to the gangplank.

The sailor squinted at the crate in the boy's arms. "That one there is like to be full of shoes," he guessed. "Got a lot of shoes this time out. And the usual—candles, pots and dishes, some cloth. Course, we're bringing a whole mess of ready-made things because there aren't a lot as is handy with a needle where we're going. Some of them big barrels is full of wine. That's always welcome."

The boy tried to appear nonchalant as he carried the crate onto the ship and deposited it in the hold. He didn't want anyone thinking he couldn't handle carrying a bunch of shoes. Secretly, though, as he took a moment to stretch out his straining muscles in the darkness below deck, he wondered how a few scraps of leather could be that heavy. What were they made of, after all? Stone? On his next trip, he sought one of the tall rectangular cases filled with ready-made clothes. He figured this would be light, at least, even if it was bulky. But this too pressed against him with surprising weight. He remembered hearing stories about a certain torture they used to get confessions out of prisoners. They made the victim lie on his back, and then they kept piling rocks onto his chest. "Confess!" they'd insist after each addition of weight. It wasn't always a very effective strategy, as the prisoner often died before he could gasp anything out. If anyone asked the boy a question now, he'd be as helpless to answer. How could the others manage that constant whistling?

The next time out, he eased one of the bigger cases against his back, stooping under it so that its weight helped hold it in place. He staggered a little when he moved forward but then steadied himself and approached the ship. He was halfway up the sloping gangplank when another sailor, heading down, bumped him lightly and set the case teetering, threatening to pull the boy backward. He fought to regain his balance but couldn't get control of the case, which finally fell away behind him with a deafening crash of splintering wood. The boy pivoted on one foot, arms flailing, and dived back toward the dock, where he landed gracelessly on his chest with his arms and legs splaying out like those of a half-crushed spider.

"Ha ha," laughed the thin sailor who had shown him where to sleep. "Good thing you're so light on your feet, boy!" he called. "Tomorrow you climb the ratlines." The man motioned to the intricate webs of ropes that extended high above the deck like great ladders to the sky. Starting out wide at the bottom, they narrowed as they angled up through the levels of sails toward the tops of the masts, where the smallest sails, the topgallants, perched at a dizzying height. The boy gasped for breath as he stared up at those white-gray sheets, each limp and heavy looking now that the ship was docked. *Climb the rigging?* He gulped.

"Back to work now!" somebody ordered. The boy went to find another crate of shoes. When, late into the night, he was finally allowed to retire to the hold for a few hours of sleep, the boy was too exhausted to notice the unappealing smell of the place or even the cramped position of his mattress. He slept deeply and dreamlessly, and when he awoke the ship was already moving out toward the open sea. He clambered up on the deck and watched with fascination as the land receded. It seemed not so much that the land was getting smaller as that the sea and sky were growing larger, rolling together into one gigantic spread of color that would soon swallow up the thin gray coast. The boy turned into the wind and felt it whip about him, and to his surprise he found himself laughing with excitement. Perhaps it was the overwhelming sense of relief that flowed over him almost as tangibly as the breeze. When you have dreaded something for as long as the boy had dreaded the precipice that was his future, there is bound to be a sense of release when it actually happens, when you take the first tentative step off solid ground. For at least now you are facing it, you have the thing itself to contend with instead of the fear. For too long the boy had been haunted by the specter of what was to come. Now he savored the moment, not thinking about past or future, but only the present. The horizon still showed the gold and pink of dawn; the ship seemed to move as freely as the orange-tipped clouds. The wind blew cold but bracing. It was beautiful and glorious. Perhaps Chadwicke had been right after all. Perhaps he would learn to love the sea.

That afternoon, as promised, he made his first ascent into the rigging. A young man named Fithers accompanied him, alternately offering encouragement and rolling his eyes with impatience as the boy moved cautiously upward. The ropes criss-crossed in a grid, providing hand- and footholds, but the empty squares in between were large so that the boy was constantly stretching. Once, about halfway up, he glanced down and then shut his eyes quickly to block what he'd seen.

"Don't look down," advised Fithers, too late. "Or up."

"Right," said the boy, opening his eyes again and keeping them focused on the ropes in front of him, trying to forget how vast the sea had become beneath him and how tiny the ship seemed in comparison.

Fithers helped him work on adjusting one of the topsails, which were in the middle of the three levels of sails. When they had finished and climbed back down, the boy stifled a great sigh of relief and locked his knees to ke ep from crumpling gratefully onto the deck.

"How often do we do that?" he asked, trying to keep his voice from sounding tremulous.

"Oh, it depends on the wind," Fithers said. "But I'd say maybe two, three, five dozen times a day."

"Oh." The boy wiped away the sweat that had accumulated on his brow and followed Fithers resignedly to where a group of sailors was busy pounding oakum into the deck. Did Chadwicke know anything about sailing? He had promised that it would be a lot of work, and he had been right. The sails needed regular adjustments to make the most of the wind, the network of ropes had to be maintained, and there was always something to be done to the ship itself. That was on a normal day. It was a grueling routine at the best of times, and the boy soon understood why most of the crewmen were young. Few were more than twenty years older than himself. The work was too strenuous for older men, and besides, Fithers explained, sailors didn't get to be old men. Either they left the sea for a safer occupation on land, or—

"The sea will never run out of ways to kill a man," Fithers told him one day as they worked among the sails, spreading them as wide as they would go in an effort to capture even the faintest of breezes.

"Why did you become a seaman if it's so dangerous?" the boy wanted to know.

"Don't have any family," Fithers said. "Don't have a home. Might as well be out here." He gestured toward the great spread of glassy water around them. At this height, every movement of the ship was exaggerated and they swung gently back and forth through the sky. It used to make the boy sick, but he was getting more accustomed to it now.

"What became of your family?" he asked.

"Died," said Fithers shortly, clamping his mouth shut on the word in a way that let the boy know he didn't want to talk about it. They worked together quietly, pitching and swaying all the time as the ship rocked in the water. They seemed to have lost connection with anything solid, throwing themselves on the mercy of the moody sea.

A few weeks into the voyage, a storm caught them, black and towering in its fury. Sheets of icy water lashed the deck like ends of a giant whip. The boy helped work the pumps throughout the night, keeping the ship alive and the crew with it. When dawn broke, smooth and peaceful, Fithers informed him that it had been a mild episode. Even so, it seemed to have ripped them to pieces. When the boy climbed up to do repairs that afternoon, he found bits of rope that had been torn loose by the storm and shredded so that they looked like they'd been clawed by wild beasts. He'd found the real sea monster, and it didn't have green flesh or huge, dripping teeth. It was nothing but water and air, and it could be deadly.

During those first few weeks, the boy's muscles ached constantly, and when he slept it was always in profound oblivion. The men were divided up into watches, each group manning the ship for four hours at a time, so the boy never had long to rest.

He would awake without the thinnest memory of a dream, without a single image left over from sleep. And then one morning, after nearly a month at sea, he had gone to sleep in the dawn after the last watch of the night, had pulled his coarse blanket tight around him against the damp chill that seeped into the hold even when air could not. And he had been asleep instantly. But instead of sinking into darkness, he felt himself rising. He dreamed that he was swimming through the night sky with the air threading through his fingers, a little softer than water but nearly as dense and with the same way of flowing. Around him the stars glowed gently, small and round, as they looked from earth, and he found that if he reached up he could catch one in his hand. It glimmered and twinkled against his skin, radiating a warmth that spread through his chest and down into his feet. He swam on, gathered up more handfuls of stars, and when he had enough he put them together to build a boat. He found more stars and built two oars and then rowed himself across the dark, silent sea, across the gleaming path of moonlight, and bits of moonbeam clung to his oars and shone out like a luminous tail as he raised and dipped, raised and dipped. He hadn't thought about where he was going, but gradually he realized that he had a destination, one that had guided all his seemingly random movements and that now pulled him swiftly across the sky. At length he spied something white and shining, which as he drew closer revealed itself to be a sort of pavilion. The boat bumped gently up against the lowest step; the boy climbed out and mounted the remaining stairs. In the middle of the pavilion, a man in a long robe waited with an arm outstretched. His hair shone like fire and his robe was whiter than anything the boy had ever seen, even whiter than the starched sheets of the sick ward and more brilliant than snow in sunshine. As the boy came near, the man spoke to him in a deep, quiet, melodious voice that made the boy think of rushing wind, or water swirling over rocks. "I know your name," the man said. And he looked at the boy as if he saw his face, as if he *knew* his face. For no reason at all, tears stung at the boy's eyes, and he felt as if he held one of the warm stars against his chest. He found himself stretching out his own arm and opening his mouth to greet the man, to call him . . .

He awoke suddenly to find himself cramped up in the very solid ship. The dream had been so vivid, the feeling so intense, that he was flooded with a sense of disorientation as he blinked dumbly at his surroundings. The word he had been about to say remained on his tongue; his lips were ready to form the first sound.

"Father," he whispered softly to himself, just to find out how the thing would taste on his tongue. He had never called anyone that in all his life. But even now, with the undeniable and prosaic reality of the ship all around him and the stench of unwashed bodies filling his nostrils, he felt the rightness of the word. It carried with it a sense of belonging, and besides that a queer sort of pain—something like what you might feel watching the last dying beauty of a sunset: a mixture of awe, joy, and loss, because in a moment it will all be gone.

That afternoon he climbed higher up on the rigging than he ever had before, right up to one of the topgallant sails at the pinnacle of the mast. In his month at sea he had grown more sure of himself as he repeatedly scaled the spider web of ratlines that carried him high above the water, and even the feeling of spinning out of control as the masts twirled through the sky and the way the horizon kept shifting crookedly no longer frightened him. He even found himself looking forward to the moments he spent above the deck. Today he paused in his ascension to look about him. It must be like flying, he thought, and he recklessly took one hand off the rope to fling his arm wide. The sleeve of his shirt caught the breeze, and for an instant he believed that if he just opened his other hand and stepped off the rope, the wind would lift him up and over the sea. He remembered the dream from last night, the exhilarating freedom of floating through the sky. And then reason took over. He put his free hand back on the rope, finished his work, and descended.

By the next month the memory of the dream had faded a little, and climbing had become almost routine, if that were possible. One afternoon he was high up among the ropes readying the ship for what looked to be a mild storm—everything had to be tied down as tight as it would go. The crew had spotted land earlier in the day, and from his elevation he could see it well—the dark, solid mass that waited for them across a stretch of still, smooth water. Behind him a thin bank of clouds threatened to stir things up, but only a little. Nothing to worry about, everyone said. He felt light-hearted and nimble as he navigated the ropes, and perhaps that was why his foothold was a little less sure, his grip a little less strong than it might have been. A wind had come up. He turned to gaze out over the water just as a wave approached the ship, and he watched it with disinterested curiosity. It wasn't unusually large, really; nothing they hadn't seen before. The ship pitched slightly as it made contact. A second or two passed before the boy realized what had happened. His tether to the ship was so frail that he didn't notice at first when it was gone. He seemed to hover there stupidly, not falling, just suspended. And then he was moving through the air. *It must be like flying*, a part of his brain thought idly. *Only it's the wrong direction.* Though he picked up speed with every instant, he seemed not to be going very fast. He had time to register a cry from somewhere below and even to see the same shocked expression mirrored on a dozen upturned faces. It was almost comical. He almost laughed. And then, suddenly, he hit the water.

With the impact came an explosion of pain. The icy coldness beat at him from every direction. Instinctively, he opened his mouth to scream and gulped in a spray of salt and foam. He thrashed about wildly, helplessly. If this were like his dream, he would swim through this water, back to the ship and safety. But he might as easily fly back up to the ropes. Swimming and flying were things that only witches did, not mortals. Inside his chest, his lungs burned horribly. Once, his head broke the surface and he gasped hungrily at the air, but soon the sea was sucking him down again, and his thrashing only carried him deeper. Beneath the surface, the sea was dark, with the sunlight coming through muted and unreal and penetrating only a short way into the gloom. Dark, everywhere it was dark . . . he had been trapped in this prison forever. He couldn't remember when the pain began to ebb—time seemed to have lost its relevancy. But he felt himself moving easily, carelessly, through the dimness. And then, to his surprise, the water began to fill with light . . .

"I've found him! Come and see, I've found him!" Judith woke with a start and sat up quickly, groping in her mind for a memory of where she was. She couldn't see anything in the intense blackness except the bright rectangle of the open doorway, which threw the rest of the room into deep shadow. She glanced quickly around, expecting to see the boy she had been speaking to only moments before. It had only been moments, hadn't it? He was going to explain why they were the ones he had been waiting for . . .

Gradually her eyes adjusted, and she became aware that the person standing next to her bed and waving wildly was not the ghostly companion from the garden, but her father.

"Who have you found?" she asked after a long pause, during which she had dug up the recent tumble of meaningless sounds and made sense out of them. "The boy? Did you see him? Did he talk to you?"

"The boy? You mean Nicholas? That's who I've found! Nicholas Casey, our ancestor. Come and see." He didn't wait for her to slide off the bed and follow but launched himself out the doorway like a competitor in the long jump and went off to wake Lori. A moment later she heard his voice in the room next door. He was almost shouting.

"I've found him, Lori, I've found him!"

Facing the inevitable, Judith pushed back the blankets and padded out into the hallway. David came out of the room next door, holding Lori by the arm. "It's in the kitchen," he told them. So the three of them squeezed into the narrow room and huddled around the table. An ancient-looking book lay open, its pages yellowed and fragile. Judith wondered that they hadn't crumbled under her father's touch.

"She let you bring that up here?" Lori asked, while one of her eyebrows arched up. "That guardian of time's treasure let you bring that up here?"

"Well, sure," said David, apparently flabbergasted that his wife should dwell on such details at a time like this. "You just have to know how to talk to her. Now look, here it is. This record right at the top." Judith and Lori leaned obediently over the book, but the loopy handwriting was too much for Judith to decipher in the middle of the night.

"'Admitted from the parish of St. Saviour's Southwark,'" read Lori. "'Apprenticed for six years to Mr. William North of Gray's Inn for the purpose of studying the law.'"

"Well? Isn't it fantastic?"

"Hmm," commented Lori.

"Hmm? We find the key we've been looking for for years, and all you can say is 'Hmm'?"

"It's a little disappointing, you have to admit," Lori explained. "After all, it doesn't name his parents, as we hoped it would."

"But it tells us right where to look. All we have to do is get the parish records."

"If they still exist."

"Of course they do. I believe this is all part of a miracle, 'oh ye of little faith.' Do you think we came all the way here and found this only to be stopped now?"

"I don't know, David, but I do know that it's three o'clock in the morning." Lori turned with a sweep of her robe and strode regally back to her room. Judith hung about for a moment before following. Though she still felt disoriented after waking so abruptly from a vivid dream, she was lucid enough to notice the hurt look on her father's face.

"This is great, Dad," she said before stepping through the doorway into the hall. He smiled at her. "You know, time only is measured unto man."

"Right." She watched him sit back down at the table and settle himself as if he meant to stay there for a while.

"Aren't you going to bed?"

"What? Oh, no. I think I'll just look at this a few minutes longer." So she left him there, sitting alone in the ugly glare from the overhead light, and went back to bed. The rest of the night passed dreamlessly.

Part Three: Chadwicke
London, 1725

Chapter 11

For the next several weeks, David's family saw very little of him. Occasionally he drifted in and out, more aloof than a statue and with about as much appetite. At dinner he sat gnawing absently on whatever was placed before him, including once, by accident, a pencil. Judith swore he had almost bitten it through before he realized.

Most of his time was divided between the Guildwell archives and other historical collections throughout the city. He was determined to find more information about Nicholas, and soon the portion of his time dedicated to working at Guildwell shrank down to nothing. Lori took up the slack.

"Every researcher has to be flexible," she told Judith one afternoon as the two of them made tuna fish sandwiches for lunch. Juice from the pickle Judith was slicing squirted up into her eye, and she grimaced.

"It's true. There's no need to make faces about it," scolded Lori. "You never know what you're going to find. You may have your own agenda, but the records aren't interested in it."

"So you think Dad's wasting his time?" Judith surmised. "I know he's a bit more of a genealogy freak than you are, but I thought you wanted to know about Nicholas, too."

"I do," said Lori, signaling with a lift of her eyebrows her disapproval of the word "freak." "It's just that your father can take things a little too far. This microfilming has to get done, whether we find Nicholas or not."

Ironically enough, it was Lori who encountered the information David was looking for. She had taken on his microfilming responsibilities in addition to her own research, so she spent most of her waking moments in the archives. One day, there it was, tucked in with some other notes about a change in headmasters. She waited until David was there for family home evening before breaking the news.

The four of them started the evening off by singing the Primary song "Hearts of the Children," and then David opened the lesson by saying, "I think we should all pray that I'll be able to find more information about Nicholas."

"Or we could just say a prayer of thanks," interrupted Lori. She held up a piece of paper with two lines of notes printed across it.

"What?" gaped David. He reached out for the paper as if he had never seen anything so beautiful—or so fragile. He couldn't have handled the Hope Diamond with more care and attention. "But this—this is amazing," he breathed.

"You recognize the surname of the bride?"

"Of course."

Lori gave him another moment to marvel over it before she snatched it out of his grip and tossed it at Judith. "See if Judith recognizes the name. I haven't had time to quiz her lately."

Judith took the paper and studied it. "See who Nicholas married?" Lori prodded from across the room. "Do you know who that is?"

"Yes," said Judith.

The candle on Chadwicke's desk sputtered and hissed, then went out altogether. Startled into action by the sudden darkness, the schoolmaster uncurled himself from his hunched position, blotted the page he had been writing on, and closed his ledger. Then, noticing his own stiffness for the first time, he flexed his shoulders and laid a long-fingered, clumsy hand across the back of his neck, which felt as hard and unyielding as a piece of old leather. Rising slowly, he fumbled his way over to the bell cord in the corner and tugged. A moment later the door opened to admit a young man. He held a candle and a cup of tea.

"Wind's come up," remarked Chadwicke to the clerk. "Sounds like the beginnings of a fine storm."

"The wind's been howling like that for hours, sir," replied the young man.

"Oh," said Chadwicke. "I must not have noticed it earlier." The clerk said nothing but set the teacup down on the desk.

"Anything else, sir?" he inquired, stifling a yawn and already turning to go. Chadwicke opened the cupboard and took out a fresh candle. "Only a bit of light, thank you." The new flame wavered hesitantly, then grew more confident, and Chadwicke withdrew to place it on the desk. "That is all, now. You may go."

The clerk took a few steps toward the door but paused on the threshold. "You're not going to keep working, sir? It's late. Nearly midnight."

"You may go to bed, of course, son," Chadwicke responded by way of dismissal. The clerk shrugged slightly, then continued out into the hall and closed the door behind him. Alone again, Chadwicke paced back and forth before his desk, sipping the tea absently. It was tepid, a fact that his brain registered indifferently, as if he were making notations in a ledger: Tea, one cup. Cold.

He paused as he passed his desk, peering down at the sheet he had used to blot his last page of work. The final sentence stood out clearly, even if he did have to read it backward: "Killed by Turks." A decisive end to this particular entry—no more payments to be sent to the captain, nothing to settle. Chadwicke sighed. The book was peppered with such entries. Oh, not that being killed by Turks wasn't unique. It just proved that life could always get you with a new hazard while continuing to menace you with the same old dangers that had been around from the beginning. Many of the entries ended the same way: "Drown'd." Only the place made them different. One entry, a few years old now, recorded the fate of a boy who had long since been forgotten by everyone, except perhaps Chadwicke and Nicholas Casey. "Drown'd off the coast of Newfoundland," it read. Another decisive ending. Another account settled.

And Chadwicke was a practical man. It was not out of callousness or greed that he tallied the funds that could now be redirected, that could be sent off to other apprentices or used to buy coats for the students in residence. For thirty years now, the school had been Chadwicke's life. Fifteen years ago or so, when his funding and staff had been at their height, he had employed two treasurers and various clerks to carry out the daily recording and accounting that a well-run establishment required. Yet even then, he had gone over all their work himself. He had known the source and destination of every penny, and as for the students, he knew every record by heart. He had had employees to scout for potential sponsors and masters and to maintain a long list of contacts, but it was he who made all the final decisions. No student was apprenticed without Chadwicke's knowledge and approval. Such involvement required time and study, but he felt it was part of his duty. How could he call himself the master of this school if he didn't know everything that went on? And with so many students coming and going, so many contracts to be worked out and sponsors to be prodded, he couldn't always afford to rely on written information. If he didn't have the contents of his ledgers in his mind, one day he might forget to glance over his notes. Someone's birthday would pass, the treasurer would make a contract, and the child would be sent away without Chadwicke noticing. Then how easy to become less and less involved, to let the others take over while he became careless, until one day he woke up and realized that the school was going to pieces around him and all his good intentions had ended in chaos.

He didn't know his students' faces; he couldn't have picked out a six-year veteran from a roomful of strangers. In Chadwicke's estimation, the face was the least relevant aspect of a person, and he couldn't spare any mental effort on irrelevant information. There were too many necessary facts to know, all the details of a student's origin and prospects, the real meat, the stuff that mattered. Lucky for him that memorization had always come easily. His father had meant him to study for the Church, and as a young man Chadwicke had embarked on this course. He knew the scriptures well and had received a decent education in the classics. He had even thought he might become the clergyman his father wanted, but something about the smallness and simplicity of the calling displeased him. As a student of a rector in a parish near his home, he spoke to many people about their beliefs. He saw how religion functioned in their lives. Most of them cared nothing for it, really, except in times of tragedy, and then it provided comfort; it was a blanket they wrapped around themselves as insulation against the uncertainty and harshness of mortality. When they were content, they used it mostly as a catalyst for gossip. "Did you hear that so and so refuses to go to church?" "Did you realize that so and so is a pagan?"—this after a man was heard to praise a sunset in public. "Did you hear about the young lady who walked home with a gentleman unaccompanied? Scandalous!" Then they would throw up their hands and wonder how much more wicked the world could get. Not that it mattered, truthfully, for eventually Christ would come and put an end to it, and meanwhile all they need do was say a prayer here and there and attend church regularly. Nothing more was required of them. They believed themselves good Christians, but they either ignored or misunderstood the bulk of Christ's teachings, and while they went about feeling self-satisfied the masses around them suffered bitterly.

At first, young Chadwicke had found himself slightly disillusioned. He had built up for himself a vibrant and living faith, and he expected to see it mirrored in all the good and respectable people of the earth—for good and respectable those parishioners were, in spite of all their faults. They simply partook of the widespread tradition of selective understanding, or selective hearing, or selective reading, whatever it was. They embraced the aspects of Christianity that fit easily and comfortably into their lives and ignored the rest. Probably they didn't ignore it intentionally, even. It was habitual, something ingrained for generations. Chadwicke began to feel less disillusioned. Perhaps he ought to thank the Lord that he was able to see a better way.

What he saw as the centerpiece of Christ's teachings was one word: work. Now was the time of tribulation, not the time for rest, and there was much to be done. Religion wasn't something soft that you lounged on to lick the wounds the world had given you. Religion should drive you, day and night, it should drag you out of a warm bed and a sound sleep when someone needed you, take the food off your plate when someone came to you hungry and fainting, lighten your purse until you hardly knew how you would manage for yourself. Of course, people had misunderstood Christ from the very beginning. Who was He? Not the Messiah, many said, for He brought no temporal deliverance. Where was the man who would overthrow the Romans and bring freedom to the Jewish people? Not here. The humble carpenter from Nazareth offered another kind of freedom, a better one. Why couldn't people see it, Chadwicke wondered, even all these centuries later? People still thought Christ had nothing better to give them than some kind of finite, material salvation. True, the parishioners Chadwicke spoke with weren't exactly looking for a revolutionary leader to rise up and usher in a better political system, but they were still waiting for the Lord to come and fix everything while they sat back and did nothing. Until He came, the world was hopeless, and they'd never lift a finger to try and make it any better. They still didn't understand that Christ hadn't come to change the world, but to change the individual. And then it was up to the individual to change the world. So changing the world was what Chadwicke had set out to do, all those years ago.

He had given up a fair bit to pursue this course. Miss Emily West, for example, with her sleek dark hair and lovely, heart-shaped face. She was the daughter of the clergyman Chadwicke had studied with, and watching her, he could easily imagine what his life would be like if he did what was expected of him—marry, settle, take over the little parish and live simply and contentedly. For Miss Emily West, life *was* simple. It included an aging but adoring father, more and more dependent on her to oversee the run of the household; a modest but comfortable home filled with fluffy chintz armchairs, generous fireplaces, and calico cats; and, of course, the dutiful weekly trips to the poorer section of the village.

She always looked enchanting on these visits, in her navy cloak with its hood framing her face, her arm looped through the handle of a basket with its contents hidden by a bright checked cloth. He might have painted her if he'd been an artist. And he would have titled the work, *A Type of Christian.*

"Why must you go, Samuel?" she had asked him straight out when he had shared his plans with her. "Why must you leave here to serve God?" They were sitting in her father's study, a cosy, dark-paneled room that smelled faintly of wood polish and old leather. One of the cats shifted in its basket next to the fire, yawned, stretched, and curled up again.

"It's what I feel He would have me do," Chadwicke answered. "It's as if I can feel Him calling me to the work—the longer I stay here, the more restless I feel."

Miss West remained unconvinced. He could see her jaw tighten as she threw down her needlework—a sampler bearing the message "Blessed are the peacemakers"—and met his eyes earnestly with her round, dark ones. "But what work is He calling you to that you cannot accomplish here?" she demanded. "Do you truly believe that you have to go away to find people who need you?"

"A person cannot always stay in one place, Miss West. Think of the apostles in the Bible, how they traveled far and wide to preach the word of God."

She frowned inexplicably, turning down the corners of her pretty lips. "You are not an apostle, Samuel."

"Of course not! I did not mean to imply—I only want to serve, and sometimes that means sacrifice."

"Sacrifice for a purpose is noble, but sacrifice for the sake of sacrifice alone—" her voice trailed off, but her eyes narrowed with disapproval.

"You speak in riddles, Miss West."

"You are a riddle, Samuel," she declared.

"Then you laugh at me?"

"No. Never. I . . . I cry."

He turned his face away, embarrassed. The emotion of women

had always frightened him. "Why do you cry, my dear?" he asked carefully.

"Because of your grand plans. Because they do not and never will include a single person."

In his confusion, he met her eyes again. "Do you mean to say, a certain person?"

"No, I meant a single person, but it is one and the same. You are only interested in crowds."

In spite of Miss West's censure, in spite of his own regret at losing her company, he had made his way to London, a city which seemed to offer all the world's woes in microcosm. He was soon hired as a clerk by the former headmaster of Disciples of Christ Schoole. It was a small establishment back then, no more than sixty or seventy children, and the old headmaster spent most of his time in his private study, hunched up before the fire with a poultice on his forehead. "My faith, Samuel," he used to cry plaintively to Chadwicke when the young man would come in with a question or some other disturbance, "I've grown very old at this place, very old indeed. Leave me in peace, my boy." So Chadwicke did. He learned to run the school on his own and quickly began making improvements. And that was the beginning of his vision. He had been looking for a life's work worthy of a devoted "disciple of Christ," a cause that would take the sentiment of his faith and make it into something active and solid. Perhaps the school's name carried more of truth than he at first expected. Every midmorning when he went out for his walk, the degrading scenes of poverty pummeled him from all sides, the beggars, the prostitutes, the sick, the starving—they were everywhere. It was overwhelming, when you thought of fixing it all at once, turning back the lifetimes of bad choices, the centuries of injustice. But what if, instead of working backward, you worked forward? Took the children out of that situation and made them into self-reliant people who could care for themselves and someday for their own children? If you could do that long enough and well enough and with enough determination, in a generation you could change the face of the city. Or so Chadwicke thought, back then.

His lack of experience working with young people—he was an only child and had rarely interacted with anyone younger than himself—appeared to him as no obstacle at all. He had more to recommend him as a schoolmaster than most of the men who hired themselves out as teachers and tutors. "Respectable, genteel person well-schooled in the classics," read the ads, but so often those qualities went along with sheer meanness. Take Mr. Fortescue, for instance, who had taught at Disciples of Christ Schoole for ten years before Chadwicke arrived and was still there to frighten the children with his habitual scowl and handy whip. Men like Fortescue had been forced into the profession; they were bitter members of declining families for whom paid employment came as the shameful end of a long downward spiral into obscurity. Fortescue's family fortune had been decaying for the previous several hundred years and had finally crumbled away beneath him, leaving him no choice but to put his education and what was left of his position to work. Chadwicke knew the type all too well. The school was full of them. He figured they couldn't do too much harm, as long as he asserted his influence to counteract them, as long as he instilled in the school's students the principle that work was the very essence of salvation.

After a year or two of running the school under the frail leadership of the old headmaster, Chadwicke took over officially when the old man finally decided to retire to his sister's cottage in Kent. He immediately began a program of expansion, visiting the parish leaders himself demanding more funding. The school was an ideal recipient of their aid, after all. As the basic units of the Church of England, the parishes were responsible for the spiritual and temporal well-being of the people living within their boundaries. Their jurisdiction wasn't confined to Sundays, and their duties weren't limited to building churches. They were part of the local government, and everyone, even religious dissenters, paid them money. A few parishes still had all their members making up the vestry, the body that collected funds and delegated responsibility, but with London growing so fast this was becoming impractical.

So instead, a few of the more prestigious property owners tended to keep the parishes under their control. A lot of money poured in, and some of it poured back out. Chadwicke knew that in some parishes, there were more people to receive aid than there were to pay the mandatory poor rates, but he also knew that nothing would ever change if they didn't make up their minds to do something about it. He went to the committee that had been formed to deal with the school, and he told those representatives of the city's parishes what was what. He met with other leaders, too; the small list of wealthy private donors doubled and tripled in the first year. He knew he could never do much as long as the school was confined to a building the size of a modest house, so he chose another place for it. Guildwell Hall was quite a new structure, only a century or so old, and there was space in the back for children to exercise and room on the sides for expansion. The current owner, a rising member of the lower nobility with a pleasant country seat, was more than willing to exchange the rather gloomy-looking place for a more fashionable residence. Chadwicke negotiated a reasonable price and pushed it through the parish committee. They must have been stunned by the sudden momentum of the new schoolmaster; they all but laid down before his wishes, as if he were a careening young horse and they wanted only to get out of his way. Things had almost been easy back then.

Perhaps his real trouble now was that he was getting older. He had spent his adult life arguing and haranguing, negotiating and placating, to squeeze the resources he needed out of the vice grips of the parish leaders and the rich philanthropists. Thousands of children had passed through the school and gone on to respectable trades. He met his former students sometimes in the streets—he never recognized them, but they recognized him and greeted him warmly. And still . . . he stopped his pacing and sunk down in the chair behind his desk. And still, he would be nearing the end of his career, and what had he accomplished? He had not even assured the school's survival. The city parishes had grown weary of his endless demands. "Couldn't you feed them less? You'll spoil them," they'd protest before he even opened his mouth. His momentum had carried him so far, but eventually they had to stand up and pull the other direction. They were pulling tighter and tighter now. He had already cut back as much as he could. He had tried to recruit more donors, but it seemed that the school had been a fad among young wealthy do-gooders and had now passed out of fashion. Still, he would have to find a way. He reopened his ledger and flipped back several pages to the summary made a few months ago, at Easter. "Total enrolled: 962."

Well, maybe he should economize by saving on candles. Tomorrow a representative from the city parishes would visit him, and they would wrestle out the details of a new settlement. Until then, there was no more he could do. He pinched the flame between his fingers and then made his way by memory out through the door, across the main hall, and through a series of corridors until he entered the narrow stairwell that led up to his own private rooms. A faint glow of firelight welcomed him when he reached the top of the stairs As he had suspected, his daughter Mary had waited up for him. She would have a cup of tea to offer—a cup of *hot* tea, not the lukewarm liquid proffered by the clerk. He found her in the sitting room with a lap full of sewing and a face scrunched up in concentration.

"Good evening, young Mary," he greeted her. She glanced up with pleasure and laid her work aside as Chadwicke sunk into a chair in front of the fire.

"Father, you've worked so late this evening," she said, eyeing him with concern. "Wait here while I bring you some tea."

He sat listening to the rustle of her skirts as she moved out of the room, and he marveled once again at how much she resembled her mother. It had been one of the great blessings of his life, he believed, that after cutting himself loose from the promise of Miss West's comfort, he had encountered another young woman equally willing and far more suited to be his bride. Miss Alice Johns had been a contrast to Miss West, indeed; she had none of Miss West's showy good looks. In fact, she was unarguably plain, with very straight, dull-brown hair and a long and slightly red face. She had been nearly as tall as he was and very skinny, with nothing round or soft about her. As for her disposition, it couldn't have been more different from Miss West's—which was fortunate, in Chadwicke's view. Where Miss West was bubbly, fun-loving—frivolous, even—and too prone to speak her mind, Miss Johns was quiet, gentle, and patient. Then, too, life had schooled her in sorrow. When her parents had died, leaving her alone in the world, she had sought work as a servant. It was this experience, Chadwicke thought, that set her apart from other women. A lady like Miss West might have died of the very humiliation of being forced to scrub out someone's chamber pots. Not Miss Johns—for her it was not humiliation, but humility.

He thought now, with a familiar, wistful sort of regret, that he would have appreciated the company of his wife's unassuming presence at this time in his life. She had died long ago, after the birth of their son Christopher. Her death hadn't come as a surprise to either of them, he supposed, since she had been sickly for a long while before that. In fact, she seemed to have faded very gradually out of his life over the course of several years, so that, looking back, he could not even recall her last dying moments or the first few solitary days of his widowhood. He had known no sudden, instantaneous loss but only a long process of increasing loneliness. A week or two after her death, his foot had hit something small and light on the floor, sending it skittering across the stone to collide with the wall. He picked up the object and examined it. It was a hairpin. *I must return it to Mrs. Chadwicke*, he told himself, directing his steps toward their bedroom, where he intended to place it among her things. He was nearly through the doorway before he stopped and stared down at the hairpin again. "Oh—I'd forgotten," he murmured.

"Father?" came Mary's voice, jolting him back to the present. She stood next to his chair holding a cup and saucer.

"Thank you, my dear," he said, accepting the tea gratefully. Although it was late, Mary took her seat again and continued her needlework, and Chadwicke sipped at the steaming tea and watched her. By the standards of the day, Mary was very unaccomplished. Her stitches were neat enough, but she worked so slowly it was a wonder she ever finished anything. But then, thought Chadwicke tenderly, few people on earth worked as hard as Mary did. It had been her misfortune to be born without a right hand. Chadwicke well remembered the stir the defect had caused during her first year of life. People would turn away from the child to whisper among themselves, and their eyes would keep shifting back to Mary. Chadwicke could imagine what they were saying. He was a firm believer that on the whole people never changed, so the same topics that had stirred up the tongues in biblical times were still being hashed over today. "Whose sin is this a judgment for? What secret evil does this reveal?" Chadwicke was never disturbed for himself, because in the end the only approval he needed was from God. But he worried over his wife and daughter. He wasn't romantic enough to attribute his wife's early death to shame or heartbreak, but he was observant enough to know that the whispering pained her and that the bleakness of her daughter's future cast a gloom about her own. For what would become of a girl who had no right hand?

Years ago, when Mary was about thirteen, Chadwicke had begun to make inquiries about having her apprenticed. Though the majority of the students at his school were boys, a significant minority of girls were enrolled as well, and he had been successful at finding suitable positions for them. He knew he would have very little to leave her; he put everything he had into the school. An apprenticeship would be just the thing. Most of the girls ended up using their hands, participating in the various feminine arts of sewing, embroidery, and housekeeping. But his Mary was a hard worker. He knew she could prove useful to anyone willing to take a chance on her. He still knew it, but he had never convinced anyone else. After three years, he had given up the project. She would simply have to marry. He had better see to that soon, he thought, as Mary handed him his pipe and bent to stir up the fire. She was nearly twenty-one.

He watched for a moment as she stood with the poker in her hand while her other arm tried awkwardly to restrain her skirts from falling forward. *Christopher used to take care of the fire*, he thought. *It was his chore.* Chadwicke rarely paused long enough to think about the son who had died the previous fall. He had been too busy even then for grief, and he had a disposition not easily stirred to strong emotion. It was moments like these when he felt the boy's absence. Christopher had come home from his apprenticeship with consumption and had remained for several months before the disease overpowered him. Chadwicke had grown accustomed to having the boy around, to coming home late on nights like this and finding the young man stretched out on the sofa, his face white even in the soft light from the fire but his eyes alive with interest.

"How goes the work?" Christopher might inquire, and Chadwicke would tell him, and then they would sit up talking about religion and philosophy until one of them remembered that mortals needed rest as well as learning. Chadwicke stared now at the sofa, empty except for Mary's embroidery. Things seemed incomplete, he mused with a gentle sense of melancholy.

"What else would you have, Father?" Mary asked, turning from the fire to face him and holding out her hand in an unconscious, supplicating gesture. "Are you hungry? You ate very little at supper."

"No, child, no, do not trouble yourself. It is late. You must go to bed."

He sat up alone for nearly two hours more, thinking what he could say tomorrow to the parish representative. Before going to bed, he picked up the little crucifix that hung from a nail over the fireplace.

"Lord, allow me to do thy will," he prayed. He had done what he could. Now it was time for faith.

Chapter 12

The next morning Chadwicke rose in the first gray of dawn, while the shapes of the washstand and the chair in his bedroom were still only faint outlines in the dimness. He washed and dressed quickly, moving with a deftness that belied his awkward frame. It was habit that kept him from stumbling over things and that steered his hands in precisely the right directions to find his personal items; he didn't need to waste time groping around. He rarely saw this room in daylight, and so it was particularly important that everything have a proper place. His comb sat on the washstand exactly two and a quarter inches to the right of the pitcher and basin, no more and no less.

When he had tidied himself and finished his morning prayers, he let himself quietly out into the back garden. It was the height of summer and the garden was in full flower, the trees thick and lush, the ground a riot of color beneath a sky that blushed with the deep pink of sunrise. The storm the night before had scattered a rain of brightly hued petals across the walks, but Chadwicke trod on them without seeing them. The morning was cool despite the time of year; he cupped his hands against his mouth to warm them with his breath and strode decisively to the far end of the garden, where several tall plane-trees stood in a neat row near the back wall. These were his measuring sticks. The first spring after he had moved the school into Guildwell Hall, he had some of the older boys plant a row of tiny saplings across the edge of the property. He could still remember, across all those years, the scent of the upturned soil and the sound of the boys calling cheerfully to each other as they worked. He could even feel the warmth of the afternoon sun he had felt on the back of his neck as he had stood gazing down at the thin scraggly branches that somehow reminded him of the arms and legs of children. He couldn't look down at the branches now. Twenty-five years had passed since then, and the saplings had demonstrated their potential, growing into the giants of the garden, the sentinels that watched over the doings of all the thousands of children who had tramped across these grounds during midmorning walks. Chadwicke approached one of the trees and placed a hand on the trunk. Solid, strong, unmoved now by the passing of time. He liked to think that these trees would stand here long after he had gone, and then as now boys would climb them and hang from their branches, viewing the world from an unaccustomed perspective.

But the children wouldn't always be like the ones who came here now, frightened and abandoned, because someday soon the whole city would be different. It would become the city of his dreams, where the only people who were miserable or hungry were the ones who had plunged themselves, of their own free will, into sin. The children who played here and learned here would be the happy and promising offspring of upstanding citizens. It was so much to hope for, but maybe it was no more fantastic than a tiny seed that sprung up into a tree. Perhaps the idea had been there in his mind when he had the trees planted. Back then the school had been as fragile as the saplings, within a quill's stroke of being reduced to its former obscurity. But over time, he had assured himself, he would build it into an institution as strong and as permanent as these trees—more so, even.

He let out the beginnings of a sigh but quickly swallowed it. He had never allowed himself the luxury of complaining. Had Christ not faced His greatest trial at the very end of His life? Had He served for all those years only to tire in the end and turn from His sacrifice? Chadwicke chided himself harshly for his gloomy thoughts. In spite of all his efforts, he must have grown complacent during the last decade, and now when he had to do a little fighting for his cause, he shrunk from it. *Lazy old man*, he scolded himself. Nevertheless, he felt overshadowed by a sense of foreboding, and all his self-discipline hadn't been enough to overcome it. The school's recent financial troubles seemed to be the manifestation of an opposition that had been smoldering for years. The institution was already suffering a decline. Oh, he could manage well enough with a reduced staff; he didn't mind the work. But still you reached a limit. Children had to eat.

You reached a limit. That was the core of it all, and Chadwicke hated it. The parish leaders had reached their limit. For years he had demanded "More, more," and they had given it. Their reluctance had grown with every transaction, their patience wore thin till he could see their faces closing like locks on a treasure chest whenever he approached. And still they had given, a little less and a little less, but enough to keep things running. Then they had written him to schedule this meeting. A strange time of year to work out a new arrangement; usually they met just after Easter.

The morning bell chimed out confidently into the stillness, calling the children to their prayers. Chadwicke left his troubles in the garden and entered the dining hall looking entirely unruffled, as he always did. He scanned the long rows of faces as he made his way toward the far end of the room. Children fell silent as he drew near, and those who had not yet seated themselves scurried to get out of his way. As the schoolmaster inspected them silently, he saw that they were all clean and neatly dressed, all meek and well-behaved as children should be. These were the 962. He couldn't put a single face with a name, but he knew everything about them. He could have stood there and recited where every child was from, the name of every child's parent, living or deceased, the general consensus of the instructors on every child's academic performance. He would not send these innocents out into the world again unprepared. Once, before he reached his table next to the fire, he glanced toward the tall windows and caught a quick glimpse of his trees, their stately forms towering above the other inhabitants of the garden. He felt strangely reassured, and as soon as he had taken his place and the prayers had been said, the business of running the school crowded out any vain worries or imaginings. He opened the ledger that one of the clerks brought for him and became entirely engrossed. Ten children were to be apprenticed in the next month, and he must see that everything was in order.

Mr. Tuttle arrived shortly after breakfast. A clerk showed him into the schoolmaster's office, where Chadwicke was waiting with his ledger open on his desk. He shut it and rose to greet the man. He had done business with Tuttle before and knew him to be a person of no extraordinary appearance, yet Chadwicke found his eyes taking stock of him in an unaccustomed and critical way. The man who had come here as the voice of the city's churches had a fringe of reddish hair edging his round, shining head and great bulging eyes that were a prologue to his bulging stomach. Tuttle's plump hands rested complacently across his belly, and as the man approached, Chadwicke caught the gleam of a small colored stone. A ring worth . . . how many pounds? Chadwicke could only guess. How many children could it feed? Again, only a guess. Chadwicke shook his head slightly to clear it. He had never used to be covetous. If Mr. Tuttle wanted to wear a jeweled ring, that was his business. Oblivious to Chadwicke's stern appraisal, the representative lowered himself into a chair, and the schoolmaster resumed his seat.

"Chadwicke," Tuttle huffed, "I suppose you know why I am here."

"Indeed, no," countered Chadwicke. "I can hardly imagine to what I owe this unexpected pleasure."

"How old are you, sir?" Tuttle demanded suddenly. "I'm sure I will not offend you when I inform you that you look to be rather—shall we say mature? A man who has had some experience."

Chadwicke nodded his assent. "I assure you I take no offense, sir. I am growing older, and as I have worked hard all my life I am not ashamed of it."

"Indeed, indeed. But I wonder that you have lived so long without learning certain fundamental truths."

"You must speak more clearly, Mr. Tuttle. Perhaps my intellect, as well as my appearance, is not what it once was."

"Must I say it? I am speaking of money, Chadwicke. In spite of all your years, you seem to have no understanding of it."

"Perhaps that is so, sir. I am not a man of business. I have no interest in money for its own sake, for me its only value is in what it can do. If used wisely, it can make the child of a beggar into a prosperous citizen and, even more, into a man who is favored by God."

Tuttle sighed. "Spare me, sir, spare me. I have spoken to you before. I have heard you boast of the miracles worked by your institution until I could recite them back to you, word for word."

Chadwicke gazed levelly at the man seated across the desk from him. Slowly he laced and unlaced his fingers, a gesture he often performed in times of stress when he needed to gather his thoughts very carefully. "I am pleased to know, Mr. Tuttle, that you have given my words such devoted attention."

"Oh, blast, Chadwicke!" erupted Tuttle, slamming a fat hand down on the schoolmaster's desk. "You may have the cunning of the devil, but we are tired of your snares. I am here to inform you officially that from this time forward we will give you half of our previous contribution. This new agreement is effective immediately."

"Perhaps a cup of tea . . . "

"Ah, tea! You offer it as if it's your own to offer, but do you know whose it is, sir? Why, it belongs to me and to the other good people of this city who have already denied themselves of more than can be reasonably asked of any civilized person so that these dirty, lazy children of beggars and prostitutes might go masquerading about as respectable citizens. No more, Chadwicke, no more!"

"Then you mean to say that you prefer the children to become beggars and prostitutes themselves, Mr. Tuttle? Is that what the good people of this city would have done with them?"

"Have done with them? Why, that is exactly our wish, to have done with them. And I'll tell you, Chadwicke, they needn't spend six or seven years here having their heads filled with arithmetic just to be shipped off to Barbados to perform hard labor under a master's whip. They can go straight to Barbados."

"Mr. Tuttle, you forget yourself. As a Christian, you must be as aware as I am of a Christian's responsibility toward the innocent poor. I cannot believe you wish these children to remain in ignorance rather than be taught the true gospel."

"You don't spend seven years teaching them the gospel, Chadwicke. Why, if anyone needs that long to learn it there's likely no hope for them in this world or the next."

"On the contrary, sir, I find that a lifetime is barely sufficient to learn the gospel of our Lord. Nevertheless, after six or seven years, one might be ready to study on one's own."

Tuttle uttered a soft "Hmph" and raised his eyes to the ceiling. "You digress, Chadwicke. I have no intention of entering into a discussion on religious learning. I am here to tell you what is real. Far be it from me to complain of sacrifice for the sake of my fellowmen, but you have been wasteful with our offerings. You have proven very skillful at obtaining your designs, but we are now unanimous that it shall happen no more. We will give you half. That should more than discharge our obligation to care for these poor. Why, we've hardly enough left for ourselves. Would you have *us* become beggars?"

"What is your obligation?" exclaimed the schoolmaster. "Can you name a certain sum, as you seem to believe, and say that it is enough, that you have 'discharged' your obligation, as you call it? Do you not walk out in this city? Do you not see the ugliness, the horror?" Chadwicke's voice remained low and controlled even though he felt more passionate about this subject than about any other that had ever occurred to the mind of man. "This is our torment as long as we believe we have done enough, to live with this wretchedness on our very doorsteps every day of our lives. 'For what is a man profited, if he gain the whole world—'"

"You are a pessimist, sir," returned Tuttle. "You misjudge humanity. You think that no one can take responsibility for himself. If these children of yours cannot take responsibility for themselves, then they deserve nothing better than to work out their lives under somebody else's whip. Pray send as many away as necessary. There is a great need for labor in many of the colonies, and no one will be testing them on their knowledge of the classics. Good day, Chadwicke."

Tuttle rose with effort and showed himself out, leaving a stunned and suddenly elderly man in his wake. *Half?* Chadwicke's mind fumbled numbly with the idea. Throughout his thirty years with the school, the parish contributions had been the sturdy backbone he could trust to bear the school's weight. He had fought for the funds before; he had known that the leaders begrudged him the sums he asked. But it was their obligation, legally, morally—in every way that counted. It was their duty to assist the poor and he had faith that they would not shirk it. The private donations given directly to the school, the sponsorship of individual children—that had all been the flesh on the skeleton. Without the skeleton, it couldn't stand. The school couldn't stand . . .

Chadwicke got to his feet without consciously making up his mind to do so. There were certain things that became natural after so many years of life, at least that was one advantage of growing older. Threatened now with an emergency, Chadwicke reacted instinctively. This wasn't something he could confront from the chair behind his desk. He took up his hat, offered a hasty and uninformative explanation to the nearest clerk, and marched out the front door of Disciples of Christ Schoole. As he walked briskly along, deaf to the numerous greetings called out to him from street merchants and passersby, his mind began to function. As clearly as if he were in his own office with all his ledgers before him, he reviewed the names and addresses of all the gentlemen who had given donations to the school during the past decade and a half. The nearest address, he realized with satisfaction, was not more than two miles away. He altered his course slightly. In just under a half an hour, he stood before the large mahogany door of the townhouse belonging to Mr. Wight. He rapped vigorously. Nothing. He knocked again. Finally an impeccably dressed white-haired old man opened the door. He examined Chadwicke slowly and deliberately, his eyes lingering over the schoolmaster's heavily patched coat. Clearly not the sort of person his master would have business with, but Chadwicke refused to be put off. Perhaps it was presumptuous of him to come here unannounced, but what were social conventions worth against the fate of a thousand children? More, against the soul of an entire city?

"I should like to see Mr. Wight right away. I have a most urgent matter to discuss with him."

"Mr. Wight is not receiving callers at present," protested Mr. Wight's butler.

"Is your master at home?" The butler nodded a reluctant assent. "Then I must request that he make an exception, for this is no social call."

"This is most irregular," complained the butler. "I am not in the habit of admitting any person off the street who pretends to require an audience with the master."

"Be so good as to give him my name at least, and convey to him the urgency of my request. Let him decide if he will see me." Chadwicke had prepared himself to be assertive, and now he reached for the door, blocking the old man from shutting it, and put one foot over the threshold. "Samuel Chadwicke," he said distinctly. "Tell him Samuel Chadwicke wishes to speak to him on a matter of some importance." The butler eyed him contemptuously but decided against a struggle. He opened the door a little wider and stepped back.

"If you will be so good as to wait in here, I will inquire of the master." He motioned toward a small room off the front hall and disappeared into the house's interior. Chadwicke refused the invitation into the sitting room but paced the hall instead. He remembered Wight well, though he had not dealt with him for several years now. Wight was one of those flimsy sorts who took up new causes on a whim and dropped them for no more substantial reason, but he had extensive resources and might be cajoled into making a sizable donation in one lump sum. It had happened before . . .

"Chaddy, my dear, I'm so bored," Wight had moaned plaintively the last time he had met with the schoolmaster. "I can't think what to do with myself." They had been standing in front of the fire in the sitting room, the same room whose doorway now gaped open as its intended guest stalked back and forth in the hall. Chadwicke had regarded his companion soberly and held out his hands to the fire. He had walked here that time, too, only then he had sent a letter first. "I confess the school amused me at one time," Wight continued, "but one can only be interested in such things for so long."

Chadwicke shifted his weight from one large foot to the other. "One of the children you brought is still there," he had explained patiently. "Surely his future is of more weight than a day's amusement."

"A day's amusement? Or a day's boredom? Hah! It's more than that, my dear fellow." Wight sighed and flung himself carelessly into a chair. "I had thought of going to the colonies myself, at one time."

When he didn't go on, Chadwicke had felt obliged to ask, "And you no longer entertain such a plan?"

"No! Not at all. That's a relic from my reckless youth. No man of sense considers such a prospect. What do you take me for?"

"I'll take you for a man of sense," replied Chadwicke evenly. "And in so doing, I reproach myself for having doubted you before. A man of sense must also be a man of duty, and so I know that you will pay the money you promised for the boy."

"I tell you, it no longer interests me. I won't bring you anyone else."

"Fine, fine. You've done much already. But this boy, you brought *him.*"

"How does he get on?" asked Wight, brightening a bit.

"He is solid, sir. He—"

"A scholar then?"

Chadwicke hesitated, wary of losing Wight's attention. "No. I must confess he is not one of our brightest students. But he . . . looks after himself well. He causes no trouble. He is a person of honor."

"Ah," said Wight, as if that concluded the matter. "Then I had better pay you what I owe you right away and hear no more of him. He is sure never to bring me a moment's amusement." Wight rose abruptly and summoned a servant. "Yes, yes, that's the thing to do.

Finish this business and move on to something else. Perhaps a hunting trip." Within a few moments Chadwicke had been paid the promised sum. "Tell that boy a bit of mischief might do him good," Wight instructed the schoolmaster in parting. "He'll need it if he's to go to the colonies."

"Sir, you are under a false impression. We do not send all the boys to the colonies. Why, one of the boys you presented a few years ago is now apprenticed with a confectioner only a few streets from here. Perhaps if you were bored you might drop in and wish him well."

"Hah!" laughed Wight. "Do keep your sense of humor, Chaddy. Perhaps I should have you call on me more often." In his coat pocket, Chadwicke tightened his fist around the money. Then he bowed slightly to Wight and walked out the door. That had been eleven years ago now, and the boy in question, the last student Wight had sponsored, had been dead for nearly ten of those years. But *the school* was alive, and Wight's contribution had helped. *Like air to a drowning man*, thought Chadwicke. Only the school was more than a single life. Much more.

"Mr. Chadwicke?" a voice asked. The schoolmaster started, then silently scolded himself for being caught off guard. Wight stood there in the hallway clothed in turquoise silk and looking a bit like a cake that has been left in the sun too long and has begun to slump beneath its finery. He now scrutinized Chadwicke in much the same way that the butler had done, apparently reaching the same disdainful conclusion. "I came down out of curiosity. I thought the name sounded a bit familiar, but I can't think how I could ever have known a person such as yourself."

"Mr. Wight, permit me to reintroduce myself. I am Samuel Chadwicke, the headmaster of Disciples of Christ Schoole. I am not surprised that you do not remember—we have not met for many years—but you were at one time among our more generous private donors."

"Disciples of Christ Schoole? You mean to say that's still going on? Hah! I'd never have thought it. Well, let me see." Wight moved closer to Chadwicke and peered at him intently. "Samuel Chadwicke, you say? Perhaps . . . it is possible that I recollect you. Yes, there was a head schoolmaster, quite a pompous sort if I remember. That couldn't have been you, could it? You could never be pompous in that clothing."

"That was I, sir."

"Ah. Well, perhaps it was after all. Let me not forget, you are now standing in my hallway without an invitation, so you may be rather pompous despite appearances. What do you want with me? Do hurry, my head aches abominably."

"I wish to speak to you about a philanthropic matter. You did much good for the school at one time, and we are now in a position to require—"

"Hmm, of course. To require more money?"

"Yes. As you may remember, we care for a large number of children, and certain expenses are unavoidable."

Wight giggled. "Yes, yes, I'm beginning to remember you now, Chadwicke. You were always a very serious-minded person, never one to admit the absurdity of the whole situation. What was it you intended to do? Put an end to poverty? Hee hee. Well, I admit I admire you for pursuing the ideal for so long. But give it up, old man. You must see there's no hope."

"With your help and the help of others—"

Wight held up a hand to silence him. "No. I'm finished with all that, Chadwicke. I'm no longer a young man, and such fancies are for young men. What, did you really think you'd make any sort of difference? These wretches, these poor, they are what they are, you see? Well now, don't look disappointed. I'll wager all those plantation owners have been grateful for the supply of cheap labor you've given them. That's something."

"Sir, if—"

"Coates!" called Wight. "Show the gentleman out." And he was gone with a swish of bright silk.

In his mental ledger, Chadwicke crossed out Wight's name and moved on to the next.

Chapter 13

It took the schoolmaster two and a half weeks to work completely through his list of past donors and another week and a half to personally visit the potential sponsors he had thought of while traveling between residences. At the end of it all, he had secured enough money to make up for about a fifth of what the school had lost. As he left the last house after speaking with the last person on his list, his mind wrestled with the problem of how to stretch the resources to meet the school's needs. He had hardly slept during the past month, and when he did his dreams were all about the school. Sometimes in these night visions a group of prominent gentlemen came to pledge a substantial contribution, sometimes Chadwicke discovered a cache of money buried in the back yard or otherwise hidden, and once, he returned from an outing to find the school empty and the building a crumbling ruin. In this dream, the sign had been all that remained true to its proper form. "Disciples of Christ Schoole," it still proclaimed, while the wreck behind it made an ironic tableau.

Chadwicke was not dreaming now, but he was so intent on finding a solution to his problem that he might have been sleep walking. He had gone several miles before he came to himself again and realized that he was not following a direct course back to the school. Instead he had wandered into the heart of the city's slums. Large, hollow eyes stared at him from gaunt faces, and ramshackle buildings stretched their foreboding black forms toward the sky as if to shut out the sun. It did seem darker here, though the hour was not late. A permanent shadow hung upon this place.

Chadwicke had not intended to walk through this part of the city—he had not been here for many months, though he used to come several times a year. He had fetched a number of his present students from conditions such as these, but when he looked at the schoolchildren now he saw no shadow of these slums. He saw only cleanliness, order, and obedience, and so it was easy to forget that these places existed, that it had been the sight of them that had sent Chadwicke on his lifelong quest in the first place. Or maybe he had not forgotten the slums after all. Had he been hiding them from himself? Had he filed the images away in some safe cabinet of his mind? Whatever the reason, they shocked his senses now like a slap across the face. Everywhere he looked his vision was filled up with thin bodies and wretched, empty faces, until he feared he might suffocate from their closeness. *This might be an image of hell*, he thought. Only there was one thing here that shouldn't be in such a picture: children. Everywhere he looked, children. He felt a tug at his coat and gazed down into the face of a dirty toddler. "Please," the child begged, though it was too young to articulate the word correctly, so that it came out as "Peeze." Chadwicke never remembered a face unless he meant to, but he had a sudden impression that he would carry this one with him forever. He bent down to lessen the distance between them and placed his two large hands on the child's cheeks. He couldn't tell if it was a boy or a girl. It was old enough to have hair, but the hair was sparse and patchy. Sections of scalp showed through like they did on the heads of old women. Feeling indecisive for perhaps the first time in his life, Chadwicke wondered what to do with the child. Give it money? What would that solve? Take it to the school? He couldn't. There was no room. He stood up shakily and glanced around him. He had drawn the attention of a small circle of children who scattered like a flock of young birds when he rose. From a distance they eyed him warily—and hopefully. What could he give them? He felt stupid and useless. He wanted to explain to them that they weren't supposed to exist at all. Thirty years ago he had set out to change things. The slums should have shrunk by now. These children shouldn't be here.

"You mustn't stand there like that," he croaked from a throat gone inexplicably hoarse. Then he walked on. He walked and walked for miles and the slums were endless. It was dusk before he left the worst of them behind. Breathing a sigh of relief, he began to watch eagerly for the first sight of the school. Its vast, towering silhouette would reassure him. But the silhouette he sought never appeared. In its place he found a tiny building, not so much bigger than a house after all. Not so important after all.

Once inside the school Chadwicke went directly to his office. He opened the cabinet that held his ledgers and took down one of the books. It was not one of the most recent, but as he flipped through it he recognized the names. How many had there been in all? Perhaps four thousand? What difference did it make among so many? He replaced the book, locked the cabinet, and went to bed. He had never felt so exhausted before.

He slept soundly, but when he awoke he felt no more rested than he had the previous evening. He moved tentatively. His arms dragged heavily across the straw mattress and his head ached. He lacked the strength to keep his eyes open. He let them fall closed and slept again.

When he awoke again it was full daylight, and Mary's anxious face peered at him from a few inches away. "Father?" She laid her hand across his forehead. "Shall I call the doctor?"

"No," he protested, twisting fretfully away from her touch. "Nothing wrong. Only tired. Must rest." She continued to stare at him nervously for several moments. He closed his eyes again and didn't open them until he heard her leave. Then he examined his surroundings, which looked unfamiliar in the bright sunlight. He moved his hand across the coverlet on his bed. Mary had made the quilt for him, and he had never noticed what color it was. He saw now that it was pale blue, almost the same shade as the sky that he could see through the round window high up on his wall. His wash-stand was a dark, dull brown. He turned his head on the pillow to examine the floor. A red and blue rug covered most of the stone. He knew exactly how the rug felt on his feet, but he had never known what it looked like. Always before it had appeared to be a mix of various shades of gray.

In this light he could see the dust as well, the tiny floating particles that filled every available space and the thin layer of gray that had already settled. He knew Mary cleaned this room every day, but this was all the effect her effort had. No matter how often she dusted it, the dust would always come back. No matter how much she cleaned away, there would always be more. Some things were eternal, but they weren't the things you wanted to count on. He was tired of fighting a hopeless battle. Let the dust fall. All he wanted was to sleep.

The next time he awoke the doctor was standing over him. "We'll put you right in no time, old man," the doctor assured him. "Never fear." But Chadwicke was afraid. He didn't want to be put right if that meant going back to his old life. He just wanted to lie here, floating aimlessly. It was so much easier. From the corner of his eye he could see Mary standing in the doorway, but he avoided looking at her. Everything would be simple, if not for her. He had meant to take care of her. How had the time got away from him?

On the third day of Chadwicke's illness, the doctor appeared less confident. "It has taken hold," he said to Mary. "He has a strong constitution, but it has taken hold." Chadwicke thought he heard Mary whimpering. He turned his face miserably toward the wall. How could he have been guilty of such hubris, he wondered. To think that he could fix a whole city—what was he, a god? An awful thought pounded at him, but he tried to shut it out. He scrunched his face together to crush it.

"He's in pain," he heard Mary say. "You must do something."

The doctor sighed. "I'll bleed him again. It's all I can do."

Chadwicke felt the sharpness of a blade against his arm, and then, mercifully, came blackness.

But the thought followed him. "You were going to save the whole city," it told him, "and you couldn't even save your own child." His whole life now seemed empty of purpose. The only thing he might really have accomplished was to assure his daughter a secure future. Why had he given up so easily? Why had he put off making a match for her? He had sacrificed her to his own obsession, and that had turned out to be a lie. He had failed. He tossed fitfully in his bed, and his mind burst into fragments, like a prism. On every face the same words were written in his own best handwriting: "You didn't even save your own child."

"Father, Father," cried Mary, and the tears on his cheeks might have been hers or his own. He felt the softness of her face against his rough skin. "Please try, please fight."

"The will of the Lord . . . " he muttered thickly.

"No!" Mary protested vehemently. "People say that when they're too frightened or too lazy to help themselves. That's what you taught me. You have to fight as hard as you can if you want God to help you."

"Child, perhaps I . . . perhaps I was wrong." He chuckled softly to himself at the irony. Wight had spoken truth—all his life he had been too serious-minded. He hadn't recognized the absurdity before, but now he could see it. And it wasn't dying that was absurd, it was ever having lived at all.

The next day the vicar came. Chadwicke knew him well and was accustomed to thinking of him more as an adversary than as an ally. He was just another person who had to be convinced that the school was worthwhile. Chadwicke had spoken to him recently on the matter that dominated all their conversations: money.

"You must use your influence to get the others to reconsider," he had argued after his disastrous visit with Mr. Tuttle. "You are more familiar with the school than any of the others as it lies in your own parish. You know what the needs are, and you see the miracles."

"I commend you for all you have done, Mr. Chadwicke," the vicar had responded diplomatically, "but I'm afraid you have already squeezed out all there is."

And now here he was, pretending to offer solace. Chadwicke opened his eyes fully to study the man's face. He was younger than many of the other clergymen in the city, and as he gazed unself-consciously at the schoolmaster, his eyes suggested a kind and gentle nature.

"My dear Mr. Chadwicke," he began softly when he saw that he had the schoolmaster's attention, "I hardly need ask this question of you. Everyone knows that you have labored all your days in the service of your fellowman. But the time draws near, and if there is anything you would like to confess, I am here to listen. Have you reconciled yourself with God?"

Chadwicke nodded. The word "reconcile" offered him a loophole. The vicar hadn't asked him if he had done everything necessary to get to heaven, he had only really asked him if he was willing to accept his fate. God could not be ignorant of his failure, of his incredible conceit, but Chadwicke was no longer ignorant of such either. Whatever punishment God chose to consign him to, Chadwicke would not complain. God was just, and Chadwicke was reconciled.

It wasn't until the very last moments that he felt the need to explain. "I wanted to serve God," he murmured, no longer sure who was in the room to listen, "but I wanted to do it alone. If I had been a better man, I might have helped the Lord to save this city . . . "

His last thoughts before dying were of Mary. She was reading a Psalm, and she seemed very far away: "Though I walk through the valley of the shadow of death, I shall not want . . . the Lord is my Shepherd."

Judith opened her eyes slowly in the darkness. She lay quiet and still for several moments before she began to wonder what had awakened her. She turned her head on the pillow and raised up a little to stare out into the garden, but everything appeared as it should be—no suspicious shapes crept around through the trees. Then she heard it again, a soft, plaintive moan. She tossed the covers aside and padded out into the hallway. Everything was dark and silent. She groped her way to her brother's door and pushed it open. A shaft of moonlight from the round window fell across his bed, illuminating him with a pale glow. "Gabriel?" she whispered. He turned fitfully and moaned again. She knelt by his bed, rubbing his back and murmuring soothing nonsense. He rolled over beneath her touch, found her arm with his fingers, and followed it down to her hand. Then he curled his fingers around hers and lay peacefully still. She sat frozen, unwilling to disturb him by moving, even to shift her weight from one knee to the other.

She wasn't sure how long she had sat like that when she heard her parents' door open and, a moment later, her parents' voices. She had shut Gabriel's door part way behind her but not enough for it to latch, and the voices, though low, carried plainly into the bedroom.

"It's these hours you've been keeping, David," scolded Lori. "You get yourself on an absurd schedule, and then when you try to go back to normal you complain because you can't sleep. What do you expect when you're used to staying up until half past three?"

"I don't know, I guess I expect my wife to get up and make me warm milk, so it looks like it's working." In the brief silence that followed, Judith could imagine her mother's expression: eyes rolling up to the ceiling, corners of the mouth pulling down. A why-do-I-have-to-put-up-with-this-nonsense expression.

"Well, sit down," Lori said finally, "it will take a minute." Judith heard the clank of metal as her mother dug a pot out from one of the ancient cupboards.

"Lori—" her father hesitated. "I think we may have to cut this trip short."

The clanking stopped abruptly. "Short? How short?"

"I think we should wrap up what we can in the next two weeks. At least we've got the most important thing—we've got some information on Nicholas that we can take to the temple."

"And now Gabriel's getting worse," said Lori flatly, while the pot jiggled and hissed over the heat.

"Yes—you've noticed it too, then," sighed David, sounding almost relieved. "We'll have to go home soon."

"Yes, you're right. Two weeks, you think?"

"Yes. If we work hard, we may be able to finish the microfilming by then."

"All right. I'll make arrangements in the morning, then I'll come down and help you with the records."

Judith eased her body forward until her forehead rested against her brother's bed. She felt strangely comforted by her parents' words, by their acknowledgment—finally—of Gabriel's needs. Now surely they had come to their senses. They would take care of things as they should have done all along.

She could remember a time in her life when she believed her parents had the power to make everything all better. She had been very young then, and somehow their family had been different. There hadn't been so many walls between them; she hadn't felt separate from them the way she did now, almost as if they were characters in a movie she was watching and not liking very much. Back then they had been the heroes of her existence, flawless, all-knowing, and above all, invincible. She had trusted them unconditionally. But even then she had been a little afraid of them, and so the rare instances of her mother's tenderness had always surprised her. Like the time Judith was sick with a high fever—she might have been four or five, but she still had an impression of the oppressive pain and of her dim, fuzzy surroundings, which wavered and stretched and grew dark with her fear. Lori had sat up with her two nights in a row reading to her from some long-forgotten story book. The words had faded in and out of Judith's mind but her mother's voice was always there, low and rhythmic, a raft bearing her up over a boiling sea, a curtain shutting out the reddish glare that scorched her eyes and lips from inside her head. Lori had caressed her little girl's forehead and murmured some endearment, "my precious" or "my sweetheart" or something else as uncharacteristically sentimental. "You'll be all better soon," Lori promised, and Judith had known then that if her mother said it, it would come true. "Everything will be all right, darling. I won't let anything bad happen." Judith's mother loved her. Yes, it was a surprise.

And if she loved Judith, she loved Gabriel also. In the morning—

they couldn't do it now, because they'd wake him—Lori and David would take Gabriel in their arms and comfort him the way Lori had once comforted Judith. "We're going home now, son," they would tell him. "Don't worry, we're taking you home." They were no longer the omnipotent beings of childish fantasy, but they were her parents. They and Gabriel were all she had. And soon she wouldn't even have Gabriel.

Part Four: Mary

Virginia, 1725-1733

Chapter 14

Mary lay curled up on her father's bed watching the progress of dawn through the round window high up on the wall. It was the morning of her father's funeral, and Chadwicke had been removed to one of the lower rooms to await the burial. The bedroom had been fastidiously cleaned since the schoolmaster's death and now had nothing to say for itself. It had always looked a little stark to Mary, and now it seemed even emptier than before, as if nothing that had happened in it had made any impression. Maybe it was a good representation of her father's asceticism, but when Mary wanted to feel close to her father it was his office she went to. The rows and rows of ledgers testified of his existence, whereas this room denied it.

The patch of sky she could see through the window had no proper respect for Chadwicke, either. It promised a fine summer day when it should have been rainy and bleak. A funeral on a sunny day? Though she knew it was unreasonable, Mary resented Nature for acting as if nothing had happened and the world could go on just as happily as before.

Mary's world would not go on—not the world she was accustomed to. Since her father's illness had taken a turn for the worse she had been forced to confront the precariousness of her situation. She would not be allowed to stay on at the school much longer. She had already tried to find some way in which she might prove useful; she had offered her services to the kitchen staff, the nurses, even the mistress who taught the girls their sewing. She wasn't surprised to be turned away. Many of the staff expected to lose their own positions soon, when the new headmaster took over. They would all have to find work somewhere else.

When she was a child Mary had sometimes asked her father if she was pretty. Being a matter-of-fact man, Chadwicke had always answered "no." But he hadn't left it at that. He had always gone on to explain why prettiness wasn't desirable anyway and why Mary was blessed to be exactly as she was—wide, awkward frame, colorless hair, clumsy features, and all. "Everyday tasks are more difficult for you, Mary, so you grow well-acquainted with hardship. You struggle with it constantly, and so it is no stranger to you. You will never be afraid of something you know so well. You are not pretty, but you are strong, and no one could wish for more."

"But Father," Mary pressed, "is it not better to be pretty and not so well acquainted with hardship, who's not a friend anyone ever hopes to have?"

"Not at all," Chadwicke would exclaim. "Some people believe one can avoid hardship, but they deceive themselves. Every person must face it someday, and the butterflies who know nothing but how to flit about letting people admire them will have their wings torn apart. How much better to be without a hand and have your soul intact."

Mary believed her father to be one of the wisest men on earth, but she wasn't sure she agreed with him, especially now. If she had been pretty, her defect might not have handicapped her quite so much. A fine nose and a delicate mouth wouldn't make it any easier to embroider handkerchiefs or scrub floors, but they would make a difference nevertheless. Helplessness became appealing when mixed with beauty. If people perceived her as frail and tragic, they would line up to offer her shelter. As it was, Mary only seemed grotesque, and no one wanted her. She shuddered, giving way momentarily to her worst fear: herself, alone, sunk irredeemably into the poverty from which her father had rescued so many.

Once or twice she had accompanied her father into the slums, and she had stared with horror at the wretched creatures who flung themselves against the carriage to plead for food and money. She had pitied them, but she had never dreamed she might become one of them any more than she thought she might someday wake up as a cat. She knew they were as human as she was, but she couldn't seem to focus in on their faces, to find anything that distinguished them as individuals. They were as alike as a herd of sheep, and so though they possessed all the requisite parts, they weren't really people. The students at the school looked that way when they first arrived. Only after they had been scrubbed and dressed in the school's blue did they begin to have faces, and with faces, names. Mary always knew everyone at the school, at least after they had been there a week or so.

But the school wasn't her place anymore, and the slums couldn't be either; it was time to venture out, to make use of the strength that was supposed to be worth so much more than beauty. Chadwicke had taught her to take action, not to sit around waiting for someone else to rescue her. So Mary went over in her mind the plans she had for the following days. She would choose a number of her father's friends and associates and write to them about possible employment. Maybe one of them had a place for her, or maybe they would know of someone who did. She knew her father had tried this before, years ago, and failed, but he had not been desperate then. If Chadwicke had ever indulged anybody, it had been his daughter, and she suspected that he had turned away offers that threatened a too-harsh transition to the outside world. She could not afford indulgence now. She would accept any respectable employment.

When the window showed that it was full daylight, Mary arose and went to dress herself in her black mourning clothes. The hearse arrived at midmorning and the procession set out in silence, a somber cloud that looked inappropriate on such a bright day. Once at the churchyard, Mary inspected the gathering crowd, searching for familiar faces and sorting through her memory for nearly forgotten names. She was pleased at the number of people who had turned out to pay their respects to the old schoolmaster. Chadwicke, of course, would have thought it a vanity to take pleasure in such a thing, but Mary didn't care. She was proud that her father had helped so many people and glad that so many of them acknowledged his contributions. She wished he could have been there to hear the way they talked about him: "a tireless man," "never thought of himself," "cannot be replaced." Listening to the fragments of conversation, Mary suddenly feared that she would burst out with uncontrollable sobs. She watched men lower her father's coffin into the earth and couldn't believe that he was really inside, that they were about to cover his hands and face and heart with dirt and darkness. She bit her lip and looked away, letting her eyes sweep over the churchyard. A tall young man with dark curly hair met her eyes across the grave. He nodded slightly and continued to stare at her, but she glanced quickly away. When she looked back again, his eyes had not left her face.

As soon as the service ended and the crowd began to disperse, the young man approached Mary with a determined stride, threading deftly through the tangles of people without ever taking his eyes off his destination. "Miss Chadwicke, I presume," he called out when he was still a few feet away. Mary had been turning to go, feeling unprepared to make conversation. At his greeting she stopped and faced him, and her eyes explored his countenance inquisitively. If he was going to force her to speak to him, she might as well know who he was. He seemed familiar, as many in the crowd had, but she couldn't come up with a name.

"Forgive me for addressing you without an introduction," he began, fingering the hat he held against his chest and raising his eyebrows apologetically. "I was hoping to find someone to do it properly, but I was afraid you would slip away. I could see that you meant to."

"Yes, I am feeling a little unwell at present," said Mary. She hoped he would excuse himself and let her go. It was the polite thing to do—but no such luck.

"We have met before, you know," he continued, "but I cannot expect you to remember me. I was at your father's school six years ago. My name is Nicholas Casey."

"Ah, yes, Mr. Casey." Mary recalled him being a rather small boy. "You've . . . grown," she stammered, hating to state the obvious but not feeling sharp enough to be witty.

"Yes, thank goodness." He flashed a quick, good-natured grin.

His teeth were startlingly white against his lightly tanned face, and Mary was acutely aware of his good looks and, as always, of her own homeliness. She wished more than ever that the interview would end.

"I wanted to tell you, Miss Chadwicke," said Nicholas, "how very indebted I am to your father. Though perhaps I cannot say it, as there are really no words which do it justice." Nicholas paused to review the powers of his vocabulary, and his large, expressive eyes held Mary captive. "I owe him what I am," he concluded finally. "I finished my apprenticeship earlier this month and was on my way to thank him personally."

For a moment Mary had no idea what to say. The emotion that had threatened to gush out at the sight of her father's coffin now throbbed against her chest and the insides of her eyes. She hesitated, struggling inwardly to hold her grief in check, not wanting to hear the quavering voice that she knew would come out if she spoke. She didn't realize that a single tear had leaked out until Nicholas touched her cheek to brush it aside. The feel of his hand caught her off guard; she jerked her face away instinctively and took a step backward. "I appreciate your telling me this, sir," she managed. "I only wish you could have told my father yourself. It would have cheered him. I believe he—that is, I am afraid he died feeling unsatisfied with what he had accomplished."

"Perhaps the only ones who are ever satisfied are those who had no ideals in the first place. Forgive me, Miss Chadwicke, if I have made you uncomfortable. I shouldn't have taken the liberty."

"I understand that you meant to be kind. As I told you before, I am feeling unwell. Thank you for your thoughtful words, Mr. Casey. Good day." She began to walk unsteadily toward the gate that led out of the churchyard, intending to leave Nicholas behind, but he leaped over the distance between them and reached out as if to catch at her arm, restraining himself at the last moment.

"I must ask you, Miss Chadwicke, if I might be permitted to call on you at the school tomorrow? There is something I must discuss with you."

"What could you possibly have to discuss with me, sir, more than what you have already told me?"

"If you'll allow me to come tomorrow, you will know then, and perhaps I'll have the opportunity to make an excuse for my bad manners. I shall not be in London long, Miss Chadwicke, and I must make use of my time here. I wouldn't trouble you now if it were not a matter of importance."

"I shall see you tomorrow then," Mary conceded wearily, wanting more than anything to be left alone. She cherished the praise Nicholas had given her father but disliked his overbearance, his insistence that she keep up her public show of control and politeness when she should already have returned to the solace of solitude. Ordinarily she enjoyed chatting with students and former students, but today was not an ordinary day. In fact, she didn't know if life could ever feel ordinary again.

Back at the school Mary let herself cry while she made up some tea, and she didn't reproach herself too severely for continuing to sniffle and whimper while she drank the tea. But once the cup was drained and washed, she wiped her face resolutely. She had no more time for tears today. She made her way down to her father's office and shut herself in with his ledgers. No one had cleaned off his desk since the last time the schoolmaster had used it. A small pile of letters awaited his inspection. His quill sat on one corner, near a candle that was nearly burnt down. Mary perched carefully in Chadwicke's chair and looked about her. She felt almost as if she were disturbing a shrine. Cleaning his bedroom had not upset her as that room had always felt impersonal, but she hesitated to move a single item here. It would somehow seem more final than today's burial. The silence draped thickly about her until she grew annoyed at the sound of her own breathing. *He is gone*, she thought. *He is truly gone.*

Trembling, she pulled out the shallow drawer in the middle of the desk and extracted a sheet of paper. She wrote until it was too dark to see her own handwriting.

She would have forgotten all about Nicholas if he hadn't made his promised visit the next morning. She had been at work since dawn cleaning the suite of rooms that she and her father had occupied—they had to be ready for the new headmaster, and though she may be destitute she was not sloppy. She would prepare them to hold up under the harshest scrutiny. To avoid spoiling her mourning clothes, which she could not afford to replace, she had put on a faded old dress that had once been dark blue. The day was warm and her hair spilled out of its bun and stuck to the back of her neck. When the clerk popped his head in to inform her that a gentleman was waiting downstairs to see her, she made a hasty attempt to tidy her appearance, cursing herself for her passive agreement to Nicholas's request. She knew that at her best she looked plain, but maybe at her worst she bordered on frightening. She imagined Nicholas turning to greet her and gasping at her red face and wild hair. She was not in the mood for such humiliation.

Luckily, Nicholas was not as faint-hearted as Mary had feared. He put on a charming smile of welcome as soon as she appeared on the landing above the entrance hall and beamed at her while she descended the final flight of steps.

"I was afraid you would refuse to see me after yesterday," he confessed. "I could not blame you if you did. I did not give a very good showing of my manners. You'll think my time at this school was wasted."

"I could not make any such judgment as that, Mr. Casey," said Mary, her voice betraying a hint of coolness nevertheless. "I'm hardly in a position to make pronouncements about you. I may have known you by sight when you were at school here, but you are a stranger to me now, and I do not make a habit of judging strangers."

"Very Christian of you, Miss Chadwicke," declared Nicholas cheerfully. "Will you walk with me in the garden?"

They let themselves out into the bright sunshine and began to saunter along one of the paths. "I was very sorry to hear of your father's death," Nicholas said. He reached out to pull aside a leafy branch that hung across the way and held it while Mary passed by. "Mr. Chadwicke always seemed a little less mortal than the rest of us. We had lost our families, our homes, but he would always be there, steady and reliable." He spoke gently, thoughtfully, turning his face about him to take in the sights of the garden and seeming to see, not what was really there, but a vision from the past. "When I heard the news, something within me refused to believe that he was subject to illness and death, just like everyone else."

Mary kept her head down and concentrated on the patterns of the stones in the path. She groped in her mind for some gracious and commonplace response but found only feelings that were too real for polite conversation. In the silence that stretched between them, she reflected that Nicholas already knew what it was like to lose a family. His bright smile and dark eyes hid a memory of sadness and fear, a memory of a time when he had confronted a worse situation than Mary did now. It was that memory that brought him here, because if he didn't remember what he had been saved from he wouldn't remember to be grateful to the man who had saved him. Chadwicke had intervened in his life and made a difference. No wonder he had placed the schoolmaster above mortal men, and no wonder Mary still staggered under the shock of losing the man she could always put her faith in. She cast a sidelong glance at Nicholas, taking new interest in his face now that she imagined what it concealed.

Though they had moved slowly, the two were now nearing the edge of the garden, and Nicholas advanced toward one of the tallest plane-trees.

"This was my favorite tree," he told her, slapping a hand onto the trunk and staring up toward the giant's top. "I don't know how many times I climbed it."

Mary smiled wryly. "This was my father's tree. He had this row planted when he moved the school here. He was very proud of them always."

Nicholas instantly sobered. "Yes, well, your father had much to be proud of." Both were silent again for a moment. "Miss Chadwicke, I criticized my own bad manners just now, but I am afraid I may not make any better showing today. I must speak plainly to you. Do I have your permission to do so?"

Mary took an uneasy step backward and glanced around the garden. She saw with relief that several students were outside, taking advantage of the break from routine that Chadwicke's death had brought them. She looked back at Nicholas with more confidence. "Yes, Mr. Casey. Please speak your mind."

"The reason I pursued you so rudely in the churchyard yesterday, the reason I must speak bluntly now, is that I am in a hurry. I told you yesterday that I would not be in London long. What I did not tell you is that I am leaving England altogether." Nicholas's words conveyed his sense of urgency by tumbling out faster and faster. "As I said, I have finished my apprenticeship, and my former master has connections in the colonies. He has helped me to secure a position in Virginia with a former colleague of his. The man who is offering the position has made a notable reputation for himself as a lawyer there, and I will be assisting him with his work and also serving as a clerk for the county. I sail at the beginning of next week." Nicholas paused for breath while Mary muttered something vaguely congratulatory. "Yes, I am pleased," said Nicholas. "It is a very fine start. Mr. Worthington, the lawyer who has been good enough to give me this opportunity, will help me to acquire some land. I will build a small house and will be able to live quite comfortably."

Mary began to wonder if there was a purpose to this boasting. "This is all very good news, Mr. Casey. My father would be happy for you. I sometimes think he wished to visit the colonies himself."

"Without your father, none of this would have been possible. I can't think what would have become of me." Nicholas smiled, and this time the expression was self-deprecating. "Well—perhaps I know, and it isn't good. For the last several months, I have been asking myself if there is anything I could do to begin to repay my debt to Mr. Chadwicke. I could think of nothing. I entertained the idea of offering my time, serving as a clerk, perhaps, without pay, but my circumstances do not allow that. I came here to thank him and to ask if there was anything I could do, but I no sooner arrived in the parish than I was confronted with the news of his death. I feared I had lost my chance. But now I think perhaps I was *given* my chance, instead."

"What do you mean? You thought of something to do for the school?"

"No, not exactly. Miss Chadwicke, I am grateful for my position, and I am not afraid to sail to Virginia. But it is very far from home, and I will be alone there. I should like very much to have a companion, a wife. You said this morning that I am a stranger to you, and even now I can give you no reason why you should think well of me. A declaration of love on either side would be absurd at this time. But—forgive me—I know that your father was not wealthy and that he invested all he had in the school. He must have been worried about your welfare. At least I can offer you security, and although the conditions may be a little rough at first, I believe I can give you a pleasant home. For my part, I will feel that I rendered some small service to your father, and as I said, I would very much like to have a companion in this adventure."

Mary gaped at him. Could he be . . . was it possible that he had just proposed marriage? Suddenly feeling disoriented, she put out a hand to steady herself against a tree.

"Miss Chadwicke, have I made you ill? I confess that is not the effect I hoped my words would have."

"If you would be so kind as to give me a moment—" Mary's head swam in a whirlpool of thoughts. This was unexpected, unconventional, *impossible*. "I appreciate your concern for me, Mr. Casey," she stammered, "but I am not yet in need of being adopted as an object of charity."

Nicholas's forehead wrinkled with anxiety. "I expressed myself badly. I was afraid I would do so. I only wanted to explain how the idea came to me in the first place. I didn't wish to insult your intelligence by pretending to have fallen in love with you at first sight, on the day of your father's funeral no less. But I wanted you—I *want* you—to consider my offer. Please, Miss Chadwicke. I don't ask you to marry me out of pity—"

"Out of what, then? A noble if misdirected desire to manifest your gratitude to my father? My father is in no position to benefit from your efforts, and though I sincerely appreciate your sentiments toward him, I also have no need of your assistance." Mary took her hand off the tree and straightened her shoulders as if ready to demonstrate her strength.

"Do not let your pride get in the way of the truth," argued Nicholas. "Unless you have extensive resources that I am unaware of, a marriage with a hard-working person of amiable disposition—such as myself—would be the best way to assure your continued financial security. You may be quite capable of managing without it, but why reject the possibility when it is offered to you? And you would be helping me as much as I would be helping you. I would like very much to have an English wife, and I have no time to pursue a proper courtship with you or any other English lady. My only hope is that you will overlook the clumsy manner in which I have explained myself to you and do what logic decrees."

Mary raised an eyebrow skeptically. "From what one hears of the colonies, I cannot be certain that going there is logical under any circumstances."

"The colonies are not all the same, though many ignorant people would have you believe that they are. The Caribbean may be a bit rough yet, but Virginia has become quite genteel."

"Then why not find a wife there? You would not have need of such haste in that case."

"True. If you reject my offer, that is what I shall have to do. But, Miss Chadwicke, how much better to have as a companion a person familiar with the place where all my best memories are from! If I start thinking of home and wish to reminisce, I need only say, 'Remember that tree in the garden,' and you will instantly know what I am speaking of. No young lady of Virginia, no matter how desirable in other respects, can possess that quality."

"But a young lady of Virginia would have two hands to work hard with, whereas I have not. Mr. Casey, you have spoken plainly, and I wish to do so as well. I do not wish to be a burden to you or to anyone else. Perhaps I am less able than others to do useful work, but that is why it is more important for me than for others to *try* to do useful work. If I were honest with myself, I might find myself in greater need of your offer than I would like to let on, but that only makes it more important for me to refuse it."

"I do not understand you, Miss Chadwicke. Do you feel that life with me would be too difficult or too easy? Make your objection clear, and I will explain to you why it is no objection at all." Nicholas surprised her by winking at her. His dark eyes sparkled.

"Is this a trifle to you?" she queried disapprovingly.

"Not at all. Please continue. You were saying that you would consent to be my wife and sail to Virginia with me, there to face a few hardships, no doubt, and ultimately prosper."

"You are a very optimistic young man," Mary remarked.

"What is the purpose of not being so? I do everything in my power to assure the outcome I want, and if it does not work out the way I wish it, at least I have saved myself the trouble of worrying over some hindrance I could not prevent."

"Mr. Casey, I have *no* dowry. I have nothing at all to bring you. You might have expected a little something—"

"I did not."

"If I were to marry you, I would work very hard, but I could not truthfully promise that you would never suffer from my defect, that you would never see imperfection where a better equipped young lady might have created perfection . . . "

Nicholas placed a hand on each of Mary's shoulders and stooped a little so that he looked into Mary's eyes from across a very narrow distance.

"I have thought of all this already. It is your turn to think now—not about whether I will be happy with you, for that is my concern, and I have made my decision. Your concern is whether you will be happy with me."

"May I have a day then?"

Nicholas released her and stepped back. "Of course."

But underneath, Mary already knew her answer. That evening when she returned to the garden to enjoy the sunset, she experienced a strange, pricking pain. How many sunsets had she viewed from this very spot, she wondered. Thousands? But now they were numbered.

Soon she would find herself adrift on a sea that appeared to extend forever in every direction. She would watch the sun dip into the ocean and light the water on fire, and although it would be the same sun that had shone over her all the days of her life, would she be able to help imagining that she had glided away into a separate world? And Virginia was a complete unknown. Yet, she would go. Nicholas had spoken truthfully: her options were limited. She had actively tried to secure her own future, but she had prayed too, knowing that she needed a miracle. Now perhaps God offered her a solution. She would enter this new life with all her heart and all her determination, and it helped that she believed her father would have approved of her decision. After all, it would take strength to go to Virginia. And in fact it took courage, Mary reflected, to let oneself be saved.

Chapter 15

They were married quietly in the little chapel at the school the day before they were scheduled to sail. Mary wore her mourning clothes still, and both bride and groom sensed the air of solemnity that settled heavily about them like the layer of dust that overlaid the railings and etched gray shadows into the crevices of the woodwork at the altar. These were the last moments before the door closed on their old lives and shut out forever any other possibilities or hopes. With every instant the choices narrowed until finally the path stretched out straight; there could be no turning aside, no changing course. Mary heard the clergyman binding her life inextricably to Nicholas's and tried to ignore the churning in her insides that seemed to be the collective effect of all the fear she had ever felt in her life. She studied Nicholas furtively, keeping her face cast down; she noted his handsome features, his grave expression that must mirror her own. She had lain awake all night lecturing herself about her new responsibilities. She was strong, proud; she was her father's daughter, and she would work herself to death rather than permit Nicholas the tiniest moment of regret. Never would she give him the opportunity to complain that his home was not as clean, his meals not as appealing, his children not as well cared for as they might have been if he had chosen another wife. She would never allow herself to be a burden on him, and most of all, she would never be the object of his pity.

Stepping aboard the *Joanna* just after dawn the next morning, Mary squared her shoulders and kept her face turned toward the open sea. "It's beautiful," she remarked to Nicholas, refusing to acknowledge any feelings besides awe and excitement. Nicholas led her to their quarters below deck and settled them into the cramped corner that would serve as sleeping space for the journey.

"This is the worst part," he told her. "When this is over, everything will be better."

Mary smiled. "Then we have much to look forward to," she said bravely. "Even this is not so very unpleasant." They returned to the deck and stood with their backs toward England. It slipped away behind them without receiving a farewell glance.

They arrived in Virginia in early autumn, or at least back home it would have been autumn. Here the trees retained their leafy greenness and the heat still pressed in from all sides. As they rode from the dock to Williamsburg, the capital of the colony, Mary marveled at the wildness and mystery of the landscape—the tall slender evergreens pointing skyward like sharpened arrows, the dense underbrush, the whirs and plopping sounds and rustlings that told her the forest pulsed with unseen life. She shivered in spite of the heat and scooted a little closer to Nicholas. He had reassured her before they sailed that she needn't fear an Indian attack. "It's been years since there was any danger from Indians," he had declared confidently. "If we were the sort to push on to the frontier, it might be different. But Williamsburg is as safe as London—safer even, for there aren't so many thieves about." Mary believed him, but she had lived all her life in a great, teeming city, and the very emptiness of this land frightened her. How far did it stretch to the west, with its vast wilderness that no white man had ever set foot in? It was almost unimaginable, but it was exciting too, so Mary laughed up at the trees to show she wasn't afraid. "It's a different sort of place," she said to Nicholas.

He nodded. "Yes, it's all its own."

They had traveled a few miles when the forest began to give way to wide tracts of farmland. "What are they growing?" Mary asked, eyeing the unfamiliar crop.

"Tobacco. It's what makes Virginia profitable." Mary could see people with dark complexions moving about in the fields.

"And slaves?"

"It's the nature of the crop," Nicholas reasoned. "It requires labor. One man working alone doesn't prosper."

"Oh." She had been right—it was a different sort of place.

As they approached the outskirts of Williamsburg, tidy rectangular gardens replaced the tobacco fields, and neat white framehouses interspersed with sturdy-looking edifices of orange brick blocked Mary's view of the farmland. The carriage turned onto a busy street and rolled slowly westward. "This is the Duke of Gloucester Street," the driver informed them. "It's not far now."

"The Duke of Gloucester Street?" Nicholas turned to Mary. "This is the main street of the town," he said. "Mr. Worthington described it in his letter." He raised up a little and looked around eagerly. At either end of the street, an imposing structure asserted the growing importance of the little city. The two buildings, both of orange brick, could have held their own in England, though their newness would have distinguished them. "That's the capitol," Nicholas explained, motioning toward the building on the east. "And that's the College." He indicated the building on the west. "They say it was designed by Christopher Wren." Nicholas's dark eyes sought Mary's. "Someday our sons will go there, and they'll receive as good an education as they ever could in England."

The driver showed them the Governor's palace and the church before leaving the main road for a narrow lane lined with painted fences and meticulously kept homes. He pulled up in front of one of the larger residences, then jumped down to open the door and haul the luggage to the ground. Little white fragments that looked to Mary like broken eggshells crunched under her feet when she stepped down.

"Sea shells," the driver explained in answer to her puzzled expression.

"Goodness," Mary marveled, "there are so many of them." A white path ran the length of the street, with branches like tiny tributaries of a stream breaking off here and there to lead up to each home. As Mary's eyes traveled the path up to the green-painted door of their boarding house, the door opened, and a plump woman in a frilly white cap and apron stepped out onto the porch and held out her arms. "Come in, come in, dears, and rest yourselves," she called. She had a hot dinner waiting for them, and after that a soft bed—the softest she had ever slept in, Mary thought dreamily in the brief moments before she succumbed to exhaustion.

Before the last of the leaves had fallen to make way for winter, Nicholas had built them a little house of their own. Mary was amazed at how quickly the structure went up. They had plenty of help, with all the neighbors pitching in to complete the task, but in Mary's experience construction was a nearly interminable process. She hadn't expected to move out of the boarding house before spring.

"It's simple," Nicholas warned her before taking her to see the finished house. "I'll build us something better as soon as I am able." It *was* small, just two rooms, one private, one for company. But Mary liked knowing it was their own. As soon as they had acquired a few necessities, she set up housekeeping feeling quite satisfied with her new situation. She had only two real concerns. First, she was lonely. The neighbors had proven their generosity by helping with the house, and now and then they offered Mary advice on adjusting to her new surroundings. One woman, Mrs. Justis, even gave her some fabric after counseling her that her clothing was unsuited to the Virginia climate. But—was it just her imagination?—they all seemed to hold her at arm's length. They were courteous but cool, helpful but not friendly. With all the labor required just to keep herself and Nicholas clean, fed, and clothed, Mary scarcely had a free moment, but whenever she could squeeze out a half hour from her workday she went visiting, hungry for even a few scraps of conversation. The women received her politely but did not return her visits. At the school Mary had never been alone unless she chose to be. There were always young people around to play with or talk to. Not so here. Nicholas worked long hours and came home tired. She didn't want to bother him, anyway. There was just one issue that she couldn't help speaking her mind on, and that was her other concern: Nicholas refused to accompany her to church.

He had attended the first week or so after their arrival in Virginia, but since then he had sent Mary on alone with Mrs. Byrnes, the owner of the boarding house. At first Mary interpreted his reluctance as exhaustion; no wonder that building the house and learning his new duties sapped his strength, and Sunday was his only day for rest. Still, she nudged him gently toward his duty, hoping that when they moved into their own house he would join her for a proper Sabbath Day observance. But instead he only became more entrenched in his determination to stay at home. Week after week Mary trudged to church without him, truly alone now that she no longer had Mrs. Byrnes for company.

One Sunday Mary had had enough. She had never uttered a complaint since the day of their marriage, and she hated to do so now—in every other way, Nicholas deserved her admiration rather than her scorn. As she wiggled into her cloak and began to squirm into her mitten, she kept her lips clamped shut. They seemed to fly open of their own accord when she stepped past Nicholas toward the door.

"I suppose you are staying behind again?" she snapped, her tone sharp and accusatory.

"Yes, my dear," replied Nicholas mildly.

"Why? Laziness does not seem to be part of your disposition the other six days of the week. Why then come Sunday do you refuse to fulfill your responsibilities?"

Nicholas's expression remained bland. "What responsibilities are those? I am aware of none."

Mary exhaled through clenched teeth. "Do not pretend to misunderstand me," she said, and she started at the volume of her own voice. Had she been shouting? "At least offer some explanation," she added hastily. "Do not send me on alone as if it were the most natural thing in the world." She paused, but Nicholas made no response. "No, never mind, any excuse would be tiresome. Do not explain, only come. You know it is right."

Finally Nicholas stirred. He unfolded his arms and stood up. "No, in fact I think it is better to stay at home," he said quietly. His eyes had a hard look; beneath his calm voice lay an iron resolve. Mary understood: if she chose to pry, she would only make sparks. "You know why those people go," he went on. "Hoping the Lord will bless them or curse them as He will, just so as they can turn the accountability over to Him. It saves them ever having to make decisions for themselves. If you wish me to be like them, you make a foolish wish. I work for what I receive, and whether I succeed or fail, I take the responsibility."

Mary stared at him with astonishment and dismay. She hadn't heard him say anything so shocking since the day he proposed to her, a near stranger. "You cannot believe that, Mr. Casey," she protested vehemently, ignoring his warning look and addressing him formally, as was her custom. "If you do, your education at my father's school was wasted. Why, did you never learn anything that he strove to teach you and all his students? *He* wanted you to work hard, as you do, and let your faith in God be as active as your own hands. *He* didn't worship in order to relinquish his accountability. You know he took such a burden on himself that he refused to rest until he had worked his strength away! And do you think he gave up making decisions? Do you think it never took any mental effort to do what he did?" Angry tears had sprung up in her eyes and now burned her cheeks as they trickled down to drip off her chin. She brushed at them impatiently while the echo of her tirade lingered in the silence that ensued.

"I did not intend to distress you, my dear," said Nicholas, still quiet, still calm. Suddenly his self-control irritated her. *How reasonable I am,* he seemed to say. *How wise, how unclouded by emotion.* Next to him, she appeared cursed with all the fabled frailties of her sex. Any impartial observer would conclude that if one of them knew what was what, it was Nicholas. And yet, that impartial observer would be wrong. Mary had made a mistake in letting her temper get the better of her, but she would stand behind what she said. Maybe Nicholas could convince himself that he was too logical and hard-working for religion, but he would never deceive her.

"Go now," he urged. "You'll be late."

Mary whirled on her heel and rushed out into the fresh, crisp winter air. The cold soothed her hot cheeks. How could he have said such things? How could she have gotten so angry? Even now her heart still slammed against her chest and her mind refused to think clearly.

She could not have repeated what was said in the sermon that day. All through the service she struggled with her dilemma, with the apparently mutually exclusive goals of keeping the peace and making Nicholas see reason. She trekked back home without having settled on any satisfactory course of action. All she knew was that she must try not to appear sullen or sulky while she continued to think the matter over.

She found Nicholas seated at the table fingering a small object that she had never laid eyes on before. It gleamed in the firelight, and as she stepped closer she saw that it was a silver heart on a chain. Nicholas glanced up at her with eyes drained of their usual sparkle.

"Forgive me, Mary," he whispered. He set the heart on the table and pushed back his chair to stand up. "I was not honest with you this morning. Come, sit, I have a long explanation to give." Mary had not expected such a greeting, and so she stood dumbly as he removed her mitten, cloak, and hat and guided her into a chair at the table. When he had resumed his place, he took up the heart again and turned it over absently against his palm.

"What I said today . . ." he began hesitantly, "it was cowardly. I lied to cover my own misgivings. The truth is—well, that is my long explanation." He put the heart down, laced his fingers together, met her eyes. "When I was six years old my family moved to London. We had been turned off our land. My father and mother tried to find work in the village nearby, then in the cities, but finally there was nothing left but to go to the biggest city of all. We had nothing—I do not know how my parents paid for the room we lived in. It was not much, just a bit of space in a dirty, crumbling building, but my sister Anne and I managed to be happy there. Anne and I had always been happy. We knew we had the kindest parents in the world and that everything would always turn out for the best. Anne was . . ." he seemed to cast about for the right words. "She was a very merry creature, a person always full of joy and hope. I can still hear her laughter." He paused as if listening to an echo that lingered across nearly two decades. "We did not live in that room long. The typhoid was going around. My mother fell sick first, then my father. Anne and I nursed them the best we could. And then Anne fell sick."

Mary reached out her hand to lay it across Nicholas's. He started a little at the touch. The past engulfed him, and he had nearly forgotten her presence. "I did what I could for them. It was so little. I've wondered now and then over the years if I might have done something different. I went looking for help, but everyone shooed me away. They were so afraid of getting sick themselves. So my family died, one by one, within a few hours of each other. I sat there alone with them. I didn't know who to go to. I was with them for three days." Nicholas shook his head as if to rid it of the memory. "Who knows how long I would have been there, what would have become of me, if not for your father. I had gone into the street to beg for food, I was so hungry. He was passing by in a carriage. He got out and spoke to me. I told him everything, and he told me not to worry. He took me to the school, fed me, gave me the uniform to wear. I was never alone again." His fingers curled lightly around Mary's.

She let the silence stretch on for several moments before venturing, "And this morning you were thinking of that experience?"

Nicholas sighed. "Yes. You see, I told you that I work for what I receive. I implied that I was superior to other people because I take responsibility for my own destiny rather than crying to God. But that was a lie I told myself. That time when I was six, I was helpless. I did not work for what I received. A man came and saved me. What I have, I owe to him."

"He put you in the school, he gave you an opportunity. But you, by your diligence, made it worthwhile. If not for your own effort you never would have bettered yourself."

Nicholas offered his self-deprecating smile. "A pleasing way to think of it," he agreed. "But then there is this." He picked up the chain that held the heart and dangled it for her to see. "The person who gave me this saved my life, and I do not even know his name."

"How did you come by it?"

"It was given to me. Years ago, I was sick with the fever. I was quite ill, I believe. I think they put me out into the corridor to die. And then suddenly there was someone. I've tried so hard to conjure up an image of his face, but all my memories are distorted. I know that he gave me water to drink when I thought I would die of thirst alone. He spoke to me. I was frightened, and he stayed with me. I feel certain I would have died if not for him. When I awoke from the fever, he had left me this." He dangled the heart again. "I tried to find out from the nurses who he was, but the poor dears had been so busy they hardly remembered their own names."

"That's a beautiful story, Nicholas," breathed Mary, unaware that she had used his given name. "How could it possibly have hurt your faith?"

"Don't you see? Twice, I was helpless. Twice someone saved me, gave me my life. You might say that God saved me. I would not dispute it. But it frightens me, you have no idea how much. To acknowledge one's own helplessness is to relinquish all that is comforting in life. Every day I lie to myself. I say, 'If you work as hard as you can, you will succeed. You will prosper.' Today I have a tiny two-room house, but in two years I will have something better. Today I have a wife, and next year I will have a son. The progress is simple. When I think that way, how easy it is to see to my duties, to go about whistling, even. And all the while, underneath, I know that nothing is so certain, that no matter what I do, I may find myself . . . in need of help, again. What am I to do if I have so little power to act for myself?"

"But you do have power to act for yourself. God does not sport with you as if you were an animal in a trap. When you reach the end of your own resources, He is there to guide you."

"Perhaps. But then there is the issue of debt. I wished to be free of debt, and so I tried to repay your father. I wanted peace, you see—to know that I have earned what I have. But you cannot repay a person whose identity you do not know, and if you accept God fully along with all of the implications, well then you can never repay Him. Or at least, it would mean giving your whole life to Him. I do not know if can ever do that. How does one let go of all one's own desires and ambitions? Many people say, 'Thy will be done,' but you observe, my dear. They say that when it is already clear that they have no choice in the matter. They praise Job for his integrity and forbearance, but who would volunteer for his difficulties? Not I."

"But it is simple, Nicholas. You make it more difficult than it is. God is not your enemy, and you already do so many things right—if you would only come to church . . ."

"No, Mary." His voice sounded low but firm. "You must go for us both. You must be the keeper of the faith for us both."

Mary opened her mouth to say that that was impossible, that there are some things one person cannot do for another, no matter how much they want to help. But at the pleading look in Nicholas's eyes she closed it again and sat for a long time holding his hand in silence.

"Mary," he said at last, "this should belong to you. It's the only thing of any beauty that I own. I should have given it to you from the beginning." He arose and came around behind her to fasten the chain about her neck. The heart glowed orange in the light from the fire, and Nicholas's fingers were warm against her skin.

"Thank you," she said.

In the spring, when everyone's garden bloomed with tulips and patches of wildflowers burst out as purple, yellow, and white surprises among the green of the countryside, Mary's stomach grew as round as a globe. "You remind me of a bumblebee," Nicholas told her after studying her with his head cocked to one side. "Round and busy."

She spent part of every day fumbling with small bits of material in an effort to produce miniature clothing. Her handicap had never frustrated her so much.

"We'll pay someone else to make them," Nicholas had suggested one morning when he observed Mary scowling over a scrap of linen. "You have enough work already."

"So does everyone else," she replied. Her back throbbed from the double strain of carrying the baby and bending over tiny stitches, so she answered Nicholas without straightening up to look at him. Sometimes she thought she would never be able to straighten up again. Her back and neck felt numb and heavy as if they had been turned into iron weights. "I shall have everything finished in time," she declared boldly, defying her body to hold her back.

By the time the pains began in earnest one warm April night, she had completed half the items she had intended to make. It would have to do for now—at least there would be a warm blanket to wrap the child in and a little nightgown to dress it with. Nicholas galloped off to fetch the midwife and returned with two other neighbor women in tow. The women swept in with an air of calm authority, assigned Nicholas a list of chores, and shut him out of the birthing room.

"Poor dearie," cooed Mrs. Burges, "the first is always a bit difficult. But don't you fret—Mrs. Woodley will take good care of you." Mrs. Woodley was the midwife. She showed Mary a confident smile.

"Why, she has delivered the last six of mine," piped up Mrs. Stuart, "and not lost a single one."

Mary tried to smile back at them, but the pain tore her apart. She couldn't seem to find the two corners of her mouth at the same instant. Even so, she could still sense her secret fear, cold and wet around her heart. Would this child be whole, like its father? The backs of her eyelids wore an image of Nicholas's face as it bent over the bundle. The eyes held excitement, then surprise, then horror. A broken child, like its mother. *No, please, God,* Mary prayed, *not that.*

Mrs. Stuart bent close to wipe Mary's face. "The pain will end," she promised. "There is an end, Mrs. Casey." Mary heard Nicholas's voice from somewhere, and it sounded anxious. *How long?* Had he asked it or had she?

And then, finally, there came a new sound. The pain was still there, had always been there it seemed, but Mary felt as if she had been lifted above it. She could hear her baby crying.

"Tell me, tell me," she demanded breathlessly.

"A fine boy," exclaimed Mrs. Woodley, holding up a small squirming creature.

"But tell me," Mary persisted. Instead, Mrs. Stuart wiped her face again and smoothed her pillow. The fear around her heart began to pulse. Were they avoiding her question?

"Here he is," said Mrs. Woodley, and Mary opened her arms to receive the bundle. Anxiously, clumsily, she pushed back the blanket Mrs. Woodley had wrapped him in. Two hands, two feet.

"It's a miracle," Mary cried, and the women smiled at each other.

"It always is," they said.

And then Nicholas was standing over them, looking down and beaming. "A fine boy," he pronounced. "A perfect, fine little boy."

Chapter 16

"Good afternoon, Mrs. Casey," called Mrs. Justis, rounding the side of the cabin to find Mary dragging a comb through a mess of flax. "I've come to sit with you for awhile." Mary set the comb aside and straightened up, her hand flying instinctively to the small of her back, which throbbed in protest of the movement. She didn't have to pretend to be pleased to see Mrs. Justis; she always enjoyed company, and the tedious process of making linen from flax included many of her least favorite chores. She had spread out a few finished pieces where she could see them to remind herself that the end result, if not the means, was rewarding.

"I'm glad you've come to see me, Mrs. Justis," she smiled. "I've been wanting to show you the dress I made from the material you gave me." Mary scooped up little Samuel Nicholas from his cradle, which she had placed outside under a makeshift tent, and led the way to the door that gaped open on a dim interior. Inside, the cabin was hot and dark, like a shroud.

"I'll hold the little one while you fetch it," Mrs. Justis offered. She opened her arms to receive the baby and stood in the rectangle of sunshine from the doorway, cooing at Samuel and shifting her weight gently from one foot to the other. Mary went into the other room and opened a chest that Nicholas had finished making for her only two months ago. The dress lay just inside, carefully folded so as not to crease.

"Here it is," she announced, returning to Mrs. Justis.

"Ah," approved the lady. "That is right for this sort of weather. When you live here you cannot dress as if you were still in England."

Mary replaced the dress, and the two women went back outside, where breathing was a little less like trying to suck air through a wet cloth. From the sound of Mrs. Justis's speech, Mary knew that she had lived in England, but many of Mary's other neighbors had not. She tried to imagine what it would be like to be born here and to know only these high, skinny trees, these fields, these ripples of heat that carried on them the voices of Englishmen, Scots, and Africans.

"It's good of you to come," Mary remarked as the two sat down on the bench that ran along one side of the cabin. "I was a bit lonely when I first arrived here. Silly of me, I suppose. Still, I like to have visitors."

"Yes, it can get lonesome, if you ever find you have a moment to think about it."

"It seems as though I have more visitors now." Mary hesitated, half hoping the older woman would supply an explanation. "It's Samuel, I reckon. He charms everyone."

"Mmm," conceded Mrs. Justis.

"How long have you lived in Williamsburg, Mrs. Justis?"

"Oh, as long as ever it's been a city worth living in. Let me remember—it had just been made the capital of the colony when my Jonas and I arrived. That was years back, that was. Nearly thirty years."

"You must have been very newly married."

"Yes, we were wed less than a month before we embarked. Much like you and young Mr. Casey, I should imagine."

"And what did you think of the place when you first came here?"

"Oh, it pleased me well enough. Though I cannot say I was as wild about it as Jonas was. Yes," she said, settling herself more comfortably on the bench and warming up to the topic, "I remember the way he would talk about it. 'Nothing like this in England,' he'd say. Everything he saw—the forest, the fields—'nothing like this in England.' Well, one day I spoke my mind. I told him, 'Jonas, they have things exactly like this in England, and you know it as well as I do. You talk as if you had never beheld a tree before in your life.'" Mrs. Justis grinned to herself. "Stubborn man, he was. And still is. 'I may have seen trees before,' he told me, 'but never so many at once.'"

"It does seem different here—like a different world, almost. Was it difficult to settle in?"

"Yes, I suppose we had our 'seasoning time.'" At Mary's inquisitive look, Mrs. Justis explained, "They call it that here—the first year or so. It takes time to get accustomed to things. So many people never make it past their first summer. You'll see in a few weeks, this time of year is the worst for sickness. The churchyard is never so well visited as in September and October. Ah, well, people grow to expect certain things. Most don't bother to get acquainted with new arrivals until they've weathered the climate for a while. It's the same with children," she said, gazing down at the infant that still lay contentedly against her chest. "With a new baby, you want to imagine its future, make plans for it. With my first boy, I would say to myself, 'This baby will be a good horseman, like its papa.' And with my girl, I thought of her wedding day. Who would she marry? I would make her a beautiful dress. I could see it already in my mind."

Mary could see her own dreams, too, the plans she had for Samuel. She and Nicholas often lay awake talking about his future. The shadowy ceiling above their bed became a blank canvas on which they projected their brightest images, pictures of a once small, chubby creature grown tall and strong. "Do you want him to be a lawyer, like you?" she had whispered to Nicholas one night, and he had surprised her a little by saying, "It makes little difference to me, as long as he has plenty of land." So as Mary lay on her back looking up, she saw the future Samuel moving with long, graceful strides across a field that appeared to stretch forever in every direction. And then, without meaning too, she thought of Nicholas—the past Nicholas, the small boy who had come to London because his family had nowhere else to go.

"Did I set you to dreaming, Mrs. Casey?" asked Mrs. Justis gently. "It comes naturally, you see."

Mary blushed. "I beg your pardon, Mrs. Justis," she apologized.

Then, with a quick spark of curiosity, she asked, "Did your son become a good horseman? Has your daughter married?" Mary knew that there were several Justis children, but she was acquainted with very few of them.

A shadow seemed to pass over Mrs. Justis's face. Mary glanced instinctively behind her to see what could be casting it, but she saw only sunlight and open air. "No," the older woman replied, and her voice sounded matter-of-fact. "My first son and my first daughter both died before they were ten years old. It's what I was telling you, Mrs. Casey. You never know. But some people are so afraid of what will happen, they comfort themselves by expecting the worst. They don't let themselves dream about their children. They don't make friends when someone new comes over from England. They find it easier that way. Perhaps it is."

Mary couldn't think what to say. Finally she murmured, "I'm sorry to hear about your loss, Mrs. Justis," and the older woman crinkled up her eyes in a half-smile and handed Mary the bundle in her arms.

"'Twas long ago. Not that one forgets, ever. But the feelings change. Now and then I think of my little ones and smile."

Mary sat on the bench after Mrs. Justis had gone, rocking Samuel gently and staring absently at the shifting patterns of sunlight at her feet. A tiny breeze, barely as strong as a breath, had tickled the leaves of the dogwood tree that grew a little way from the cabin, sending shivers of shadow across the grass. Human life could seem almost as ephemeral, she thought, remembering the morning when she had risen to find her father still in bed. She didn't need the doctor to tell her that something momentous had happened; even the few times in his life when Chadwicke had been seriously ill, he had forced himself up in the predawn and gone staggering about until he fainted from sheer exhaustion. In that moment when Mary stood uncertainly on the threshold of Chadwicke's room and saw him prone and unresponsive, everything had changed. Her sense of security was revealed to be false. Her identity was called into question, because who would she be when she was no longer "Chadwicke's daughter"?

Samuel wiggled against her and began to fuss. Mary smiled down at him serenely. He was not as strong yet as his namesake—maybe he never would be, because if everything could change in a moment, tomorrow her arms could be empty. She knew that little children died all the time. Life was uncertain; she couldn't argue with that or change it. So what could she do? She thought about the people Mrs. Justis had spoken of who chose to keep everyone at a distance. Should she accept Samuel's loss right now, as if he were already dead? Then there was Nicholas, pretending that he had complete control over his future and afraid even to acknowledge the existence of a Higher Power for fear he might need to ask for help. Mary sighed. If she wanted to spare herself pain, she had to sacrifice her joy as well. There was no other way around it.

Samuel waved his small fists about. His fussing hadn't gotten him what he wanted, and he was working himself up now for a hearty cry. Mary smiled at him again. "Hungry, are you?" she said, and suddenly the moment—screaming baby, suffocating heat, dreary cabin, and all—seemed so beautiful that her breath caught. If she could take this memory and fold it up in all its brightness, she would slip it inside a mental treasure chest for safekeeping. She would put dozens and dozens of moments in that chest, and now and then she would take them out very carefully and look at them. And no matter what happened in the unknown future, how could anyone ever feel sorry for her? With such a treasure as she would have, she would count herself as one of the richest women in the world.

When Samuel had been fed and put back to sleep, Mary returned him gently to his cradle and went back to combing flax.

By the next spring, Nicholas was ready to begin work on what he called their "true house." This turned out to be a two-story white frame house with rows of tidy windows that made the inside light and cheerful. When Mary walked into it, she wanted to spread out her arms and twirl like a little girl, but she found it hard to do with a small child attached to her hand and another soon-to-be-born

Casey kicking against her stomach. So she confined her expression of delight to a smile.

"It's so large," she exclaimed. "And grand."

"Have we really been away from England so long?" Nicholas teased. "You could have fit this house in the front hall of your father's school."

"No," Mary disagreed. "Not in the front hall. Perhaps in the dining hall." But the school was not as fresh in Mary's mind as their cabin, and compared to that the house seemed as big as a cathedral. Four rooms opened off the entrance hall and a steep staircase rose up a few feet from the front door. It would take a while, Mary mused, to fill all the bedrooms on the second floor.

Time passed quickly, though. After little Elizabeth was born in November, Mary found herself caught up in the rhythm of domestic responsibilities, with dawns and dusks following on each other so quickly that she never had time to pause and reflect. It was not an unpleasant rhythm; it gave meaning to every hour of the day, for each had its own specific set of chores. Every evening at dusk, Nicholas returned home to find a hot meal set out on the dining room table and clean little children neatly bundled in their beds. Mary would pretend to be irritated when Nicholas found the little ones still awake and, rather than wishing them goodnight, roughhoused with them until long after the sky had deepened into black. But she didn't mind, really; she approved of the counterpoint they made together, with Nicholas boisterous and charismatic, blowing through the house like a fresh spring wind, and Mary calm and organized and acting as if the skillful maintenance of an orderly household required no more effort than the lifting of her little finger. It seemed like the right combination, somehow, though she never thought about it consciously; rather, her satisfaction with her life was like a gentle humming beneath the current of her thoughts, like a regular rocking of waves that buoyed her up as if she were a little boat on the surface of the sea.

Two summers after Elizabeth was born, baby Christopher came to join them, and two autumns after that Mary hoped for another girl. When the baby died inside her, she cried openly, but her tears were without bitterness or despair. Every woman who knew what it was to be a mother must also know what it was to grieve. And by the time of Samuel's seventh birthday, her stomach had grown round with a new hope. At dinner that night she sat with her hand resting on her belly and her eyes resting on her eldest son. He had dark hair and eyes like his father's, but something about his mouth and chin reminded her of Chadwicke. He had this way of pressing his lips together when he was considering a problem, whether it be an exercise in arithmetic or an attempt to coax a small animal out of its hiding place to play with him. In those moments, he made her think of her father bent over his ledgers.

Samuel caught her watching him and flashed her a grin. "The baby will be sad it missed this when it finds out," he said, digging into the bread pudding that she had prepared tonight because he liked it especially.

"We shall all have to remember not to tell it, then," she replied, winking, and then bit her lip quickly to hide a grimace. She had been feeling pains off and on all day. It was early for the baby to come, so she hadn't asked Nicholas to summon the midwife—she had felt early pains with the other pregnancies. It was nothing to worry about, she told herself. The pain came again, twisting through her until she felt it in her teeth and in her toes. Despite her effort, her brightness must have wavered, because she looked over to find Nicholas peering at her with a frown line creased between his eyebrows.

"The dinner is excellent, as always," he said, raising his fork in a sort of salute.

"Thank you."

"Preparing it must have tired you out. Perhaps you should lie down."

Mary opened her mouth to protest that she would certainly not leave the table in the middle of her son's birthday dinner, but at that moment the pain came again, and this time she couldn't hide it. She could feel her face distorting itself into an image of misery.

"Perhaps you are right," she managed, beginning to heave herself up from the chair. Nicholas jumped up and came around to support her. He half-carried her up the stairs and helped her get settled on the bed. Mary sighed in relief as she melted into the softness of the mattress. "I am a little tired," she confessed. But when Nicholas had gone and she lay in the shadowy room alone, her mind insisted on tangling itself up in worry. She had admitted to not feeling well. Now she had put herself at the mercy of her body, for what else could she think about sprawled out helplessly on this bed while her family continued with dinner? Now she grew conscious of every ache, every fleeting sensation. If she had kept ignoring the pain, would it have taken this much hold? She twisted in agony and cried out without meaning to. The room was suddenly dark. Had she slept? Nicholas stirred beside her and rose up on one arm to squint down at her through the blackness.

"Mary, what is it?"

"Nothing . . . a nightmare perhaps. I cannot tell."

"Is it the baby?"

She tried to say no, but the sound that came out—a childish whimper—made her cringe with embarrassment.

"I'll go for the midwife," Nicholas said, and he had risen and dressed himself before Mary could form another coherent word. The next few hours passed as a nightmarish blur. Mary kept trying to steel herself against the pain, but again and again someone else's will seemed to take control of her body, making her cry like an infant when she meant to be brave and dignified. What was wrong? She had been through this before. Was it a sign, she wondered, that the baby would die? It was too early for it to come. It couldn't be healthy.

"Not again," she moaned, catching at the midwife's arm. "Please make my baby be safe."

"There, there," soothed Sarah.

When finally the baby was born, Mary thought everyone seemed strangely silent. Nicholas had come in and taken the child in his arms. He stood staring down at it with his face white and drawn. Mary whimpered again. She had known it. Something had gone wrong.

"What is it?" she asked Sarah. "Can I hold her?" She and

Nicholas had decided that if the baby were a girl, it should be called Anne, after his sister. Mary refrained from using the name now. It had to be saved for a little girl who would use it for decades.

"Not now, Mrs. Casey. You have to rest now."

"I do not want you to lie to me!" she screamed.

Sarah's eyes opened wide with surprise. "I will not lie to you," she promised, speaking in a soft, coaxing voice she might use for a child.

"Then tell me what is wrong with her."

"Why, not a thing, dear. Now rest. You really must."

By the next evening Mary understood that Sarah had not lied to her. The baby truly was healthy. She could her the little thing crying. Such a vigorous, lusty cry did not originate in a sickly chest. Somehow she was safe, even though she was early.

"We might have misjudged," Sarah explained. "It happens sometimes."

Mary nodded slightly. The movement hurt, as if she had scraped her cheek against a stone instead of a pillowcase. She tried to keep her eyes open and focused on the midwife's face, but she couldn't.

"There, now, Mrs. Casey, sleep," murmured Sarah. "Sleep is best."

It was she, not the baby, who was dying.

The idea had shocked her at first, and she had wrestled with it instinctively. But she had quickly grown too tired. Much easier to give in, she thought. If only the pain would go away, that was all that mattered.

She slept fitfully that night and awoke before dawn. Her body felt as if it had been crushed, or maybe pulled apart by horses the way they did sometimes to punish prisoners. Only now the horses had slowed down; they pulled her apart gradually. Every hour or so her hand became noticeably farther away, less attached to her mind. If she weren't so exhausted, she might be able to gather in all these floating parts and put them back together before it was too late. What if she put them together wrong, though, she wondered.

What if she put an arm where her waist should be? She smiled up at the ceiling, imagining herself as the cloth doll she had made for Elizabeth. Yarn hair. Stuffing for brains. If she pulled apart at the seams, you just stitched her up again.

I am dying.

She let her eyes fall closed and her mind drift. Dying was like being washed away on the sea. If you let yourself move with the current, it didn't hurt so much.

I am dying.

"Samuel!" she cried. She struggled to sit up. Sunlight filled the bedroom now, and she waited for the delayed sound of her own voice. She had yelled out, so why couldn't she hear anything?

"Samuel," she tried again. It came out like the mewing of a kitten.

"What is it, Mary? Did you want something?" Nicholas's face appeared above her. Why was he here at this time of day?

"Samuel, please bring me Samuel," she whispered. Then she began to cry, because Samuel would be down the road at the grammar school.

"Straightaway," said Nicholas, and he disappeared.

Whether he had run to the school and fetched him or whether Samuel had never gone to school at all, Mary couldn't tell. But soon he stood above her, looking too solemn for a seven-year-old boy. Looking so much like Samuel Chadwicke that Mary gasped.

"Father said you wanted me, Mother," said Samuel. His voice sounded unusually husky. Mary worried fleetingly that he might be coming down with a cold.

"Yes, darling. I . . . I have so much to tell you, and I do not know if I can do it. You must be patient, please, and listen."

Samuel nodded.

"Pull that chair over by the bed," Mary directed. He turned to drag a wooden chair with a straw seat away from its position against the wall. Then he settled himself and watched her with big dark eyes.

"I have been lying here thinking that there is so much I meant to teach you. So many things I wanted to tell you. If this week had been different, I could have told you a little every day for years and years, but now I have to tell you all at once. Try to remember, please, even if it is difficult."

Samuel nodded again and pressed his lips together.

"I wanted to tell you that . . . that I know there is a God in Heaven, and He knows us. He sees what we do and say and even think. Not because He likes to spy on people and tattle on them, not because He wants to punish them when they are wrong. Do you understand?"

"I will try, Mother."

"He loves us and is there to help us, but when things go wrong we musn't think He has turned His back on us. Sometimes there are things we must do for ourselves. You have chores to do, and your father and I insist that you do them even when you might wish to play instead. There are things you must learn, and you cannot learn them any other way . . ." Mary sighed and lay back deeper into the pillows. So much that she should have told him—how could she expect him to understand all at once?

"I have said too much. You will forget. This is what I want you to remember. Are you listening? Good. Samuel, I know that there is a God, and He knows that there is a Samuel Casey. You can pray to Him when you need help. When you cannot find the answer, you can ask Him. And it says in the Bible—remember, we read it together only last week—'The truth will set you free.' Search for the truth, Samuel. Promise me."

"I promise, Mother." His lip quivered.

"Your father is a good man, but even he cannot understand everything. It is up to you, Samuel. Your father might not pray with you, so you must pray yourself. Teach the little ones."

Samuel began to cry. Mary watched the way he tried to hide it, the way he stared soberly at the floor as if he were only deep in concentration. Now and then he brushed quickly at his face, as if he could get rid of the tears so fast that no one would notice.

When Mary had rested for a while, she moved her hand up to touch the silver chain at her neck. She pulled at it until she found the heart.

"Samuel, come and help me, please. Help me undo the clasp." He came and stood over her, and when he had released the catch she pressed the necklace into his hand. "This will be a token between us. Keep this and remember what I have told you. Someday, when you are much older . . ." she paused and smiled dreamily.

"What, Mother? Is there something you wish me to do?"

"Someday, when you are much older, you will marry. This is something beautiful and precious for you to give to your bride. Only do not forget, when you give it to her, what is has meant. Do not forget that your mother taught you to pray, Samuel."

This time the tears came out with sobs. And then the sobbing became her own. Or did it? It was night again, but Nicholas was not on the bed with her. Instead he knelt on the floor next to the bed, his cheek pressed against hers.

"Nicholas," she whispered. *I love you,* she wanted to say. Why had she not told him long before? She thought of their eight years together. They had passed so quickly, but even so, how could she not have realized what was happening? Why didn't she understand that the little shock of pleasure she felt when Nicholas came home in the evening was more than pride in her well-run house? Why hadn't she noticed all these years that this man had become more than a partner in adventure, more than the other half of a marriage of convenience?

"I love you," she tried to whisper, but she couldn't find the strength. All she could do was hope that somehow he already knew, and that maybe he loved her a little in return. The tears against her cheek were not her own. She lifted a finger slightly to brush it against his chin.

"Mary," he sobbed. "My Mary."

Across the room the window shone like a ghostly portal. Would her soul fly out through it before morning, leaving this man alone in the room? In her dream she floated across the ceiling, and she was part of all the images she had plastered across its shadows. The man Samuel strode past her on his way across his fields. The woman Elizabeth sat next to her, rocking a tiny baby. Christopher carried an armload of books through the halls of the College, and a lovely girl with dark hair and bright cheeks danced across the room to kiss her gray-haired father's cheek. "Anne," said the older Nicholas, beaming up at the girl. Mary didn't want to leave. If she groped about, perhaps she could find a tether connecting her to this world. If she could make her way back . . . . Her hands closed on something. She pulled and pulled, and then she began to fall away from the ceiling.

When she opened her eyes, it was morning. The pain was still there, but she could feel it receding as gradually as her body had once torn itself apart. She turned her head cautiously on the pillow. Nicholas sat on top of the covers, fully clothed, with his back propped against the headboard. Mary noticed for the first time the several days' growth of beard across his chin. She smiled up at him.

"There is something I must tell you," she said. Her voice was still hoarse and weak, but the words came out audibly.

Nicholas reached down to stroke her hair. "What is it then?" he asked gently.

"I love you."

"And I love you, Mary." He smiled back at her, then covered his eyes with his hand and turned away, his shoulders shaking gently. From the hallway Mary heard the tiptoeing footsteps of her children and, from somewhere far away, the lively wails of baby Anne.

I am going to live.

Part Five: Gabriel

Salt Lake City, February-March 2003

Chapter 17

Sunlight streamed into Judith's bedroom full-strength, pounding at her eyelids as she struggled to open them. She must have slept late. Her eyes felt dry and scratchy, as if she had been walking on the beach in the wind. She rubbed her eyes with her knuckles and lay in bed listening. Silence. Her parents must already be down in the archives.

She sat up and fished under the bed with her foot for her slippers, not wanting to press her feet to the cold stone that was covered only here and there by rugs. When she had found them, she stepped to the window and leaned her forehead against it, scanning the section of garden that wasn't blocked from her view by a corner of the building. It had become part of her routine, these past few weeks, to take up her post here both morning and night, so that the image of the garden framed her waking moments like the two covers of a book. A strange tryst, maybe; she hadn't encountered the "ghost boy," as she thought of him, since the night he had told her his story. A few times, during her nightly vigil at the window, she thought she caught a flicker among the trees, a faint shifting of light or a flowing movement. It might have been him, but then it might not have been. In her dreams she had often walked through the garden in the moonlight, and twice it had appeared to be full of boys and girls, all with strange clothes and all watching her expectantly. That was the funny thing about dreams, though; you didn't always act like yourself. So Judith, instead of shrinking from them or asking them questions, had ambled calmly up and down the paths while the children parted like the Red Sea to let her through.

Oh well, strange dreams were to be expected, she guessed. From the first moment she had laid eyes on Guildwell Hall, it had haunted her imagination. These conversations in the garden with a nearly-three-hundred-years-dead boy might be a natural enough fantasy. After all, she had to remind herself that it was a dream, that she had never seen him while she was awake—or at least, she couldn't be sure that she had. Daylight couldn't dispel the memory of him, though, or of the way he had looked at her most cherished possession, the little silver heart. She grasped the trinket now and studied it closely. It had a past beyond anything her family could remember. Maybe it was all a dream, but if that boy in the garden was real, this heart had belonged to him. She couldn't look at it now without thinking of him, however fleetingly. She had become suddenly conscious of the feel of it bumping gently against her skin as she walked. *You are the ones I've been waiting for,* he had told her, and because her father had wakened her that night with news that he had found Nicholas, she had never been able to find out why. Why hadn't he come back then? If he was simply a product of her subconscious, she wished her dreaming mind would at least put an end to her suspense.

With nothing unusual making itself visible in the garden, Judith turned away from the window, pulled her door open gently, and stepped into the hallway. Her father sat at the kitchen table eating absently from a yogurt carton.

"Morning, Dad," Judith said, continuing on down to Gabriel's door and pushing it open a crack. He lay curled up in a circle like a kitten. Well, she wouldn't disturb him then. She closed the door again and returned to the kitchen. The red numbers of a digital clock read 10:07.

"I don't know why I slept so late," Judith remarked as she dug some bread out of the cupboard and lowered it into the toaster. "Is Mom microfilming?"

"Yeah," said David. Judith could hear his spoon knock against the empty carton, but he raised the spoon to his mouth again anyway. She watched him take a bite of nothing and then glare at the utensil as if it had stashed its contents on the way up just out of spite.

"Would you like some more yogurt, Dad?" Judith offered sympathetically.

"What? Oh, no." He tossed the sneaky spoon into the sink just as Judith's toast popped up. She spread orange marmalade across both slices and sat down at the table. The chair made an awful screech as its legs ground across the floor.

"I just came up for an early lunch," David explained. "I got started pretty early. We've got to finish up quickly now."

"Oh?" Judith remembered the conversation she had overheard about leaving in two weeks. She wanted her father to confirm that now, in daylight. But instead he pulled a folded sheet of paper from his pocket and spread it out on the table. Judith recognized the notes Lori had taken about Nicholas's marriage.

"So he married the daughter of the schoolmaster," Judith said, even though they had discussed it before. Something about the silence had seemed uncomfortable. "It might be romantic if you think about it. Maybe they were childhood sweethearts."

David snorted. "Things like romance weren't so important then. I doubt they even knew each other that well."

"But why? She grew up here. He was at school here. They must have known each other to get married, or why wouldn't both of them have married someone else?"

"Oh, I don't know how it went," David conceded with a sigh. "One thing about history you gotta keep in mind: you can't know how many details the records *aren't* telling you. But I have my suspicions."

"About what?"

"Well, from what we do know, it looks like a pretty good marriage of convenience. Nicholas went to America not long after this. He probably wanted to get married before he left his home and take something with him that wasn't foreign. And with the marriage following so close on the death of Samuel Chadwicke, it makes me think Mary didn't have many other options. It was hard for women back then if they found themselves on their own."

"Hmm. So they were desperate young people fleeing their pasts to start anew . . ."

David grinned at her. "OK, say it like that if you want to."

"So what happened after this? I should know it all, I guess, I'm sure you've told me. But help me get it all straight."

"Well, our line comes down through Nicholas's oldest son, Samuel. He started moving out west, toward Kentucky, and then north. A couple of his sons fought and died in the Revolutionary War. His youngest son, Henry, was born during the war. He was the only one who lived long enough to have children. He moved around a bit, too, like his father, but he ended up in western New York in the 1820s."

"Ahh—providential."

"Right. He became one of the early converts of the Church. Several of his kids were grown by then and living in the same area, and they joined too. His son John was our ancestor."

"So it goes Samuel, Henry, John—great names, huh? At least they go that many generations without repeats."

David was looking thoughtful. "It's interesting," he mused, ignoring Judith's comment, "that for so long we didn't know Mary Chadwicke's name, but we knew something about her."

"What? I've never heard that before. I thought she was a total mystery."

"No, not total. I guess I just never honed in on this tidbit before because her name was a blank. But John mentions her in his narrative."

"John left a narrative? What was he, a novelist?"

"No, a lawyer. But he wrote the story of his conversion. Oh, it was years—decades, even—after the fact. A lot of people did stuff like that for posterity."

"What did he say about her?"

"He gives this sort of genealogy of prayer. He says how his father always talked about finding the truth, how his father taught him to pray. I thought that was odd at the time, because usually that would be something the mother would do. But he says prayer was important to his father—that was Henry, remember—because he had learned it from *his* father—Samuel—who believed that prayer would lead him to some higher truth. John recounts this almost as a family legend, something that went from grandfather to father to son. But the grandfather, Samuel, he didn't get it from *his* father—Nicholas—he got it from his mother. 'Whose mother had ever taught him to pray for the truth,' he writes. The mother—that was Mary."

"Oh," said Judith, a little disappointed. Of course all those old dead people were pious. She'd hoped to hear something more exciting. But her father was excited, all right. He had this sparkle in his eyes that some men got when they were showing off a new motorcycle.

"This is the kind of thing that always fascinates me about history: the why of things. The little tiny things that make all the difference. Of course, you never know for sure. But it looks to me like Mary Chadwicke had a big impact on her posterity. We'd probably have been born atheists on the East Coast if not for her."

"Is anyone born an atheist?" teased Judith.

"Ah, you know what I mean. And not to discount the agency of Henry and John. They had to be fertile fields to nourish the seed Mary planted. Maybe they would have joined anyway, who knows. But you gotta wonder."

"Yeah, I guess." The two sat in silence for a moment as Judith munched her toast. "Maybe I should go check on Gabriel again," she said after a while. "I guess we were both extra tired this morning, but he doesn't usually sleep so long all in one stretch." She pushed back her chair and padded out into the hall, then opened Gabriel's door softly and peered in. He hadn't stirred since the last time she looked in on him. She stared at him for several moments, waiting for the twitch of a finger, a sigh, something. She tried to ignore the cold feeling that began around her stomach as she stepped all the way into the room and bent over him.

He was breathing. That was a relief, at least. But she wanted him to wake up now, reassure her by opening his eyes and smiling up at her. "Gabriel," she whispered. Then "Gabriel, wake up," a little louder. He didn't move. His eyelashes remained perfectly still against his cheek.

"Gabriel," she said out loud, reaching down to nudge his shoulder. "Gabriel! Wake up!" Even when she yelled at him he didn't move. His breaths were shallow and far apart. "Dad," she cried, but when she turned David was already in the doorway. "I'll get your mother," he said. "Put your clothes on and be ready to leave for the hospital." He disappeared, and Judith stood like a statue, hearing his footsteps grow fainter as he raced down the spiral staircase. When they had died away completely, she sprang suddenly into action, as if she were a battery-operated toy and someone had pushed the 'on' button. She dashed into her room and began pulling on her jeans over her pajamas. They wouldn't fit.

"Blast, oh blast," she cursed. "Why didn't I get the silky ones?" She kicked the jeans off and removed her pajamas before putting the pants on again. Why was it that you could never do things as quickly when you were in a hurry? When she had finally gotten everything on in more or less the right place, she dragged her bag out from under her bed and began running through the rooms, gathering up the most important things to throw into it. Who knew when they would be back from the hospital? She didn't even want to think about it.

Outside, a drizzle of half rain, half snow pelted the ground and coated the roads and sidewalks with a sheet of icy slush. The four of them piled into the car, soggy and with their breaths puffing out in thin white clouds. Lori pulled out her cell phone to call the hospital. She'd had the number on speed dial, Judith noticed. Always prepared.

The car wheels screeched as they pulled away from the curb, and Judith glanced up to watch Guildwell Hall recede into the distance. It looked exactly as it did when they arrived, she mused, as if they had never been there. On the roof the goblin-chimneys still posed like frozen dancers. The tree branches still stood out as bare and desolate as skeleton fingers. So many things had already happened there, maybe the old building couldn't bring itself to care anymore. Judith wondered as they sped down the street if the ghost boy was there now, somewhere, if he watched and puzzled vaguely over what all the fuss was about.

The car skidded twice on the way, but David drove on without comment. Around them the city appeared choked with gloom. Too many dark-colored buildings that looked black in the rain. Too few people out on the roads, and everyone seeming to move in slow motion. Above it all, a thick, dark, lowering sky. But the inside of the hospital looked like every other hospital on every other day. Judith recognized the smell instantly. Maybe you left the place and didn't think about it for weeks, but when you came back you realized the memory of it had been there all along. You could snap back into this environment as easy as a joint snapping back into place, and it was as familiar as home. Only not as comfortable.

After the initial bustle of getting Gabriel admitted, there was nothing to do but wait. Judith's body wasn't getting the message; her muscles remained on the alert, so she couldn't seem to keep still. They settled themselves in the waiting room and Lori flipped idly through a magazine with a headline about celebrity hairstyles on its cover. David picked up the sports section of a paper that had been left on an end table. *He must be really distracted*, Judith thought. He didn't know much about sports. Judith paced back and forth until Lori glared at her, then she took a seat. She had found a ponytail elastic in one of her coat pockets, and now she sat twisting it around her fingers, watching them turn red and then white. A TV set was mounted high up on the wall. A woman with shiny brown hair and red cheeks was smiling and mopping her floor. "What would I do without Lemon Wonder?" she asked. She was a pretty good actress—she made it seem really important. Judith imagined her pulling out her trusty bottle of Lemon Wonder only to find it empty. She could see how the woman's face would scrunch up in dismay. It might almost qualify as an emergency. She would jump in her car and speed to the market to pick up another bottle. Maybe she'd be having guests over that night. Judith could hear her telling her guests over dinner, "And that Lemon Wonder saved my life. Really, I can't think what I'd have done if I hadn't made it in time to get that last bottle." That was the kind of emergency you could deal with. You could keep it contained within an hour or so, not let it seep out to destroy other parts of your life. Maybe the woman wasn't acting. Maybe she really couldn't think of anything worse than not having enough Lemon Wonder.

It was possible to exist in this sphere, Judith thought, where commercials like these seemed to represent real life. Where a major issue was whether you could get your parents to stop for fast food instead of driving home to eat bologna sandwiches, where you got impatient waiting in traffic not because you were in a hurry but just because you craved the thrill of driving fast, where you knew life was overall fun and if you weren't having a good time at the moment things were bound to pick up. Where having a floor cleaned with Lemon Wonder counted for something. In this sphere, everyone was happy most of the time, and nothing that went wrong was very important. Judith thought of the Relief Society women making wreaths at Enrichment Night. Making a wreath seemed a very Lemon Wonder Sphere thing to do. After they finished praising Lori's amazing pioneer-esque faith, they probably swapped cleaning tips. Either that or casserole recipes.

So was that sphere real? Because it had seemed that way once. And now that she was outside of it, Judith felt like a child locked out of its home, gazing wistfully through the window at a model 50s-style sitcom family who somehow couldn't see her. That fun, carefree life went on without her, and no one who was still a part of it even acknowledged the other sphere, the one where terrible things happened and you couldn't do anything to stop them. The one that now held her and everyone else at this hospital captive. She imagined the waiting room enclosed in a giant glass bubble, breaking off from solid ground and floating randomly through the universe while she and the others pressed their hands against the glass walls like mimes.

Judith stood up abruptly and went over to stand by one of the narrow, rectangular windows. The drizzle had stopped but fog was moving in, gradually shutting the hospital into its own little world. She became aware of her own reflection in the glass. A pensive face with wide, scared-looking eyes. *What am I afraid of?* she asked herself. *What scares me most?*

She heard her parents talking to a doctor behind her and turned back to them to listen to the conversation. A physician who looked to be in his early thirties was explaining the situation. Yes, Gabriel was stable for the moment. No, there was nothing they could do. Well, they could make him comfortable. It wouldn't be long now. Underneath his words, Judith could sense another meaning. *Why did you even bring him in?* he wanted to ask. *Don't you know he's dying?* Of course they knew. They'd known for months now, and since their decision to come to London, Lori and David had acted as if he were already dead. Did they care after all? Maybe they thought they'd come to terms with it, but now with death lurking about as an almost-visible specter, they'd fight for him until the very last moment.

Judith turned to the window again. *Father in Heaven,* she prayed fervently, *please help us to get through this. I won't ask for a miracle: I know that isn't always in the plan. But I can't keep from hurting, and I don't know how I'm going to get through the next few days. Please help me to be strong for Gabriel, and please help Gabriel not to be afraid.* She didn't exactly feel a burning in her bosom, but when she turned back to the room again she felt better.

"We can see him now," Lori told her. "He's awake." As soon as they went into his room, her parents pasted on fake plastic smiles.

"Hello, son," said David. He sounded like he was greeting a group of Cub Scouts at a pack meeting.

Gabriel smiled up at them weakly, then stretched his hand out to Judith. She walked over and perched very lightly on the edge of his bed.

"I brought you something," she said. She reached into her coat and brought out a little dinosaur figurine. "I saw this yesterday when I was out walking."

"It's a T-rex," murmured Gabriel.

"That's right. It's the biggest and the meanest. But this little dude is so small, I think maybe he's just a kid still."

"Tell me a story about him."

"A story? Hmm, let's see. First we need a name. What do think is a good name for him?"

"Mmmm, maybe Max."

"All right, Max it is. Well, even though he was a T-rex, Max was a pretty nice kid. He mostly did what his mom said—kept his cave clean and all, ate his leafy greens. But he liked adventure. See the twinkle in his eye? He didn't mean to be naughty, but sometimes he would wander off. His mom worried about him all the time, because it could be dangerous for him to be out alone. She told him never to get so far away that he couldn't hear her if she called. Max tried hard to obey her, but one day something happened. He was just about as far away as he could go without disobeying his mother when he saw one of his friends running along toward some quicksand. Max knew his friend didn't know where the sand was or how to avoid it, so Max ran after him. By the time he caught up with his friend, the kid was already starting to sink. But Max was smart. He grabbed a tree branch and pulled his friend out. When he got home, his mom yelled at him. She said, 'I called you and called you, and you were nowhere to be found. I was so worried.' Max felt bad that he had made her worry. But he explained what he had done—how he didn't have time to get anyone else's help. Do you know what his mother said then?" Gabriel shook his head. Judith cleared her throat and, with an effort, kept her voice steady. "She said, 'Son, I was wrong to yell at you. I guess I have to learn that I can't always have you with me, even though I want to. If anything like this happens again and you need to go, it's all right. Go if you have to go.'"

Judith looked around. At some point her parents had drifted out of the room—she and Gabriel were alone. She smoothed his hair back from his forehead and bent to kiss the pale, smooth skin. When she looked at his face again, his eyes were closed.

"Sing to me, Juice," he whispered.

"OK," she said. She used to sing to him a lot. What was his favorite song? "Hush bye bye, don't you cry, go to sleep ye little baby. When you wake you shall have all the pretty little horses . . ." Her voice quavered on through several verses, and it seemed to become an entity unto itself, a thin silver ribbon that hovered in the air above two children caught between this world and the next. She stopped singing before the end because there was no one left to hear. Gabriel had gone.

In the first seconds of silence, she kept her mind a careful blank, afraid to think or even to move. The room in all of its hospital whiteness seemed frozen in time, or perhaps just outside of it. She seemed to have left both spheres behind. And although she was alone, someone seemed to have tiptoed up to drape a fuzzy gray blanket around her shoulders. Not just any blanket, this; its threads bore a balm of peace and comfort. "Go, Gabriel," she whispered. "Go and be free." A few tears spilled out smoothly, unaccompanied by sobs. She rose, and the blanket rose with her. She walked slowly out into the hall. Her parents were waiting several yards away, their heads down. They didn't look at her or at each other. She approached them with a sort of detached compassion, and when she was close to them she held one hand out to each, as if they were small children that she could soothe just by gathering them into her embrace. "He's gone," she said quietly. "It's over."

Neither of them had taken her hands. Lori squared her shoulders, glanced up at the ceiling, and then excused herself to go fix her makeup. David stood staring blindly at some spot on the wall. "Dad," Judith said, touching his arm. He placed his hand over hers briefly and then began pacing up and down. Lori was back in a few minutes, her lipstick fresh and her eyes betraying no signs of tears. "I'll get the arrangements made, " she said. "We'll want to get home right away." She took out her cell phone and palm pilot and began speaking in her most business-like voice. David lingered around her looking lost. Judith lingered for a while too, trying to decide if she could help. When she decided that she couldn't, she wandered back toward the waiting room. After a while the Lemon Wonder commercial came on again. This time, something about the woman's smile made Judith look closer. *She knows it doesn't really matter*, she realized with surprise. *She knows.*

Chapter 18

The odd thing about funerals, Lori reflected, was their resemblance to weddings and various other family celebrations—baby blessings, missionary farewells, and reunions. The clothing and the menu called for thought and preparation. You greeted family members you never met in regular life, had to try to remember the names of small children you hadn't thought of since reading their birth announcements. The only difference between a funeral and a wedding, really, was the receiving line. In one, the guest of honor was allowed to lie flat on his back, while the other required standing for two hours straight.

In her brusque and efficient way, Lori had taken care of all the details for this particular family gathering. She had purchased tickets for herself, David, and Judith to fly home to Salt Lake immediately and had Gabriel's body sent home as well. Fortunately, because of their rather abrupt departure for London, they hadn't let out their house for the season. It waited patiently for their return, its shelves and dressers coated with dust and a few of its corners shadowed by cobwebs, but otherwise in good shape. Lori dusted and scrubbed for two days, in between calls to a caterer, a visit to the hairdresser to touch up her highlights, and trip to Nordstrom for a new dress (muted blue-gray silk, mid-calf length, with a jacket to match).

"What's the occasion?" the sales associate had asked innocently as she and Lori stood admiring the dress in front of the mirror.

"Oh, nothing much," Lori had hedged. "A family party of sorts."

Now here she was in the midst of the production itself, leaning over a platter of tiny round chicken salad sandwiches. The caterer had done a fine job—after all, you really couldn't expect perfection from everybody—but Lori thought she might be able to make to the arrangement look just a little better. If she moved this one like so . . .

"Lori, here you are," called her mother's voice. Lori glanced up almost guiltily to see her mother gliding through the swinging door into the kitchen. Funny that Emma Mackay could glide when she was so plump and well-satisfied looking, but there it was. She wore a rose-colored dress that matched her lipstick and a string of pearls that matched her white hair. She might have been on her way to a Valentine's Day tea. The fact that it wasn't customary for Mormons to wear black to funerals didn't give her mother any excuse to show up dressed as a gigantic box of chocolates, Lori thought. But that just exemplified the mystery of her mother's world. Mrs. Mackay didn't believe there was anything wrong with wearing a rose-colored dress to her grandson's funeral, and her belief seemed to make it true. All the whispered comments Lori had heard about Mrs. Mackay's dress were in praise of it. A group of ladies from her mother's ward oohed and aahed over how fine Emma looked all during the bishop's talk.

"I started to think maybe you were hiding out," said Mrs. Mackay. "But here you are fussing over the refreshments. I should have known."

"They just didn't look quite right. There, I've finished. Would you take this out for me?"

"Well, it's nice to be away from the crowd for a minute, isn't it? It's been a long day. I think maybe you should go up and lie down. Judith and I have got everything under control, and I'm sure there's nothing left for you to rearrange or adjust."

"I don't need to lie down. I'm fine."

"Of course you are," her mother agreed a little too enthusiastically. "But you needn't tire yourself. You've put so much work into things as it is."

"So I may as well stay to enjoy the fruits of my labor."

"Oh, it's only the tail end of things, anyway. Judith and I are just waiting for everyone else to leave. You don't have to wait, though.

Go on up to your room and take a little rest."

Lori was tired of arguing. Her mother was as stubborn as she was, in her own way. She allowed herself to be escorted through the dining and living rooms, both of which were still filled with people talking quietly in little groups. She spotted Judith in the living room at the center of one of the larger groups. The girl's hair was loose, and it caught the light of the late winter sun. She looked like she had a golden waterfall on her head.

At the foot of the stairs, Lori protested again. She didn't want to go upstairs where she'd have nothing to do or to think about. "Mom, do I have to be sixty years old before you stop treating me like a child?"

"No dear, I'm never going to stop treating you like a child. I'm your mother."

Lori sighed and began the ascent. Soon the house would empty out and she would be left alone, anyway. She might as well face it now. She brightened at the thought that her drawers probably needed to be organized. She and David had unpacked in a bit of a hurry.

Once in her room, though, she couldn't focus on the drawers. She sagged onto the foot of the bed and stared at a little statuette that had sat on top of her dresser ever since her wedding. Or at least it was always there when they were home. It was one of the few possessions kept permanently at the house, dutifully packed away to make room for tenants and just as dutifully taken out again when the family returned. The statuette had been a wedding present from her mother. It was a porcelain figure of Christ kneeling at a rock in the Garden of Gethsemane. In the light from the window Lori could see the iridescent glaze, the hints of rainbow tones gleaming here and there above the smooth white surface. She wasn't a big fan of porcelain. It somehow suggested a Victorian house filled with picturesque clutter, a wife in a ruffly apron. Probably the woman her mother had wanted her to be. So why had she kept it? Who was she trying to impress? Some sense of loyalty to her mother had prevented her from throwing it out, but she realized now that her mother probably thought she had already gotten rid of it. What good did it do to keep it in here? Her mother never came in her bedroom. She would have been looking for it out on one of the bookshelves or on the mantelpiece. The one thing Lori did to please her mother, and no one even knew about it.

But that was life. Things didn't work out the way you intended. Lori had prided herself on being a sort of renegade, a brave enough person to do what she wanted even when it went against other people's expectations. She thought she was different from everyone else, but now that she considered her life from the perspective of nearly fifty-one, it looked more like a model of conventionality than a pioneering trek into the unknown. Sure, going on a mission was a little unusual back then, and so was grad school. But how neatly everything had fallen into place. She came back from her months in South America to start graduate school at Brown and met David in time to be married the next summer. Perfect timing. They didn't have to wait for each other through missions or try to set up a household as undergrads, but thank goodness (from her mother's point of view) they got together in time to save Lori from a serious case of old-maidhood. What an orderly course her life had followed. But wait, she didn't have to be disappointed. The Lord would let her be different, just not the way she had planned. Losing two out of three children, now that wasn't something all her neighbors had done. That was worth a little Relief Society gossip.

She'd had a scripture in mind for the past few weeks. When she got up to speak at the funeral today, it had almost come out. "Let me explain why this has happened to me, " she had wanted to say. "Then you can be wiser than I have been. See, you might think this is just one of those things, or that our family is just being tested. You wouldn't blame it on us, you wouldn't say it was a judgment come upon us for our sins. You don't think like that. But you're wrong, you see. Maybe it is a judgment. Don't you all know the scripture? I found it in Nephi, but it's everywhere: 'From them that shall say, We have enough, from them shall be taken away even that which they have.'" OK, maybe it was talking about knowledge and spiritual understanding, but it could mean children too. Because that was where she had really diverged from the path. When Elijah was born, she'd never known greater joy; she loved taking care of him, getting to know him. That surprised her a little because she wasn't one of those women who cooed and gushed over every baby they saw. She wasn't cuddly or particularly motherly, but she was *his* mother, and that pleased her. If she hadn't waited so long to have more, maybe she could have felt that way about the other children, too. But instead she had let their family drift complacently; Elijah seemed to complete them, and though they never actually decided against having more kids, they never decided to have them, either. Judith was a surprise—a mistake, really. Lori didn't kid herself into thinking she felt the same about both children. Elijah was the golden boy, pure and simple. Then he died and Gabriel came along. This time Lori got all the advantages of motherhood and hardly any of the work. She didn't have to set her career aside to tend to a small child; Judith took care of that, and all Lori had to do was sit back and watch him become whoever he was going to become. If she had let herself develop into a different person twenty years ago, maybe she would still have him with her. If she could have opened her heart and her mind, loved all her children as unreservedly as any mother should, maybe she could have been spared this lesson now. When you tried to hold on to something too hard, when something was too precious, it was bound to be taken away.

She reached out and picked up the statuette. *Sure, pretend to be noble and blame yourself.* In her mind she saw Gabriel lying in bed in a London hospital and reaching out to Judith, Judith sitting next to him and speaking naturally while Lori and David watched through masks of optimism as unrealistic as the faces of clowns. "Big joke on me," she whispered to the figurine. "I wasn't as smart as I thought, so just take it away. Take it all away. That's how it works, right? No second chances." Maybe Gabriel *was* the second chance. Well, what about third chances? Whatever happened, the figurine didn't care. It remained cold and aloof in her hands. Without a conscious thought, she hurled it against the wall, then picked up the largest piece and slammed it against the edge of the dresser. BANG BANG BANG. The pulse in her wrist and neck throbbed with emotion. CRASH SMASH. With all the racket, she didn't notice that someone was knocking at the door. The thumping from the hallway blended with the pounding in the bedroom. When she chanced to turn around and see Judith standing in the doorway, her mouth fell open with shock.

"Mom?" The word came out as a question, as if Judith really wasn't sure whether the woman throwing bits of porcelain around was her mother or an imposter.

"Um," said Lori. What could she say? "I noticed this statuette had a crack in it." Judith gazed at her with an expression of—what? Pity?

"Oh, Judith, I can't lie to you now. All I can do is bribe you to keep your mouth shut."

Judith took another step into the room, apparently convinced that this was no imposter. "Mom, no one will think less of you if you're upset. *I* wouldn't think less of you."

"Who cares what people think?" Lori collapsed onto the bed and covered her face with her hands. "I'm so stupid, you wouldn't believe it," she moaned. Two moments of uncomfortable silence pulsed by. Lori couldn't take it. She steeled herself and looked up. "I'm fine. Just fine. Forget this." She hoped Judith would leave her alone, but instead the girl knelt down and began picking up the pieces of porcelain.

"Don't do that," Lori scolded. "You'll cut yourself." *You'll see what I broke. You'll see the worst part of me.*

"I'll be careful." She didn't say anything when she picked up the figurine's head, just set it gingerly into the wastebasket along with the other fragments. Maybe she already knew. Maybe Lori had figured everything wrong, and Judith had seen through her all the time.

When Judith had finished cleaning up the pieces, she sat down next to Lori on the bed. "I'm fine now," Lori told her. "You can go."

"Oh, OK," said Judith, but she didn't move.

"I guess you want an explanation. Well, it was my bit of porcelain, and I was tired of it." Judith watched her with wide blue eyes.

Or were they blue? No, Lori remembered now—they were blue from a distance, but up close you could make out a dozen distinct shades. Lori used to study them when the infant Judith lay pressed against her breast. The eyes were endlessly complex. Only from a couple of feet away did all the shades appear to blend together into a uniform color. "I underestimated you," Lori said suddenly.

"What?"

"You heard me. I thought I was so strong, so in control. Well just look at what I've done! I'm angry, OK? Do you want me to admit it? Here all the time I had more faith in myself than in anything or anyone else. But you know what?" Her voice cracked. She was trembling. She stood up, wrapped her arms around herself, and faced the wall, away from her daughter. "You're stronger than I am," she admitted. "You're stronger."

"What?"

"I've been watching you these last few days. These last few weeks, really. You may think I couldn't tear myself away from the phone long enough to notice anything, but I saw you. I saw this dignity that you seemed to pull out of nowhere. But you had to get it from somewhere. So I started thinking. I thought about the last six years, and I realized that you've been more of a mother to Gabriel than I ever have. That's why he reached out to you at the end, that's why it was fitting that you were the one watching him go. I had put myself out of the picture. Somehow I've gotten exactly the opposite of what I wanted, and it's all my own doing. And you—I love you, Judith. I'm your mother. I held you in my arms when you were a tiny baby and promised you the world. Problem was, you didn't want it. I thought I could see everything there was to you, and I thought . . ." she turned to face the girl on the bed. Judith had her head down, her expression hidden behind a cascade of hair. "I was wrong. I didn't know how strong you were." Lori stepped slowly back to the bed and sat down again. Through the window she could see a rim of orange sunshine edging the mountaintops like a fringe of fire. "Would you rather see the end of every day or the beginning?" David had asked her when they first moved into this house.

"The end," she had answered. "That's when you have time to think and everything becomes clear."

"Judith?" she asked now, her voice coming out horribly thin and childish. "I've gone too far already to save my dignity now. So I have to ask you for, uh, help."

Judith brushed her hair back from her face and gazed at her mother inquisitively. "Oh?" came her noncommittal invitation.

"Yes. I see how you've kept yourself together this week, and well, I thought keeping myself together was my forte. I've worked long and hard on it." She allowed herself the hint of a laugh. "Trouble is, there are these pesky feelings that keep working their way out in the most tiresome manner." Her eyes focused on the wastebasket. She couldn't see its contents from here. "I'm angry. I'm so angry at God I can't even bring myself to pray. But you aren't. You never have been. Tell me the secret, Judith. Tell me how to stop feeling this way."

Judith stared at her with unconcealed astonishment. "You? You want me to tell you how to fix your relationship with God?"

"Well, yes. No. I just want some input, OK?"

"OK. Well, let's see. I've been thinking things over, too, but I never was angry at God, so I don't know how to fix that. I was angry at other people, though."

"Really? Who?"

"Oh, lots of people. The women in the Relief Society here in our Salt Lake ward. The pioneers. Everyone in the Church who's ever been held up as an example of stoicism and endurance."

"Hmm, I guess that's a lot of people."

"Yeah, I would say so. Especially when you throw in all those pioneers. That's a few whole generations, right there. And I really was mad at them. I mean, I wasn't just tired of hearing stories about them. I had a real attitude about it. Here's how it is. When I was a kid and I'd get hurt somehow, falling off my bike or something, I liked to go to Grandma Mackay for comfort. But I hated it when Grandpa Mackay was there, because he'd always call me a baby and tell me how minor my wounds were and how he'd never let something like that stop him. So then it's not just the pain itself, it's the guilt—because you shouldn't be upset about this, and if you are, you're just bad or cowardly or something. That's what I felt about the pioneers. They were just one big huge guilt trip. You couldn't come up with anything that would rival what they went through. No matter what you're upset about it, count on it they had something worse. But *they* never complained, oh no. So not only do you feel bad, you feel bad for feeling bad. Ugh—that's the worst."

"And how did you resolve that?" Lori asked, a touch of sarcasm creeping into her voice mostly as a cover for her earnestness.

"Oh, I'm not even finished telling you the problem yet. Then there are these people in the Church today who never get upset about anything and are never even stirred up or caught off guard or disappointed. They've got everything together. And they don't understand why *you* don't. Or at least that's what I thought."

"Well? How are you going to turn this around now? What's the solution?"

"I figured something out. I can't tell you exactly how I figured it out; I mean, it sort of hit me while I was watching a commercial on TV. But I think the thoughts had been brewing under the surface for a long time, waiting to come together in just the right way. See, there was this lady on TV selling Lemon Wonder—"

"Lemon what?"

"It's a cleaner. Good for mopping floors, this lady says. Anyway, I watched her and I thought, I'm outside of this world. I'm too far gone for clean floors to help me. So I watched this woman, kind of envious, and then I realized—"

"What? What revelation did you have about mopping floors?"

"Oh, nothing about cleaning. It was more about people. See, I know everything that's inside of me, but I only know what other people show me. And with the pioneers, I know even less. Most of the time, all we have are the records of the actions themselves. If there's any kind of commentary from the people involved, it's a testimony. I thought that's all there was to them—not that that isn't important, but it doesn't make a whole human being. They were these two-dimensional brownish gray figures who did things and testified of God and that was about it. No feelings beyond that. No inward struggles. I really believed this, see, that they just did what they did without thinking. It was a given. 'Move into the desert and leave all my stuff behind? Oh, sure, no prob. Let my wife and kids die and bury them on the trail? Oh, you know it, and I'll be dancing the Virginia reel the very next night.'"

"Oh, Judith."

"OK, maybe that's going a little far. And maybe it sounds stupid, but I almost didn't understand that the things they did were hard for them, that maybe they didn't always want to do them. Maybe they had to fight themselves just as hard as you're fighting now. I used to focus on the physical pain, but I never imagined there was any mental anguish. I never thought they might have been torn—as torn as I've been, and more. I was sure they never grumbled, even inside. But I started thinking, what if the whole point isn't that they were better than I am? What if the point is that they were exactly like me, and they became better? What if that's the whole point of everything? Maybe you don't have to be happy all the time to be as righteous as the pioneers—maybe if you didn't hurt, your righteousness wouldn't be worth much. If the pioneers were here with us now, I think they would be more compassionate than judgmental, because they *k n ow*. They know what it is to suffer."

Lori sighed and propped her chin on her hand with her elbow on her knee. "I don't know if that makes a difference, Judith. God knows what it is to suffer, but I don't know if that makes Him compassionate. How can He have patience for someone who resists trials that must seem miniscule to Him?"

"Oh, I don't think Heavenly Father is up there going, 'Come on, Caseys, snap out of it. Move on already.' Maybe that's what we'd say—mortals, I mean—but thank goodness He's a little ahead of us. If He can comprehend eternity, if He can keep track of worlds without number, then He can understand the tiniest pain, too. If He understands infinity, then that covers infinitely small as much as infinitely large."

"Yes, I suppose. But that doesn't justify selfishness or weakness."

"No, I wasn't saying that. But how much easier would it be to keep on trying if you believed that, not only does God know the pain you have to face along the way, He's willing to cry with you even while urging you on?"

"How did you develop this theory again?"

"Watching television."

"Oh. Well if you leave television out of it, I think you may have something." The room was getting dim. Soon darkness would hide the evidence of Lori's outburst. *How merciful,* Lori thought. *If I could sit here in the shadows forever, never face anyone again . . .*

"Judith?"

"Yes?"

"You won't say anything about this to anyone, will you?"

Judith didn't answer right away, and Lori couldn't read her expression. "Why?" she inquired finally. "Do you think it helps to pretend you don't care that your son died?"

"I don't want to talk about it."

Judith sighed and stood up to leave the room. Lori hoped she could take that as assent. She didn't know what Judith meant, though, when she paused on the threshold to say, "I get it now. They were right to compare you to the pioneers." Judith disappeared before Lori could ask for an explanation, so she lay back on the bed to await the gathering darkness.

Chapter 19

Outside, the air was stiff and cold. In London it had felt soft and flowing; it had slithered in through Judith's coat sleeves and tickled its way up her arms. Here it barely trembled as she pushed her way through it. It was as if the atmosphere itself found the cold unpleasant and had hunched itself together, not to move again until spring. The street was silent and deserted, with houses throwing out squares and rectangles of light. Families sat down to dinner in front of uncurtained windows. Judith paused once to watch one group smiling and talking. She could see them so clearly, they might have been on a stage, but the glass captured and held their words. So she turned away and continued walking in the silence, cutting diagonally across the intersection at the end of the street and heading toward the park.

Perhaps she had misrepresented herself to her mother, acting as if she had eve rything figured out. But what were you to do when someone like Lori praised you, even if she sounded reluctant and, above all, shocked? Judith hadn't lied about what she felt. She wasn't angry any more; that night that Gabriel died, so many things had drained out of her, leaving her light and clean. She had the sort of washed out, pale feeling of a person who has just recovered from an illness. She couldn't tell how long it would last. She had thought about things a lot because she wanted to remember, when life began to seem normal again, the new ideas that had passed through her mind, the old ideas that had finally taken hold. She had never learned as much in seventeen years as she had in the past week, and she kept on learning, too. Today, for instance, seeing her mother with part of her façade chipped away, seeing Lori standing scared and vulnerable with the pieces of her fortress lying broken at her feet. Maybe she wanted to believe that the statuette was all she had broken. No wonder she had begged Judith to keep silent about what she had seen. Maybe if no one ever spoke about the incident again, if the knowledge of it were contained within their two heads, it could be as if nothing had happened. *My mother is afraid of something*, Judith thought with amazement. *Of her own self.*

So maybe there really was something she could teach Lori, and what she had told her today was only the tip of it. "I know everything inside of me," she had said, "but I only know what others show me." And there were some things other people couldn't show you, things you had to understand for yourself. If they tried to explain, they only sounded absurd. Like happiness after tragedy. It was something she had heard about in church many times. People who had lost loved ones or who had been diagnosed with devastating illnesses would get up and testify that they felt blessed and joyful, as if they had been granted some special favor. Judith remembered one man in particular who had spoken his testimony into a portable microphone shortly after an accident made him a paraplegic. "I thank the Lord that He has given me this opportunity to grow closer to Him," he said from his wheelchair parked at the back of the chapel. "He's helped me to feel a joy I've never experienced before."

"Yeah, right," Judith had scoffed silently, twisting uncomfortably in her seat. A fight with Lori that morning had already put her in a bad mood, and here was this guy whose cheerfulness couldn't be ruffled even by paralysis. What did it take? How much was enough? "Must we always be the happiest people on earth, no matter what?" she scrawled across the top of the scratch paper she and Gabriel had been using to play tic tac toe. Then she immediately scribbled it out.

"What was that?" Gabriel wanted to know.

"Oh, nothing."

Then there were the Sunday School and Young Women lessons on adversity, each bursting with quotes on happiness that went something like, "My baby just died, but I'm at peace. In fact I'm rejoicing, because I know we'll be together again." *How silly*, she jeered. *Who are they kidding?* Sure, she believed families would be reunited in the eternities, but that was so far away. How much comfort could it be in the present? Even now, she found the enthusiasm of some of those quotes a little fake. Maybe sometimes people lied to themselves, hoping that if they acted brave enough long enough they'd convince their own hearts. As for her, she wouldn't pretend that Gabriel's death had not devastated her. If she had had any choice in the matter, she would never have let him go, and she would trade all her newfound knowledge just to have him here with her again, selfish as that may be. But she also knew that the joy—or maybe it was only peace—that those people spoke about was real. She couldn't understand it before because she existed in that place where nothing really bad happened, and so somehow nothing seemed all that good either. At least, not transcedently good. Not worth suffering for. It was the opposition thing, she guessed. Adam and Eve could never know happiness in the Garden of Eden, even though they lived in a sort of paradise, because they had never known sorrow.

Judith thought now that the opposition principle didn't apply just to feelings themselves, but to degrees. Her capacity to experience joy was apparently proportional to her capacity to experience grief. When she anchored her happiness on things like ice cream sundaes, a smile from a boy, or a day with no schoolwork, of course she couldn't understand why someone claimed to be happy when a long familiar piece of their comfortable world had just fallen away. No one could really explain to you the kind of joy that could coexist with sadness. You had to be brought so low that nothing on earth could comfort you. You had to understand the fragility of your boring, run-of-the-mill life, which turned out to be as easily crushed as the china teacup Lori had once dropped from an upper shelf. Fifty years old, another family heirloom, and in a moment it was gone. Only then did you really appreciate the comforts that went beyond earth, the truths that didn't spoil or crumble away or disappoint, the plan that could never fall through. Only then did you experience this depth of emotion that was half painful, half exquisite, that drew you apart from the rest of the world and at the same time warmed your insides into tenderness. Yesterday morning, as she had walked along this same street as pale and silent as a ghost, Judith had seen a little girl go racing along on her bike. The girl had smiled at her as she passed, and Judith had smiled back. Funny, she thought. She hadn't known before how to smile and cry at the same time, and mean them both.

All the principles that she now pondered with fresh amazement had been there inside her before. The concept of eternal families, work for the dead, immortality—she had known about all of it and had sincerely believed the gospel to be true. But once, listening to a missionary give his farewell address, she had found herself wondering, *Do people really need this?* She hadn't allowed herself to finish the question, because what she really meant was, *Do people really need this inflicted on them?*

She shuddered now and shook her head in the darkness. *I might as well be honest with myself. Sometimes it is just a huge chore, a list of don'ts and even more difficult do's.* She had been too caught up in the world, she supposed. She had sought after the happiness the world had to offer, and the world had grown so large in her view that she hadn't been able to see past it. Only now, with all its pleasures as empty as deflated balloons, could she push it aside and catch a glimpse of the beauty beyond. Judith wasn't happy the way she used to think of happiness; the joy she felt had tears laced all through it. She yearned to have her brother with her again, and her longing spread out around her as wide and as deep as an ocean. She might have floundered helplessly if not for this swelling of hope that buoyed her up like an inflatable raft. *There is more than this life, this visible world. We are more than this life.* The truths of eternity were sublime, and yes, she needed them, even if embracing them caused her pain sometimes. Partly *because* embracing them caused her pain. How funny that the Lemon Wonder Sphere should turn out to be her own Garden of Eden, and that only by being thrust outside of it could she hope to understand true joy.

She had been blind before, as blind as Adam and Eve were innocent. Nothing beyond this life had seemed real. Now, for the first time, she sensed her identity as a child of God, and she could almost imagine, in some tiny, mortal way, the glorious wonder of a celestial reward. Maybe everyone followed the progression that Adam and Eve had toiled through so long ago, from a pristine lack of sorrow into suffering and opposition . . . and finally, someday, into wholeness, perfection, eternal life. *"God . . . shall consecrate thine afflictions for thy gain,"* Lehi had told his son. How amazing that such a thing might turn out to be true!

Judith had reached the edge of the park now. A white gazebo stood a little way off, in the center, and a few lights glowed mistily through the trees. A fine, cold rain tingled against her face. She inhaled deeply. On a night like this, it was easy to believe in eternity, easy to think of herself as a wanderer on this planet, a lonely traveler yearning for a home that was nowhere on this earth. She had all sorts of maps and compasses to get her back where she belonged, if she'd just be patient and stay on the path. But it was such a long journey. What if her mind wandered, just for a little while? She thought of the ladies gathered at the church last fall, those women gluing dried plants while they talked about Gabriel's imminent death. Some of them probably knew what it meant to grieve; Judith understood now, especially since her conversation with her mother, that people's outward persona was only a fraction of their true selves. Perhaps many of them had experienced a night like this, a time when they stood alone beneath misty lights and glittering stars and whispered to themselves, "I'll make it home. I see the path clearly now, and I'll get there." Had they managed to stay on the path ever since, or had there been detours? Where were they on that very night? Judith almost wished she could have asked them, though she couldn't think how she would have phrased the question. "How did you stay true to your moment of truth?" she might have said. "When time had passed and you had to do all the usual things just to keep life moving along, when your days became filled again with household chores or school or work, how did you remember what was important? How did you clear a view through all those distractions so you could keep your eye fixed on eternity?"

Judith's greatest fear now was of falling away, not from the Church but from the enlightenment that this week's experience had brought her. How easy for her blanket of peace to slip off, forgotten. After all, she couldn't stand here in this park forever. She'd have to go home, and she and her parents would find a routine again. Eventually mundane tasks would snatch away bits of her day until nothing else was left, and she would go back to being exactly as she had been, with nothing more substantial to occupy her mind than new clothes or an upcoming test. On the other hand, if she kept her eyes focused too far off, she might stop caring about worldly things altogether. What if she just stopped everything? Stopped doing schoolwork, stopped helping with chores, stopped bathing even. What if she sat on her bedroom floor like some medieval ascetic, devoting her whole life to meditation? She crinkled her nose. That wouldn't work either, and not just because she'd stink. She'd lose her way by making her life too empty just as surely as she would by making her life too full. She sighed. It was a puzzle, and it might take a long time to figure it out.

At the funeral earlier that day, many of the women from their home ward had come to show their support. Or to socialize and eat free food, the old Judith might have suspected. She had studied each woman furtively, trying to peek inside far enough to determine which group each one belonged to. Who could really empathize with her family and who had no way of understanding? They all seemed too cheerful for the occasion, Judith had thought, all smiling serenely, some pulling out compacts now and then to check their makeup. Judith refused to be too harsh on them, though. What could they say or do that would be of any help? Their simple presence was the only thing that might matter. That alone said what words could not: that they acknowledged the loss and offered the family their compassion. If there were those among them who had no idea what the Caseys were going through, could Judith blame them? Would she have been any different two years ago? *No,* she admitted. *Not one bit.*

She remembered one night when her family had been reading the Book of Mormon together. They had reached the end of the book of Ether, and her father narrated the ignominious end of the warmonger Shiz, who had his head cut off by Coriantumr after everyone else in the whole civilization had been killed. The story went that headless Shiz rose up and tried to breathe, as if he wouldn't admit even then that he had lost everything. "How could he move when he was dead?" Judith had asked, and then she had laughed. It was just an entertaining story to her then, nothing more. Well, maybe even now she wouldn't feel too sorry over the death of such a man, but it went to show how easy it was not to let things in, not to let bad things be real if they didn't affect you directly. Maybe you had to be that way a little in order to survive. If you lived in the world, you heard about bad things all the time, but mostly they happened in far off countries or in cities you had never been to or to people you had never heard of and would forget about as soon as you turned off the news.

Judith had wondered before if strength could coexist with compassion without turning it cold. Everyone, including Judith, had believed that Lori was strong, and she had about as much warmth as a stone. No wonder; her outside *had* been stone, with her real self locked determinedly inside it. She was as mysterious and stoic inside her careful façade as the pioneers were in their flat, brownish gray portraits. Judith suspected that sometimes the quality labeled as strength was really only pride or fear, both of which could put up a pretty good masquerade. As for compassion, it demanded strength. Every person was basically the equivalent of a whole universe, because everyone had the concept of the universe inside of them. For each person, reality is made up of what they perceived. So if you let yourself care too much about other people, you have to let other universes squish into your soul next to your own. Maybe if you weren't strong enough, the fear of being crushed would overcome you, and you'd turn everyone else out. But if you were strong, you could figure out a way to grow until there was room enough for everyone you let in. How big would your soul have to grow to be like God's? She couldn't begin to imagine.

The rain intensified, threatening to turn into snow. Judith made her way slowly into the gazebo at the center of the park and sat down on a bench, remembering. She had come here once seeking consolation for a different loss. When she was a child, the doll that her Grandma Mackay had given her had been her most constant friend. "There, there, Lucy," she would say to the doll whenever she herself felt sad, "everything will be all right, don't be scared now." If she could help Lucy to be brave, all her own fears disappeared too. She was nine when Lucy got lost at the zoo, and she had come here the next day, the muscles in her legs a little stiff from her long search up and down all the zoo trails. Life had looked bleak.

"I'm afraid she's just gone," David had told her after they had circled the park two or three times. Gone. That was the end of it. Judith's backpack hadn't been zipped all the way, and Lucy had slipped out. At least they could explain it. How had they let Gabriel slip away? How could they have zipped him in tighter? Judith pulled her knees up to her chest, wrapped her arms around her legs, and began to cry, partly for Lucy and partly for Gabriel. But there was a difference, she realized beneath her tears. Lucy was precious, but she was just cloth. When she was gone, that was all. You had to get a new doll. A boy couldn't get lost so completely. He was more than cloth, more than flesh. He was eternal.

What did her father love to say at family home evening? "We're a forever family. We're part of a chain going forward and back, and never ending." Judith fingered the silver heart that hung from her neck. It was proof of that chain, wasn't it? People's names could be forgotten, but their lives couldn't be erased. Her family wasn't perfect, but maybe there was still hope. Thinking about eternity made everything seem different. What she had thought was impossible might be possible after all.

For Gabriel's fifth birthday she had given him a kite, a huge diamond of shiny blue and orange nylon. They hadn't flown it for a long time, but she remembered taking it out once or twice, staring up at the huge shape as it glided and bobbed and cast a shadow big enough to cover them both. If you watched a kite from a little way off, you couldn't see the string; its connection to earth was invisible. You could only see what happened on either end, the kite skating about and the practiced hand movements of the person on the ground. For all you could tell with your naked eye, they might be completely separate phenomena, but all the time the string was there making the difference. Being in a family might be like flying a kite. It took practice. There were high periods and nose dives, and sometimes you couldn't see, for all your looking, the connection that would hold you together even as you went your separate ways. That didn't mean it wasn't there, though. The bonds of family could be fragile, but they were also stronger than Judith had ever dreamed. They had to be. They weren't just for a day in the park; they didn't have to cover just a few feet of air. They had to stretch much farther, much longer, from continent to continent, over years and decades—from one world to the next.

Chapter 20

David made his way slowly through the now-deserted house, up the stairway, and down the darkened hall, pausing only momentarily to listen outside the door of his own bedroom. Nothing. He continued on down toward the closed door at the end of the hallway. When he had placed his hand on the knob, he turned once to look behind him, skulking almost guiltily into the darkest shadows in the corner next to the door. No one watched him. He entered silently, closed the door behind him, and flipped on the light.

He surveyed the room that he and Lori had come to label, when they had occasion to refer to it at all, as "the guest bedroom." The scene that met his eyes was a study in careful anonymity. The quilt that covered the double bed reminded him of a hotel bedspread, with its geometric pattern in red, navy, and khaki. Probably Lori had picked it up at a yard sale sometime; he couldn't recall when. A tall, narrow chest of drawers stood against one wall. An uncomfortable-looking chair with wooden arms and a blue vinyl seat took up one corner. A painting by a French Impressionist hung above the bed. Lori disliked Impressionist art. He didn't remember why.

He stepped toward the white painted closet door, and his stomach churned a little as he pulled it open. This room had been swept carefully clean, but in the back corner of the closet, beneath one of the shelves, sat a brown cardboard box. At first he could barely see it, with it tucked so closely against the wall and its sides drooping as if it cowered from the light. He dragged it out now and eased himself down on the edge of the bed, tugging at the cardboard flaps. Lori was usually so thorough, and she was quick too, but for once he had beaten her to something. He had recovered from his shock enough to gather up a few mementos to hoard away before she destroyed them all for the sake of "housekeeping." He had placed the items here in this box, and she had left them alone. Surely she knew about them now; she kept that closet vacuumed. But maybe she didn't know exactly. Maybe she never dared to look inside.

The first thing he saw when had pulled up the flaps was the red and white banner with the dried drips of paint. He took it out carefully and unfolded it, spreading it out next to him on the bed. "Welcome home, Elder Casey," it read. He and Judith and Elijah's girlfriend had spent the morning painting it in the backyard. The weather had turned unusually warm for October, and they were out in shirt sleeves.

"What's Elijah's favorite color?" Judith had asked that morning. They were seated around the picnic table on the deck eating bagels spread with strawberry cream cheese. "I can't remember. Is it blue?"

"No," said Melanie, Elijah's girl, who had flown in the night before from Seattle. She had long brown hair and freckles and wore a striped T-shirt that reminded David of one he had owned as a little boy. "I'm sure it's green. Like hunter green. Remember, he has that one sweater."

Lori glanced up idly from her magazine and cup of hot chocolate. She sat apart from them, on the chaise lounge, with her legs stretched out long and her knees crossed. "You're both wrong," she announced nonchalantly, pretending with all her might that she wasn't the proudest mother around. "It's red. It always has been." So they went down to the hardware store and picked up some bright red paint.

They were ahead of schedule, though. Elijah's flight wasn't due in until the next morning. They were edgy and excited. Judith wanted to put up the banner that afternoon.

"I don't think the paint is dry," Melanie warned. But they couldn't wait. They brought in the step ladder from the garage and started hanging it across the entryway. Little squiggles of paint dripped down, distorting some of the letters.

In his mind, David could see it all in three different ways. First there was the should have been. The four of them laughing and talking late into the night because they couldn't sleep anyway. Then the drive to the airport through the predawn, the early morning bustle of people going and coming, the smell of cinnamon rolls and coffee from the airport vendors. Elijah tall and lithe, his suit hanging easy on his thin, graceful frame. He would have liked the banner.

"Aw, Dad," he might have said, ruffling Judith's hair and circling an arm around Melanie's shoulders. "You guys are great. It's good to be home."

Then there was what really happened. The phone ringing, David walking casually over to answer it. How could you know that something you've done almost every day of your life is suddenly going to crush your world? He imagined the chatter growing quiet, the faces turning in his direction, the expression of disbelief mirrored three times over. Himself putting down the receiver, careful.

"There's been . . ." he stopped, cleared his throat, tried again. "There's been an accident. Elijah isn't coming home."

His memory got stuck there a lot, or rather his thoughts turned back upon themselves. The accident, that was the snag that his memory couldn't slide over without getting caught. The accident jutted up like a rock in a river, and his thoughts swirled around it and beat themselves upon it. *What was it like?* he wanted to know. The mission president offered sparse details. Elijah had been on his way to the mission home, his final stop before the airport. He had been driving along the coast of Madagascar through a landscape fit to be showcased on the travel channel—or so the pictures he had sent home during his two years there had led them to believe. He glided along between an expanse of turquoise sea and a steep rise of emerald-green hills. He probably had the window down, with one elbow resting across the top of the door, and he would have been whistling. A hymn, David supposed, since he was still a missionary. And then something had gone wrong with the car, or maybe something had been in the road. He swerved, spun off across the gravel at the edge of the highway, plummeted downward into cliffs before ricocheting off into the sea.

No, it couldn't have been like that. Let it have been fast, David prayed. He had said the same prayer so many times it was more familiar than the standard prayers from childhood, more natural than "bless this food to nourish and strengthen us" or "please bless that we can go home safely." He prayed it over and over, but how could you change what had already happened? So his mind kept circling back and back, stalled on the same few moments. The first impact against Elijah's body. The terrifying view through the windshield. "No, oh no," he moaned, standing up abruptly to shove the image away.

He paced back and forth slowly, with the heels of his hands pressed against his forehead, and pictured it the third way. This time he saw the events as they had happened, but he watched them from the outside, as an uninvolved observer—he saw himself smiling up at the banner, strolling toward the phone, then looking around stupidly as he held the receiver to his ear. If he repeated this scene to himself until all the shock had gone out of it, maybe he could extract the emotion, like drawing poison from a wound, and view the event impartially. After all, he was a historian; he valued facts and objectivity. And people died all the time. It was nothing new. Who was it that said you had to understand that you were just another specimen of the human race—not special, not exempt from the hazards that threatened humankind? If he tried hard enough, he might succeed in pushing this memory away until it shrank down to the size of the centuries-old tragedies he read about every day. Elijah's death was unexpected, but maybe that was the anomaly, that people rode in cars all the time and then felt shocked when someone they knew got killed in one. Take any average day, and the statistics would tell you that dozens or maybe hundreds of young, healthy people had gotten the life smashed out of them. Why should Elijah be any different?

Because he was my son. David covered his face with his hands, then let his arms drop to his sides. He stared down at the banner, and the red paint made him think of blood. His mind involuntarily flashed a picture of jagged rocks baking in the sun, with squiggles and streams and pools of blood hardened by the heat into a permanent stain. How much did Elijah suffer? That was what he wanted to know. He had learned as a historian that sometimes the truth lurked just beyond reach; you could find every record in existence, and they still left a gap. You had to fill in the rest with your own experience. You made an educated guess and backed it up with all kinds of sources, and people believed you. But you couldn't really forget about that gap. Some truths you could never know.

"David?" He stiffened and raised his eyes slowly to stare at his wife, who stood framed in the doorway. He watched her gaze sweep around the room and freeze on the banner. "What are you doing in here?" she asked tightly.

He closed his eyes and exhaled. He thought of all the years of silence that had stacked up between him and Lori until they could barely see each other over them. He might have lulled himself into believing that he had given in to her for the sake of their marriage, that he had avoided stirring up feelings that would only rip them further apart, but he had lied to himself. All this giving in, and soon there wouldn't be any marriage worth saving. They had both let the warmth drain out of them until this house felt like an igloo with its generic white painted walls that threw their failure in their faces. They had never made a mark on this house. The little etches in the doorway between the kitchen and the living room showed the heights of tenants' children. What had they accomplished all these years, closing themselves in with their work and shutting everything else out? They had buried themselves alive.

Well, maybe it was too late, but he was finished giving in. "What am I doing?" he repeated. "I am looking at a little bit of our family history." He picked up the banner and spread his arms wide. "'Welcome home, Elder Casey,'" he read. "Remember this? You and I are all about family history, right? Well, this is it. This is our history."

"David, stop it, you're talking nonsense."

"No, my dear, for once I have to contradict you. The nonsense is that it took us six years to say anything. What are we going to do, live out the rest of our lives pretending we never had any sons, tip-toeing around any topic that cuts too close? What kind of family is that? What kind of marriage?"

"A typical one, I'd guess," said Lori coldly.

David let the banner drop and shook his head. "Lori, tell me you're not that cynical."

"I won't tell you what you want to hear if it means acting like a wide-eyed Pollyanna."

"What's your problem, Lori?" he shouted. "What do you have to prove? Do you think a person has to be naive or stupid to want a decent relationship?" They stood facing each other in silence, like two boxers waiting for the real fight to begin. David took a step toward her and saw her muscles tighten. His instinct was to hesitate and back off. But his instinct hadn't been that great a guide so far. He kept walking toward her. He reached out for her, but she shrunk away.

"What, are you scared?" he asked, sounding to himself like a kid in elementary school. Back to the basics.

"Scared? What would I have to be scared of?" But her voice trembled slightly.

"I dunno, because all I wanted to do was take you in my arms." He studied her face for a few seconds. He was less than three feet away. "I think you are scared," he concluded. "You've been so scared of this box all these years that all you could do was pretend it didn't exist."

Lori scowled at him, and with her beautiful face the expression was as pathetic and unformidable as the frown of a child. "What's the point of all this? What can it possibly help now to pull out that awful banner?" She edged past him suddenly and went to stand over the bed, where he had let the banner fall. She snatched it up and held it ready to tear. He opened his mouth to cry out in protest, but before he could make a sound, she let it go. He moved toward her again and reached out for her, but she backed away until she stood silhouetted in the window.

"I have so many good memories of Elijah," David said quietly, "I wish I could talk about that sometimes. I wish I could turn to you and say, 'Remember when—'"

"Stop it David!" she snapped. "What good does it do to talk about things? Talking never changed anything. People always say, 'Talk about it and you'll feel better.' Well, how is that supposed to work? How are you better off when all you've done is display your weakness around to everyone?"

"I'm not everyone, Lori. I'm your husband. What good are we to each other if we isolate ourselves inside our own grief?" He took a step toward her.

"Throw that banner away," she insisted. "Get rid of this box. Make everything clean."

"Clean and empty aren't the same things."

"Empty will have to do for now." She tensed up as he approached, and for a moment she seemed to teeter between two courses of action: fling herself out of this window or stand and fight.

"My heck, Lori," he burst out, "if any woman ever should have been a nun, it's you! You're just cold and hard enough to spend your whole life looking down on human affection. You don't need anyone, oh no! You'd never lower yourself enough to ask for comfort. My heck!" he exclaimed again.

He retreated toward the center of the room, and she followed him slowly. "Watch your language, David Casey," she chided sarcastically, with an arch of her eyebrow. "Where did you learn to use a word like 'heck'? In the sandbox at preschool?"

David threw out his hands, exasperated. "For five bucks I'd yell the 'f word' out the living room window."

"Oh? And what 'f word' would that be? 'Fetch'?"

"Don't be stupid. I never liked dogs." He sank down on the bed. "Did I ever tell you about that golden retriever my dad got for me? Wouldn't come near me." He chuckled suddenly. "I guess you and it might have seen eye to eye on some things." Lori said nothing but hovered somewhere near the door. David traced the pattern of the bedspread absent-mindedly with his forefinger. "Gosh, this is the ugliest bedspread I've ever seen."

"Nah, you're wrong. Remember that bedspread in the motel where we spent our honeymoon? Green and gold, vaguely floral—now that was the ugliest."

"Yeah, I guess you're right, come to think of it. That was pretty bad."

"Maybe even that wasn't the worst, though," she said. "We've done a lot of traveling in our time." She stepped slowly over to the bed and sat down next to him. "We've been so many places, sometimes I just sit and wonder how we did it all. I guess when you're young you take a lot for granted, just figure everything's going to work out. I never was afraid back then. Now, looking back, I think I was stupid not to be. Not brave, just stupid." David glanced over at her. She had started out speaking in her usual confident, slightly sarcastic tone, but her voice had dropped until at the end it came out little louder than a whisper.

"Lori—" he reached out a cautious finger to tuck a lock of hair behind her ear. "I know you're brave." He paused. "I also know you're stupid, but the only thing you're stupid about is trying to be brave. You don't have to work so hard at it. You don't have to pretend not to be human."

"David, I can't believe you just called me stupid. Don't think I'm not going to remember that the next time you need me to finish your microfilming for you."

"Well, you can call me whatever you want. I know you won't let me down." He picked up the hand closest to him and covered it with both his own. "We're a good team. We just can't throw it away." She said nothing, and he moved closer to her, releasing her hand and draping his arm across her shoulders. He pulled her against him, and she didn't protest. She let her head rest on his shoulder. "See now, is this so bad?"

"No, this isn't what's bad," she murmured.

"What then?"

"That I need this. That I want you to hold me."

"I love you, Lori."

She turned her face into his shoulder and sobbed.

Chapter 21

Judith relaxed against the chaise longue and pulled her sweater a little tighter across her arms. After weeks of overcast skies and frigid temperatures, the afternoon sun had broken triumphantly through a bank of clouds and smiled down on the frozen city. It had shed its warmth in long golden streams across the gray glass surface of the lake and beamed down over rooftops and backyards with their long-abandoned trampolines and pink and yellow plastic play sets. It had reached into windows and scooped out children who ran about wildly with bare arms until their mothers yelled at them to put their coats back on. It had come to Judith where she sat at her desk reading, and it had spread out a long gentle finger across her cheek. Sensing the warmth against her face, she turned to the window and took in a view of azure sky. She didn't know why, but she felt lighter. She need only lift up her arms to float up into that blueness. There had been a stiffness encasing her body, a knot imprisoning her chest, and she hadn't realized it until now that she felt it softening and dripping away. This release left her legs agile and her chest free. She had cast her book aside and plunged into the darkness of her closet to pull out two square rubbermaid containers full of summer clothes. She exchanged her heavy jeans for coral-colored Capris and her brown oxfords for last summer's beat up sandals, and she rushed out onto the deck with her face and arms flung skyward. It was a beautiful day. But after all, it was still March in Salt Lake City. She had gone back inside for a thick gray sweater that contradicted her optimistic attire, and she lounged now with her bare feet pressed against the coarse outdoor material of the chaise longue and her upper body huddled into the sweater's soft folds. A collegecatalog lay open across across her lap. She watched the pages turning slowly in the breeze. Somewhere around the biology section, the wind shifted direction and the last page settled into place. *Hmm*, considered Judith. *Maybe it's a sign.*

She heard the glass door slide open behind her and turned to see her father step out onto the deck. He wore a suit and tie, even though it was a Saturday, because he and Lori had gone to the temple that day to finish the work for Nicholas and Mary.

"Hey, Dad," she called, getting up and coming to sit next to him in a green plastic chair.

"Hey," he responded absently. After a moment he focused on the book that Judith held now with one finger stuck between the pages.

"Choose a major?" he wanted to know.

Judith grinned. "I was thinking about biology."

David sighed and raised his eyebrows. "Mmmmph," he commented.

They sat in silence for a while until Judith's series of furtive glances culminated in a definite conclusion. "You don't seem as happy as I thought you'd be."

"Hmm?"

"You finished the work today, didn't you? You sealed Nicholas and Mary together."

"Yes," he said slowly, as if it surprised him. "Yes, we did. Your mother and I were the proxies."

"Well, you don't have a feeling like—you know, like it wasn't accepted?"

"No. On the contrary, I felt rather strongly that it was accepted and appreciated."

"Well, then," said Judith.

David sighed and rested his face in his hands. "I was just thinking today," he said, "about numbers."

"Numbers? You mean the book of Numbers in the Bible?"

"No," he said, looking up at her. "Just numbers in general. What do they mean? I was thinking about one versus thousands. I was trying to guess how many names were on those records that your mother and I microfilmed this winter. It isn't the first time I've thought about it. I've been like those annoying missionaries and RMs who like to brag about how many converts they've had. I've been sitting around saying to myself, 'You did a pretty fine job for all these thousands. Thousands. That's something, that's a lot.'"

"It is a lot," Judith agreed. "Just think of all those Johns, Henrys, Williams . . ."

He shook his head. "How does God do it?" he asked.

Judith studied him, puzzled. "I'm sorry?"

"Remember the individual in the midst of the millions. Remember the millions next to the individual."

"It's a lot of people to keep track of."

"Yes, but its more than that. I don't know how to say what I mean, but—well, think about the airlines. They put a price on every life. It's a couple hundred million dollars, or something like that. Nice, isn't it, if you can quantify it so simply? Then you know just what you're dealing with. If you have two hundred and fifty people on a plane, you can figure the total worth of the human life on that plane. Just pull out your calculator and multiply."

"Yeah, great. But that's dumb. It's the dumbest thing I've ever heard. Are you serious, they've got an actual figure that's supposed to be the worth of someone's life?"

"Sure they do. It's how they decide what's economical."

"OK, whatever," said Judith. "Say that's true. What does it have to do with your microfilming work?"

"Well, somehow, without using price tags, God understands how much every soul is worth. When there's a group of people, he knows how much the whole group is worth, and at the same time he remembers every individual in that group. Say you've got a thousand people. He knows every person in that crowd, and he knows the crowd as a whole. Here I've done all this microfilming, I'm bragging about it to myself, but it's all numbers to me. Thousands of people, and aside from Nicholas and Mary I don't know a single one. I see the crowd, but I can't see any single person in it. Maybe that's the difference. If my memory were big enough to keep track of ten or eleven thousand individuals, maybe the crowd would have a different meaning to me."

Judith sat taking this in and watching her father out of the corner of her eye. He had put his head in his hands again. A minute or so later he gained her full attention when a half-stifled sob startled her out of her calm. She whipped around to face him. At first she thought the sound couldn't have been what she believed. The gray-haired man next to her sat perfectly still in his neat charcoal suit. She couldn't see his face, but he seemed the same as always; he was her reserved, easy-going father, and he couldn't make such a noise, that horrible twisted cry of despair that sounded as if it had been wrenched out with force from a deep tunnel.

"Dad," she said, uncertainly.

He shook his head without taking his hands away from his face. "I couldn't have done it," he groaned, his voice coming out choked.

"What? What couldn't you have done?"

"I couldn't have given my son, not voluntarily. Not even for the whole world."

Judith felt the way she had two summers ago when she had ridden the "Rocket Racer" at an amusement park on the East Coast. You lumbered up a few stories in this little seat like a ferris wheel car and then, when you'd hovered suspensefully at the top for a few seconds, the car just dropped. Now again, everything solid seemed to give way beneath her, and she stared at her father without knowing what to say. Would her parents never stop surprising her? They had so much in them that she had never understood before, whether because they had kept it hidden or because she had refused to see. She took a breath and looked up at the sky, which was still light even though the sun had disappeared now behind the rugged outline of mountains and the shadows across the yard had grown dark. Her own lip quivered slightly as she placed a hand against her father's arm.

"The Father of heaven and earth fled to the farthest corner of his universe, so it's said, when his Son was on the cross," she said softly.

David straightened up and muttered woodenly, "He fled, but he didn't stop it."

A surge of compassion welled up into Judith's chest. Funny, she reflected, how she had hated her parents' lack of compassion, and all the while it had never occurred to her to have compassion for them. "After all, Dad," she whispered, "You aren't God."

He turned his head to meet her eyes, saying nothing for a long time. Finally he nodded. "You're right. I've puffed myself up." He took his glasses off and began to clean them with his tie. He spoke somewhere in the direction of his left shoe. "There were things I couldn't stop, so I focused on my work and told myself it was important. I felt powerless, so I relied on these ten or eleven thousand names to save me, and all the while I pretended I was saving them."

Judith stood up slowly and walked a few steps to the edge of the deck, gazing off across the lawn. A few months ago, on her family's first night in Guildwell Hall, her father had compared his and Lori's work to the work of the Savior and Judith had resented it. Who did he think he was? Just a man, a very imperfect man who couldn't even take his dying son in his arms and tell him he loved him. No, she had judged, her father was not at all like the Savior. Now here he was admitting it. But somehow, Judith couldn't agree with the verdict. She turned around to face him and saw him slumped in his chair, his hands still clutching his glasses absently. Just a man, she thought. That was it, exactly. Not a god—yet. A man. Why hadn't she realized it before? She thought she had outgrown, long ago, that childish belief in perfect, omniscient parents. Well, she had, but she hadn't outgrown the idea that they *ought* to be perfect and omniscient. She had condemned them these many years for their failure to live up to her ideal. And she hadn't just disapproved of isolated faults; she had rejected the complete package. Either they were perfect or they weren't. And they weren't.

But maybe it wasn't that simple. She felt the silver heart bump lightly against her chest. Those ten or eleven thousand names that her parents had microfilmed represented real people. Among them was the boy with the kind, green eyes, the one who had reached out to her and said *You are the ones I've been waiting for*. She had to concede that . . . that . . .

"Dad, what you do is important. It is." He smiled at her slightly, and she had never seen him look more vulnerable.

"But you find it so exciting, you're going to be a biologist."

Judith laughed. There went a little more tension being released. Today, in the sun, some of her stiffness had melted away, but there was some of it to go yet. She took a hesitant step toward her father. He replaced his glasses and stood up. She took another step. She was close enough now to put her arms around him. Luckily, she didn't have to make the first move. He pulled her in and hugged her the way he had when she was a little girl.

"I love you, Judith," he said softly from somewhere over her head. When he let her go, they stood awkwardly for a few moments. Eventually David said, "I'm going to help your mother with dinner. Don't stay out too long."

Judith went back to the chaise longue and stretched out. When she closed her eyes, the image on the back of her eyelids was that of a red bow tie with yellow polka dots. That was the kind her ninth-grade physical science teacher used to wear. He'd put it with a red sweater vest and a shirt with light blue and gray stripes. He was the silliest-looking person she knew. And he had bad breath, which she couldn't help noticing during the couple of months that the seating chart had trapped her in the first row. Thinking back on it now, she could tell he had been a good teacher, probably one of the best. The way he had explained things, really abstract things, they stuck. She still had bits of physical science facts floating around in her brain when a lot of other stuff she had learned that year had drained out long ago. Why then had she never liked him? It was the clothes and the breath. She had linked everything about him into one bundle that deserved one judgment: uncool. Yet his fashion sense didn't necessarily have much to do with his ability to explain the unexplainable. And maybe a scientist really ought to have better oral hygiene, but still—just because he might have something to learn, it didn't mean he didn't also have something to teach.

So maybe it was the same with her parents. They had a lot to learn yet, she wasn't going to change her mind about that. Still, there might be some good in them if she looked. Did their faults cancel out their righteous acts? She didn't think so, at least not completely. Dedication to family history had to be worth something.

She slipped her finger under the chain at her neck and drew out the silver heart. Over all those weeks since the boy in the garden had told her his story, he had been in her mind, rarely the main subject of her thoughts, but never completely forgotten. With the past a part of her contemplations for the first time, she had picked out a pattern, a series of images that reminded her of the descriptions of the mirrors that a couple looked into when they got married in the temple. Only these reflections were of grief. There was the boy, whose mother had abandoned him; Nicholas, orphaned somehow and sent to Chadwicke's school; Mary, who David said must have found herself without support; her parents, staggering from the trauma of losing two children; herself . . . Well, for herself she liked the phrase "sucking chest wound." That was pretty much how it felt sometimes.

Moving restlessly, she swung her legs off the chaise longue and strode across the deck. Light poured out through the sliding glass doors, across the green chairs and the picnic table and onto the grass. She stepped close to the frame of light and peered through the windows. Her parents sat at the dining room table picking halfheartedly at a roast that Lori's mother had sent home with them after dinner on Sunday. Judith thought about going in to join them, but she couldn't do it yet. Instead she padded down the stairs, seeking solace in the deeper shadows. A large oak tree, the only tree in the yard, sheltered a corner of the lawn from view and kept it dark even on moonlit nights. She ducked under one of the low branches and went to lean against the trunk. She had always felt safe here in spite of the darkness.

She couldn't help noticing, though, that it wasn't quite as dark as usual. This fact floated gently at the edge of her mind for a long time before she turned enough to face the object responsible for the extra light.

"I don't think this is a dream," she murmured. "If it is, I'm going to be awfully stiff when I wake up."

"Does it matter if it is a dream?" said the boy from the garden. "Dreams are true sometimes."

"There's so much I've wanted to ask you. But you didn't come."

"I've come now."

"And you still can't tell me your name?" He shook his head sadly. "Which name is it?" she wondered. "Which one can't you remember, the name your mother gave you or the one that Chadwicke did?"

"It's the one from Mr. Chadwicke. I hated it, you see. I never knew it would be important."

"But it's important now because . . ." she hesitated, waiting for him to confirm what she already understood.

"Because of the records," he explained. "Because it's the only name that got written down."

"You said we were the ones you were waiting for."

He nodded. "The missionary told me—he said you would come for the records, the ones with my name. I never knew how much it would matter. When they gave me that name, you see, I thought they had taken everything from me." He stared down at his feet. "I didn't understand. I thought I could have saved my mother."

"She left you because she was dying, didn't she," surmised Judith. "The necklace was all she had to give you. That man, the sandy-haired man who had the heart made—who was he?"

The boy gazed at her levelly. "He was my father."

Judith's hand had gone instinctively to the pendant. She reached behind her neck now and undid the clasp so that she could hold the heart up and look at it.

"When you told me how the heart came to be," she said slowly, "I thought it was strange. It's a family heirloom, and that makes it seem so dignified. I never dreamed this started as a gift to a pr—" she stopped, embarrassed.

"You can say it. It's the truth."

"It doesn't matter, anyway. It doesn't change the good that's connected with this heart. It doesn't change the good in you."

He showed her a self-deprecating smile. "You're a kind person."

"I know what it is to feel like no one sees you." She paused, inclining her face half-unconsciously in the direction of the house, where two strangers sat. "You thought no one cared about you," she went on, "but you still cared about someone. They didn't take away your compassion. You're more than your name—you're the things you do."

The boy looked down at his feet again. "I never did anything much."

"But you did," Judith countered. "You saved Nicholas. The consequences of that one act are huge—endless, in fact. Your legacy is still going strong today."

"My legacy?"

Judith smiled into his face. A light had turned on inside her. "I've been sitting here thinking about all the sad things that've happened to us, to you and me and Nicholas and Mary and my parents. It was like a cycle, I thought. But there was something bigger, more beautiful, that I didn't see."

"What was that?"

"I've thought about you a lot since you first came," Judith said, "and at first I wondered why it was you and not Nicholas. But now I see that the circle began with you—the circle of saving. You saved Nicholas's life. From what my dad says, Nicholas saved Mary Chadwicke from poverty. Mary saved her son—well, a lot of her posterity, really—by teaching him to pray. Eventually my ancestors joined the Church, and so on and so on, until here we are today, in a position to complete the circle." She still had the heart necklace in her hand. She held it up now with the clasp undone. "It started out as a chain," she said, drawing the ends apart so that the necklace formed a straight line. "One person saving another down through the years and the centuries. But when we find you, when we find your name, we'll clasp the present and the past together. Because the saving will come full circle . . . back to you. And the truth is, there are probably so many chains and circles that we don't even know about. Samuel Chadwicke—he had his part in it too, recording all those names. In the midst of bleakness, there was beauty, and it was better than a shiny floor. It was love and selflessness."

The boy nodded pensively. "When all you see is the bad, the hard times," he affirmed, "it's like someone telling you about the Fall and then forgetting to teach you about the redemption."

"That's it," agreed Judith. "And I've been falling for a long time, seeing only the sad, only *this side.* You know, I've been talking about my parents being able to help save you, but you've helped us, too. My family has been—well, in a pretty desperate situation. When I couldn't find anything good about my parents, you helped me see that what they do is important. When I felt like my brother was going to be lost from me forever, you reminded me that the spiritual world is real even though we can't see it. Is that why you came? Because we needed you?"

"I came to ask you not to forget me," he replied simply. "Not only me, but all of us. There are so many."

"'They cannot be saved without us, neither us without them,'" quoted Judith. "My father says that all the time. I didn't used to get what it meant, though." She thought about the dozens of children her dream mind had seen in the garden, about the "ten or eleven thousand" names her father and mother had filmed. "We will find you," she promised. "We will. And if it isn't us, then it will be someone else. You aren't forgotten. There is Someone who knows your name. He sent the missionary to you. He meant for you to be found, and you'll never be lost to him."

"He could reveal it miraculously," suggested the boy. "I hoped He would, at first. But something about all this work is important."

"Yeah," said Judith. "Sometimes I've wished there were more miracles. More obvious ones. If you think about it, there's no good reason for us to do family history—I mean, He could just reveal everything and set us to baptizing nonstop, if that was really the only point. I guess He lets us do it because . . ." Her father's words echoed in her mind: *in a tiny way, we become like Him.* "Because our salvation really is tied up with yours. When you help to save another person, you become stronger and better and more worthy—closer to your own salvation."

"Promise not to forget about me, Judy," said the boy, holding out his hand. Judith extended her arm until the tips of her fingers almost brushed against his. Almost, but not quite.

"How could I forget you? I may not know your name, but I have your heart." They smiled at each other while a thought dawned in Judith's head. *Judy*, he had said. He was only the second person in the world to call her Judy. The first had been tall and light-haired, and the last time he had said it he had been wearing a white shirt with a black name tag. She opened her mouth to ask the boy about that missionary, but he was gone. The place where he had stood was covered with shadow.

Judith braced herself against the trunk, feeling suddenly drained and pale. "Judith?" she heard her mother calling from the deck. "Judith! Where can she have gone? Did she tell you she was meeting friends?"

"No," came her father's voice. "She'll be home in a bit. Come on back inside."

"I told her this morning what time we were having dinner. If she wasn't planning to be here for it, she could have said something."

Judith left her shelter and edged slowly out of the shadows. Her parents had gone back to the dining room. She approached the band of light on the grass and watched them again through the window. Maybe it was a trick of the glass, but they looked older than usual and a little fragile. She stood there staring at them, trying to understand how they were: dedicated or neglectful, cold or compassionate, intelligent or clueless. All of those. Fallible, stubborn, prideful, blind, aloof, uncertain, angry. But they were also children of God, bearers of the light of Christ, potentially divine. On the path to discipleship there were many steps. If only perfect people could serve the Lord, what would ever get done? Taking a deep breath, she left her sanctuary of shadow, climbed the stairs to the deck, slid open the door, and stepped inside.

About the Author

From the time she was very young, Amber Esplin, born in Preston, Idaho, loved to read or hear stories read aloud. Some of the books she loved growing up, especially *Dawn's Early Light* by Elswyth Thane and *Mrs. Mike* by Benedict and Nancy Freedman, are still among her all-time favorites and have even affected her life in other ways. (For example, when she was deciding where to go to graduate school, she was partial to the College of William and Mary in Williamsburg, Virginia, mostly because *Dawn's Early Light* is set in Williamsburg during the Revolutionary War.)

Amber went to Brigham Young University and studied French and history. Later, she earned a master's degree in early American history from the College of William and Mary. While at William and Mary, she worked as a research assistant on a project involving apprenticeship records from a school in England, and the historical parts of *Leaving Eden* grew out of that experience.

Amber Esplin lives in Northern Virginia in a suburb of Washington, D.C., where she works as a copy editor for scientific journals.